Books by *Domini Taylor*

Gemini

Gemini

by

Domini Taylor

Atheneum   New York   1985

Library of Congress Cataloging in Publication Data

Taylor, Domini.
  Gemini.

  I. Title
PR6070.A913G4   1985   823'.914   84-20389
ISBN 0-689-11535-0

Manufactured by Fairfield Graphics, Fairfield, Pennsylvania

First American Edition

Gemini

CHAPTER I

From birth the twins were bathed in a kind of radiance. People almost saw haloes about their tiny heads. From their first thin cries and fluttering movements, they were blessed in the love which surrounded them. It was soon clear that they were blessed in their faces as well as their fortunes, and in the outstanding talent and originality which they both precociously showed. They were blessed in their devotion to one another.

Their spinster aunt Eleanor Collis, no less besotted than the rest, felt that the fairies had been too prodigal to the twins; they were too lucky. There must be snags. There were. The twins were dogged by the most frightful succession of tragedies. They were cursed as they were blessed, extravagantly, disproportionally, unfairly. To Eleanor Collis, as to everybody else, another blessing was revealed by the fact of tragedy: the dauntless courage of the twins. It was hard to believe that children could have such spiritual strength. Eleanor's mind, like many another's, reeled at the crushing series of disasters; and her faith in God and man, like many another's, was revitalised by the courage of the twins. It helped each, no doubt, to have the other. There were times when it seemed that the other was all that either did have.

No trace of shadow of the shocking future darkened the hospital room where Melissa lay with her twins. It was mid-afternoon in early June when Eleanor first visited her there, and the sun struck golden through half-open blinds. The room was high – the private wing of a big hospital – and the traffic was more a murmur than a roar. A slight smell of disinfectant mingled – not disagreeably, to Eleanor's puritanical nostrils – with the scent of the early roses already banked around the room. A jumbo confetti of greetings telegrams fluttered in the breeze from the open windows. Simon – Melissa's husband, Eleanor's brother, the twins' father – had been and gone, leaving behind Talisman roses and a narrow, opulent basket of quarter bottles of champagne.

Eleanor crooned over the twins, aware that she was crooning, aware that she was behaving exactly in her spinster-aunt capacity. With part of her mind she mocked at herself; with part she didn't give a damn. These scraps of miraculous mortality were her new loved ones, and it would be perverse not to show it. The twins, with crumpled faces and tight-shut eyes, were magnificently indifferent. Melissa was pretty indifferent, too. She was in a haze of exhausted happiness. She looked as beautiful as ever, more beautiful than ever, with long fair hair spread like a blessing over the pillows, and on her perfect little face an expression of unusual tranquillity. She was not often tranquil. She was an enthusiast, reaching out for life in every direction, reaching out for the moon and touching treetops, touching people and animals and flowers, sometimes like a child, like a puppy, like a leopard, taking more than she earned but giving more than she took. . . .

The twins would have fun, Eleanor thought, with Melissa as a mother. With dear old Simon as a father they would have reassurance, solidity, security, but not exactly fun. 'Dear old'? He was four years younger than Eleanor, and looked it, but what he liked was a quiet life. Melissa was good for him. He was good for her, too. She was high-octane fuel, sparking-plugs, accelerator. He was chassis and brakes. It was astonishing that they should love one another so deeply; and it was fortunate. This had been obvious to everybody, almost from the start – when both families had overcome their astonishment, they had recognized the good fortune. It made up for the sharp difference in the fortunes of husband and wife, which had not mattered when they were children playing together. The son of the Vicarage, the daughter of the great house. The tortoise and the hare. No – the tortoise and the hummingbird. But it worked. Melissa was calmer and Simon more sprightly. It worked, and it made a lot of people happy as well as themselves, and it would make the twins happy.

Eleanor picked up the scattered telegrams before she left. She knew, with only occasional bitterness, that this was one of her functions in life. Dermot's death, when his Jeep ran over a land-mine in Italy in 1944, had left her purposeless and forlorn. She fought not to be forlorn, and she found purposes. Too many purposes – a life which had threatened to be empty was over-full. One of the things it was full of was picking things up after people – after her father, her little brother, Melissa. No doubt she would pick things up after the twins, as long as her back held out.

In a mood which was drily self-mocking – better, she found, than self-pitying – Eleanor straightened with an armful of telegrams to come face to face with her reflection in the looking-glass over the wash-basin. She was amused, as so often, to observe how exactly she resembled what she was – the thirty-five-year-old unmarried daughter of a country parson, keen gardener, blue-stocking, amateur archaeologist and local historian, instructor in the local branch of Riding for the Disabled, organizer of the Red Cross socials and outings for the elderly, bell-ringer, chorister, volunteer helper in the Citizens' Advice Bureau, local stalwart of Oxfam and Action Aid, taker-round of collecting-boxes for the Blind, the Deaf, the Lifeboats. . . . Even her dog, a Norwich terrier called Charley, was almost ludicrously apt. She put on green gumboots and took Charley for walks. Walking, she botanised in the hedgerows and bird-watched in the spinneys. She carried binoculars and a tin specimen-box with a moistened pad. But when she brought an unfamiliar plant home, it was often days before she found time to identify it in her books.

Much of this could have been guessed, she thought, by anybody looking at her. Much could have been guessed about Melissa, too, even as she lay unusually languid with her babies. She was just short of twenty-eight. She was beautiful in a way that was not quite conventional at any point. She was an only child, brought up rich and pampered. She had, to Eleanor's knowledge, been spoiled rotten as a child: but with an astonishing, an almost total, absence of evil effect. Simon's tendency would still be to spoil her rotten. Past and present spoiling did have one inconvenient consequence: Melissa was whimsical, and she was accustomed to indulging her whims. Things like suddenly deciding to have dinner in the tree-house, or starting to repaint the drawing-room at three in the morning, or going for a walk in gumboots and a bikini in a cloudburst. These vagaries caused people to call her 'fey', but Eleanor thought this the wrong word. It implied a twittering, simpy quality – the P. G. Wodehouse girl who thought the stars were God's daisy-chain. Melissa was not in the least like that. Simply, she danced to music which other people didn't hear.

Her mother, it seemed, had danced more wildly, to wilder music. Would the twins dance? Eleanor hoped so. Seeing that Melissa was dozing, she tiptoed across the room to stare down at the fragile newcomers. The afternoon sun, a little lower, threw a splash of gold on the wall behind the bed. The twins were angels in a panel by Fra Angelico, delicate detail on a gilded ground, the painting an act of worship by the artist and an object of worship to the watcher. The twins were an object of worship to Eleanor. She tiptoed out of the room, wondering why she wanted to cry.

Simon had had to leave the hospital immediately after the lunch he had no time to eat. Even the birth of twins could not give a day's freedom to a man who was, in effect, Managing Director of a company farming nearly three thousand acres. That was the Sterney estate – Melissa's grandfather's estate.

Simon drove out of the town and back to his office with the tape of the *Siegfried Idyll*. It seemed the right music for celebrating a birth, as it had been written to celebrate a birth. Melissa always refused to have it in the car, because she said they played it ten times a week on Radio Three, which she listened to while she was painting, gardening, cooking or ironing. Simon never had time to listen to the radio during the day. If he had had time, it was one of the ways he would have used it – only music, only good music. The house overflowed with records and the cars with tapes. It was something old Eleanor could never understand. She rang bells and sang in the church choir, but she was not interested in the real thing. To Simon this was odd – it cut her off from a major segment of the world's greatest art. Because she couldn't appreciate it, she couldn't understand its importance to somebody like himself. She didn't despise it, exactly – she was not so stupidly arrogant – but she didn't take music-loving seriously. She didn't understand that, in his way, he was as serious a lover of beauty and an admirer of genius as she was; she understood how poetry and painting made you cry, but not how music did.

It contributed to something Simon was aware of – something which only wasn't irritating because it didn't matter. Eleanor had always underestimated him. It was because she was four years older, academic at school as he was not, intellectually an earlier developer, as girls often are; it was because he was her little brother, and for her the difference between them was frozen when she was fifteen and he was eleven.

He was glad the dear old thing was going to see Melissa. Melissa would be glad too. They all lived a bit cheek by jowl, like the Musgraves in *Persuasion*; it was lucky they all got on so well.

Simon thought Eleanor would be pleased with the way Melissa looked and was. The people at the hospital, ringing him up early in the morning, had said there was no problem at all. He was deeply thankful, and prayed his thanks before ringing up his father, his sister, and his grandfather-in-law. The thought of twins emerging from those delicate little hips. . . . He supposed there was risk of damage to both babies and hips. But Melissa was pretty fit. She was always active and continued to be so to and beyond the last moment during her pregnancy. She was tougher than she looked. Simon had known that about her since she was five or six. She looked frail, waif-like; but nobody frail could have had that passion for climbing trees, or been so good at it.

Wherever Melissa went there had to be a tree-house. If for no other reason, that would have stopped her from ever living in a city.

Physically, they swore everything was fine. Mentally, emotionally, Simon supposed there might still be a bit of finger-crossing to do. Girls sometimes went odd after they had babies. Melancholia, inability to cope, even nervous breakdown. Apparently it was well known. So much so that infanticide – the killing of a baby by its mother in a moment of

5

mindless despair – was more a sickness than a crime. Simon was not afraid of Melissa killing her twins – she was reluctant to kill even a mosquito – but some sort of collapse was possible. At least, it was a thing to watch out for any signs of. She must not tire herself, or worry. When there was a history of inherited mental trouble, you just had to be extra-watchful.

It was a thing Melissa relied on him to be. He was aware that he was handsome, because a lot of girls had told him so; that helped, no doubt, but what Melissa centrally valued in him – as a child, as an adolescent, as an adult – was solidity. It might not be the most glamorous or romantic thing to be valued for, but it was what he had. That was what people who were surprised at the marriage didn't realise. Melissa was far too clever not to be self-aware; she diagnosed herself and prescribed for herself, and to Simon's enormous happiness what she prescribed was him. It was something to do with her parents being dead, and something to do with her mother's West Highland oddities. 'Father figure' was putting it too crudely – Simon was only twenty-seven when they married – but it did as a kind of shorthand. In taking Melissa he was taking the responsibilities that any new husband shoulders, and a little more besides.

Melissa knew all that. In the words of the sacrament of marriage, there had been an unspoken rider.

Simon refused to allow these thoughts to spoil his present happiness. He filed them away, as orderly-minded as in his super-efficient office; they would not clutter his mental desk, but he knew where they were if they were needed, like a circular from a feed company, or the standing order to the oil-fuel supplier.

The twins were a boy and a girl. What he had hoped for. Melissa had not allowed herself to hope for anything more specific than two healthy babies.

Wagner's lyrical and passionate music seemed to carry the car out through the drab suburbs of the town and into the sunny countryside. Simon felt drunk with the music and with being the father of twins and with Melissa's safety.

He switched off the ignition at a level-crossing, thus losing Wagner. The sudden silence made him think, for some reason, of Eleanor. He compared his blazing luck to her misfortune. The love of her life had been killed, a very good fellow in the

Rifle Brigade, intending after the war to be a solicitor. She was only nineteen at the time. There never had been anyone else. Her life was full but empty. Simon contemplated this paradox, and found that it was glib but that it contained truth.

The train passed; the gates opened; Simon switched on the ignition and pushed the cassette back into its slot. Wagner, resuming, sent his thoughts joyfully back to the twins.

And they stayed on the edge of his mind – crumpled scarlet faces, smaller than his fist – while he did three hours' work in his office.

The Estate Office had been converted between the wars from a small farmhouse. The outbuildings were used as garages – a lot of cars came and went – and for the central storage of compact, high-value items like aluminium gates and stop-cocks. The five rooms of the farmhouse worked very well as an office. There was plenty of room for filing. It was convenient to have a functioning kitchen and bathroom surprisingly often. Simon's own room had been redecorated by Melissa soon after the wedding; it still worked as an office but it no longer looked like one. It looked a cross between the studio of a very tidy artist, and the drawing-room of a hostess who thought Habitat had become corny. After the initial shock of Melissa's colour-scheme, Simon liked it. Melissa's grandfather thought it was silly, until he realised how much it impressed the people – hundreds of them – who came to sell things to the estate or buy things from it. Eleanor thought it was all a waste of money, but she did not understand public relations.

A convenient half-mile from the office was the house where Simon and Melissa lived. It went with the job only in a qualified sense. There was an agent's house, in which Simon had lived before his marriage, and in which his predecessor had lived. It was a decent six-roomed Victorian dwelling, with a small garden, built for somebody's widowed aunt. Melissa would have lived there, at least for a time (there was a beech-tree in the garden adequate for a tree-house), but this was never seriously contemplated. Her grandfather let them have the Dower House, which had twelve rooms, good out-buildings, a cool 1780 façade, and a four-acre garden. It was rent-free, but the tenants were responsible for decoration. This was not mean of Melissa's grandfather – he was often generous and always fair – but it was certainly prudent.

A retired general had rented the Dower House for fifteen years, until 1955. His wife had gradually imposed her absence of taste on the decorations so that, when Melissa first seriously inspected it six weeks before the wedding, it looked like the officers' quarters of an obscure North Country regiment. The changes Melissa made were large but gradual (unlike those in the office, which were small but sudden). After three years, only seven of the twelve rooms had been finished, only two of the three bathrooms, only one of the two staircases. Simon saw that this was right – it enormously reduced the chance of expensive mistakes; but he would have liked to have seen the last of paint-pots and step-ladders and dust-sheets. It was surprising that someone as impulsive as Melissa should approach the task so gingerly, as though she doubted her judgment, as though she were frightened of decisions. Simon was moved when he discovered the reason, and could have kicked himself for not understanding it sooner. Melissa was determined not to waste his money. She had none of her own, except a moderate allowance from her grandfather. Simon had none of his own, except his salary. Melissa had a lot of points of pride, and one of them was not living beyond Simon's means. Her freakish impulsiveness, when from time to time it popped up, cost him sleep but not money.

Except the tree-house. That did. It was built on Rolls-Royce lines by an estate carpenter, but not in estate time or with estate timber. For Melissa it was not a luxury. There were some necessary things she could only do in a tree-house – listen to Monteverdi, read Herrick, write her diary, sew buttons on Simon's shirts. Sometimes she did these four things, or others, all at once, which was possible because of the magic of a tree-house. In hard weather her diary went unwritten and Simon's shirts buttonless.

She never called it a 'Wendy house' and despised the use of the phrase by other people. She did not necessarily despise the people: only their use of that whimsical bit of Barrie. That was characteristic of her. She could deliver a really funny, ruthless, contemptuous tirade about a woman's loose covers, and then truthfully say how much she liked and admired the woman.

Melissa's grandfather understood about the tree-house, although he declined to pay for it; he had had one as a child, and given Melissa her first one. Eleanor did not understand about it. There had never been a tree-house in the vicarage garden. The only tree big enough was a monkey-puzzle. Simon understood about it because he passionately loved the whole bundle of oddities and excellences which constituted Melissa. But he was not allowed in it except as an invited guest.

Simon was perfectly capable of looking after himself – he had done so in the agent's house for three years before his marriage – but he was hardly allowed to do so during the week they kept Melissa in hospital. He had supper twice with Eleanor and their father in the Vicarage. He dined twice with Melissa's grandfather in the big house. He had scrambled eggs in front of the TV with Tommy and Barbara Watkins, who were almost exact contemporaries of Simon and Melissa. The Watkins had an ancient cottage on the edge of Sterney village, cosy but cramped. Tommy sold agricultural chemicals; Barbara was due to produce their first in September. Tommy was more congenial to Simon than Barbara to Melissa.

'Agenda for semi-immediate decision,' said Simon's father, from whom his children had inherited their orderly methods of thought. 'Date of baptism. Selection and recruitment of godparents. Names of infants.'

The Reverend Jonathan Collis was seventy. Everything in his life had happened late – ordination, marriage, first and only incumbency, children – except the death of his wife. He had retired as Vicar of the parish of Sterney, but he still took services all over the diocese, driven by Eleanor to churches whose parsons were on holiday. His sermons were brief but baffling. He liked crossword puzzles. He wore his First War medal ribbons on his surplice.

'As we didn't know what we were getting, we couldn't make plans about names,' said Simon.

'No discussion, even? No speculative flights? No purview of names already traditional in the family?'

It was evident to Simon that his father and sister wanted the twins to be called Jonathan and Eleanor. It was also evident to him – although he and Melissa had not, in truth, discussed it – that these excellent old names would not be chosen. Not for any reason. They simply wouldn't be the names the parents picked. It was an area in which, ultimately, Simon would defer to Melissa, although anyone overhearing them discussing it would think it was the other way round.

Godparents were no problem, although the numbers were awesome. Four to each child meant eight. But they had plenty of friends – good blokes Simon had known at Marlborough and Cirencester and in the Army, and kept in touch with, and Melissa's girlfriends and all her American cousins.

'It might be better to postpone the Christening until people are about,' said Simon. 'Everyone's away in the summer.'

His father frowned. He appeared to be examining Simon's remark for traces of heresy or frivolity. He found none. He agreed that September would be early enough for the admission of the twins into the Church. He said that he would, if spared, perform the ceremony, confident of the complaisance of the incumbent. He put it like that: 'I am confident of the complaisance of the incumbent.'

They moved from the Vicarage dining-table into its drawing-room, which was still full of the golden light of the midsummer evening. The house was no longer actually the Vicarage, having been sold by the Milchester Diocesan Finance Committee to Melissa's grandfather, and let by the latter to old Mr Collis. The present Vicar lived in a smaller house, modern and charmless, with his study over the garage. Mr Collis's house should have been called the Old Vicarage; but there was already one of those, as in so many English villages – a big Georgian house by the church, built for a younger son who took orders at the time when it suddenly became respectable and profitable to be a parson. That Old Vicarage had been divided (by Melissa's grandfather) into flats inhabited by retired people of ample means. So Eleanor and her father lived at the Vicarage, and the Vicar lived at the Vicarage, and it was fortunate that the postman knew which was which. When he was on holiday his substitute made muddles, and there was much traffic in mail-order catalogues between the households. Often the items exchanged were identical. This was a source of mirth to the present Vicar's wife, and of irritation to Eleanor. She was too busy to be for

10

ever swapping bulb catalogues and competition entries with Mrs Evans.

Simon had substantially the same conversation with old Lord Kendall de Sterney, on both the nights he dined at the great house. It was natural enough. Paternal grandfather, maternal great-grandfather, were equally concerned about names, dates, godparents. The circumstances of the conversations were different. When Simon dined there on Tuesday, he and his grandfather-in-law were *à deux*, but they still wore dinner-jackets. Lord Kendall's was green with age. So was Simon's; he had bought it second-hand from a shop in Shaftesbury Avenue when he finished his National Service in 1949. On Friday there were a dozen people, neighbours; much of the conversation was about racing, and much about the twins, of whom some of the guests were hearing for the first time. Formidable ladies became twittery. Toasts were drunk. Simon was covered in congratulation, as though by a fleet of affable dump-trucks. He said that they had reached no decision about names.

Tommy and Barbara had already decided, but had come to different decisions. Tommy favoured names like Robert and Jane, Barbara names like Alaric and Ariadne. Simon thought compromise between these extremes might be difficult.

He went to see Melissa every day in hospital, although it was difficult to make time to do so. There were late hay and silage, selective felling in the new forestry plantations, two thousand pheasant poults, new drainage in some of the bottom land, a turn-round of dairy cows, and the continuing responsibilities of forage, fertiliser, fuel, fences. All the most bothersome things began with 'F'. Foxes, farmers' clubs, fallow. Simon did his office work at dawn, to make up for the time spent at the hospital.

Melissa emerged from her languor with amazing speed. She changed before his eyes from a pallid invalid into the gentle dynamo he knew. The twins changed too. They were people; they were beautiful. Melissa stared at them and stared at them, with a sort of incredulous adoration. Simon knew what she felt because he felt it, too; and Eleanor told him gruffly that the twins were Fra Angelico angels on a golden ground.

Simon played miles of tape on those exhausting drives to and from the hospital. It was all music about Melissa and the twins. He found it interesting to test the essence of the music he played against his feelings about his wife and children, against his joy and amazement. His friends in the Army and at the Agricultural College would have been astonished at this intellectual-aesthetic exercise; but it was natural to him to scrutinise things, to test them for authenticity and genuine merit – political platforms, pieces of four-by-four oak, agricultural statistics, Melissa's grandfather's Gainsboroughs and Cotmans. The authenticity of musical emotion, he thought, could only be tested against an emotion of your own you knew to be authentic. He tested his tapes against his joy. Bach preludes and fugues, on an organ, came out well, though they tended to blast the inadequate stereo in the car. Schubert's *Trout* quintet came out very well, a work full of simplicity and sunshine. Beethoven asked too many disturbing questions, and Chopin was sad, even in the little mazurkas. Gluck came out best of all. Simon had never seen *Orfeo*, but he had taped Kathleen Ferrier's long-ago recording of the scene where the hero emerges from the horrors into the Elysian Fields. To Simon, the music painted little pink quattrocento clouds on a pale blue sky; and on that magic background it painted the faces of the twins.

There were rooms enough in the Dower House, furbished and finished – an upstairs room for the twins at night, a downstairs room for the twins by day, a room with its own television for the nursery nurse on whom everybody had insisted.

'They won't need a day-nursery in this weather,' said Melissa. 'They can lie about on the lawn. Simon can go round them when he mows. When I was a baby they laid me out on the lawn. I had a sentimental nanny. She thought the birds would sing to me. All they did was make messes on me. And then a mole came along underneath me, and made a molehill. It hoisted me up into the air. Of course moles were stronger in those days. Nobody could understand why I was in mid-air. They thought I had the gift of – what is it when you lift yourself off the ground, without even pulling your bootstraps?'

'Levitation?' suggested Eleanor.

'They thought I had the gift of levitation. They thought it

12

was a miracle, or else witchcraft. They couldn't decide whether to beatify me or burn me at the stake. They didn't do either in the end, because it was a Bank Holiday and everybody had gone to the seaside. The twins are beatified already. Look how good they are. They like the car. I don't think they like me much yet. I ought to have been a car, then they would have liked me at once. A family saloon. I'm only just beginning to tell which is which. They can't be identical, can they, being different sexes? But they look identical to me. Don't tell me all babies look exactly alike, because even though it's true it would enrage me, and Doctor Thing said I mustn't get enraged. Or drunk. Enraged, or drunk, or both, quite forbidden for a month.'

'I've never seen you either enraged or drunk,' said Eleanor, laughing indulgently, as she did at Melissa.

'Ah, but you've never seen me at breakfast,' said Melissa. 'Somebody gave us a pot of whisky marmalade. I never knew there was such a thing. Never have I eaten so much toast.'

Eleanor was driving her back from the hospital, because Simon had had to go to a cattle-market in the next county. Melissa was in holiday spirits, overjoyed to be going home. Her abundant energy alarmed Eleanor. She was a bird let out of a cage.

The twins lay about on the lawn. They were exposed to a moderate amount of the June sunshine, rationed by their nurse. Eleanor thought it was too much sun, Melissa too little; but Melissa accepted the ruling of the nurse with a docility which surprised everybody. She accepted the ruling of the gynaecologist, enforced when he was there by Simon, that she should not dig, climb trees, move furniture, or exercise her horse. She accepted his ruling that she should not become enraged or drunk. She had never been drunk, and was in no danger of doing something she considered a waste of a precious waking moment. She had often been quietly and sometimes noisily enraged, in spite of what Eleanor said, by cruelty or treachery or unfairness.

The twins became pink-gold. They both had their mother's blue eyes. They promised to have their mother's abundant corn-coloured hair. Though by definition not identical, they were uncannily alike; their similarity was not diminished by the passage of a month, two months, three months. They were precociously aware of the world and of one another. They cried when they were separated. The nurse had never, as it happened, looked after twins before, and she reported this with amazement to Melissa. She had taken the boy out of the nursery to his bath, leaving the girl behind, and they had both cried. Reunited, they gurgled.

'It's going to make problems if they keep it up,' said Melissa. 'One bawling every time the other goes to the loo.'

They were still 'the boy' and 'the girl', because there was still a debate about names.

Melissa woke up one morning, and said, from her pillow to Simon's, 'Peter and Pandora.'

'Peter, Pan,' said Simon sleepily. 'And you're the one who won't have a tree-house called a Wendy house.'

'Not Pan. Pandora.'

'Not Dora, I hope.'

'What a great clod you are.'

He rolled over and kissed her, and they looked at one another with a love grown greater over the three years of their marriage.

Simon got up, and was replaced in the bed by the twins.

Melissa immediately began using the names. The nurse began using them. They were the twins' names.

Simon walked to the Estate Office (being able to do so was one of the joys of the job) with the names reverberating in his head. By the time he was opening his letters they had established themselves. Right or wrong – in danger or not of contracting into whimsy or tweeness – his son was Peter and his daughter Pandora.

Peter Jonathan. Pandora Eleanor. Why not? Pleasure was given to grandfather and aunt. And Eleanor was to be a godmother.

All eight godparents made it to the christening in September, including Melissa's cousin Dick Kendall with his new American wife. Dick was a lean brown man of twenty-seven, an art historian who looked like Gregory Peck. In England he seemed like an American, in America like an Englishman. Helen his wife was a little dark girl from Vermont, formidably educated, whom only Melissa, of the family, had met.

14

The twins were baptised by their grandfather. They were stoical. Photographs were taken by a man from the local paper. Old Lord Kendall was induced to pose with the others, leaning on his stick and grinning incredulously at the twins. It was a long time since he had any close contact with babies, and he had forgotten how much they resembled people.

After the service, the Reverend Jonathan Collis gave Helen Kendall a quick tour of the church. She knew about ecclesiastical architecture. She appreciated the embossed vaulting of the transept, correctly dating it at about 1300.

Dick and Helen had come straight to the church, having taken longer than they expected on the drive from London. Consequently, it was not until they all went back to the big house for tea that Helen first saw Sterney Court.

'But I've seen this place before,' she said. 'Near Padua. It's by Palladio. It's weird in this landscape. It ought to have cypresses and olive-trees. But it's very beautiful.'

Dick told her the story, counterpointed by Eleanor, who was with them in the car.

Sterney was in Domesday, and the Manor of Sterney popped up in local history in almost every generation as providing a soldier or a Knight of the Shire, or entertaining an archbishop or a royal person. It belonged from about 1200 to a family called Talbot, a cadet branch of the noble family of that name. A Talbot of Sterney had made the Grand Tour in Georges II's reign, and like so many others had fallen in love with Italian civilization. Like not so many others, he had the money and the taste to do something more about it than importing a few statues; he pulled down the Jacobean mansion built by his ancestor, and commissioned a near-exact copy of the Villa Razzari, one of Palladio's most perfect domestic creations.

That particular Talbot's grandson mortgaged himself to the hilt in order to invest massively in the railway boom of 1836; but he invested in the wrong railways, and lost the lot. Meanwhile the Kendall family, yeoman farmers in County Durham, had found that their farm rested on a foundation of solid coal. A very rich Kendall came south, to set up as a country gentleman. Sterney was the place he bought. His son supported Lord Palmerston to such effect that he became Lord Kendall de Sterney. The 'de' was in the mid-Victorian gothic-romantic mode.

'I like it,' said Helen.

'Phoney but harmless,' said Dick. 'It always makes me think of half-timbering which is actually planks stuck to the wall. But don't tell my grandfather I said so.'

'Melissa should still be living here,' said Helen. 'That amazing off-beat beauty. And those gorgeous golden babies.'

'I can't see Simon living here,' said Eleanor. 'He'd be incongruous. But I see what you mean about the twins.'

'Medieval angels,' said Helen. 'Who by, sweets?'

'Renaissance angels,' said Dick. 'By Fra Lippo Lippi.'

'Framed by Palladio,' said Helen. 'That would be exactly right.'

Eleanor thought that, when Dick eventually inherited Sterney, Helen would would want the glorious frame for herself.

Most of the party stayed that Saturday at the big house; one couple fitted into the Dower House, and two bachelors into the Vicarage. Most went to church on Sunday morning. Eleanor was there in the choir, in a purple hat and robe. Her father was there as a simple member of the congregation. The Reverend George Evans mentioned the twins in his sermon – a well-meant but infelicitous reference to seeds and growth, in connection with the following Sunday's Harvest Festival. Melissa did not come to church. She said the gynaecologist had forbidden too much excitement.

All the guests left after lunch on Sunday, except Dick and Helen Kendall. He had another two weeks before returning to his Assistant Professorship at a New England college.

On Monday morning old Lord Kendall proposed a tour of the garden to Helen. They made it as far as a wrought-iron bench in front of the topiary yews. There he said it was time for a rest. He liked the look of his new granddaughter-in-law. She looked almost English – more English than her husband, who was half-English. They talked about the garden for a time, part of which had been redesigned by John Fowler and which looked, in consequence, like a set in a Zeffirelli movie. Then he wanted to change the subject.

16

'Bore to bang on about one's possessions,' he said. 'Been doing it for the fifty years since I inherited. Bound to repeat oneself. To the same people, sometimes. Get to feel like one of those fellows who show you round an ancient monument – just bring it all out like a parrot.'

A cedar shaded part of the six-acre lawn spread in front of them. At its foot was an artificial lake, made by damming the river, spanned at one end by a bridge in the Chinese taste. White fantail pigeons went in and out of the little gothic doors of their dovecote beyond the yews.

'Melissa had a boat she used to sail on the lake,' said Lord Kendall. 'That was when they came to stay, before the war, before her parents were killed. It was a tiny little boat, but it sailed properly. She was only six or seven. The higher the wind the better she liked it. Capsized a few times. Terrified me, but it needn't have. She already swam like a fish. Better than the fish we've got in that lake. You'd call it a pond. The Germans would call it a sea. Did you know that? Every scrubby little German puddle is called the Königsee or something. When she wasn't sailing she was up trees. I had a tree-house made for her. Wouldn't be safe now, of course. Over twenty years old. The other thing she did was sit and think. Imagine it. A six-year-old. I used to ask her what she was thinking about. She told me, but it never made sense. Simon Collis used to come. There was nobody else much for her to play with. He was three years older but they were great pals even then. He was a nice lad, a very steady decent stamp of boy. Still is. I was glad he came. I got him to come here as often as possible. Sane influence. She's turned out fine –'

'Much more than fine.'

'Much more than fine. But one couldn't help wondering. Her mother was a rum one. I was dubious about that marriage. Tried to dissuade my son, but he was besotted. I daresay you've heard all this from Dick or his father.'

'No. Practically none of it. I don't think Dick knows anything about it, and I don't think Ralph knows much.'

'That might be. He was in America most of the time, for the ten or twelve years before the war. But I don't want to bore you with ancient history. Bad as banging on about one's worldy goods.'

17

'You won't bore me. I'd like to account for Melissa. In some ways, to me, she's kind of E.T.'

'Kind of what?'

'A creature from another planet.'

'Yes, always was. But a nearby planet. Something in our own solar system. Venus or Mars. Venus, I suppose. Yes, she's a creature from Venus. But Isobel came from a lot further away. A planet near one of those stars the light takes a million years to get here from. I always find that incredible. Extraordinary notion, to be seeing something that happened a million years ago. All that twinkling is a lot of incandescent gas that was burning a million years ago. Isobel was incandescent. A lot of chaps fell for her besides Herbert. That was my older boy. A lot of girls fell for him, too, from all the stories I heard. Odd. He was a solemn fellow. I thought they were shockingly mismatched, but I believe they were very happy, the few years they had together.'

'Tell about them.'

'I hope I can. I haven't talked about all this for years, not since my wife died I suppose. Nobody else I've wanted to confide in.'

'I'll be proud if you'll confide in me.'

'You're in the family, a most welcome recruit. Especially if you're a good listener. Well, Herbert. Born the year the old queen died. Very normal lad, active, liked ratting and rabbiting and so forth. Went off to private school and Eton. Just too young for the war, thank God. Went up to Oxford just after the war. Then London. He could have lived here – I could have found him plenty to do, on a place of this size – but he wanted his independence. I daresay he was right. He went to a lot more parties than he would have here. He had a job in a private bank. I was glad about that. A drone in the country's bad enough, but a drone in London is terrible. I suppose he knew all the debutantes. They still had them then. I'm told they don't any more, and a damned good thing. I had to give a dance here for Melissa. Nightmare from start to finish. Anyway, in London he met this girl Isobel Raden. She came from the West Highlands, from Sutherland. Brought up at home, with a governess. In a sort of castle, with moss growing inside the walls. I promise you. The rooms were like caves, only colder. The governess was a witch. I met her. Isobel's mother was a witch. They all had second sight. They were as daft as weasels. But, by gum, Isobel was a beauty. Melissa's very like her. When Isobel went back to Scotland at the end of the London season, Herbert went with her. He wrote to us. We thought he'd gone to catch trout, but he'd gone to catch Isobel. He stayed there and stayed there. Chucked up his job. Sat there like a siege engine. The old governess consulted one lot of fairies, Isobel's mother consulted another lot, Isobel herself floated about in a dream, listening to – damn, my memory's going. I'm too old to be telling stories. Tennyson. Something about fairy trumpets.'

'The horns of Elfland, faintly blowing?'

'Isobel went about in a dream, listening to the horns of Elfland faintly blowing. Well, the fairies and the governess and the mother approved of Herbert, as well they might, and he and Isobel got married. We went up there. Spring of '29. Marvellous country. And mushrooms growing downwards out of our bedroom ceiling. Those people are too remote. They get neurotic and introspective. They surround themselves with crazy old retainers, and get worked on. Nobody could be normal, living there all year round. Inbred too, I should think. Herbert's mother and I were very dubious. Melissa was born in 1932, wasn't she? Yes, she's almost twenty-eight. Isobel had a crack-up. They had to put her in hospital, and take Melissa away from her. Herbert brought Melissa here. She was tiny, almost new-born. It was a terrible time for Herbert. Isobel couldn't have any more children after that. Herbert looked after her. He was infinitely patient. I hadn't realised what a good man he was. That's a curious sensation, you know – discovering your son is a hell of a good man. They came here a lot. The quiet was good for Isobel. She still looked stunning, and she could be damned funny. A very kind girl she was, very gentle. But you never knew what she'd say or do next. Can you imagine a gentle unexploded bomb? That was Isobel. I got very fond of her, but I never understood her. She and Melissa were very close, but I was never sure Isobel had what you might call a stabilising influence.'

'But her father had?'

'Oh yes. Thank God, yes. And he was an outcross to all that inbreeding, if I'm right about the inbreeding. And I think I must be. Until the railways went up there, how could they

19

ever meet anybody but each other, just a few families within a day's journey. . . . They sent Melissa down here with a nanny at the beginning of the war. Herbert was sucked into the Army. He'd been in the Yeomanry for years. Isobel worked in a hospital. She wanted to drive an ambulance, but they wouldn't let her. Herbert had a leave in London. They were killed by a bomb on a nightclub in the blitz. And here Melissa was, and here Melissa stayed.'

'You could have sent her to America, to Ralph. He is her uncle.'

'We might have in 1940. Not by the summer of 1941. No children were crossing then. The Atlantic was crawling with U-boats. Besides, we thought she was better here. We thought we understood her. We knew the background. We never did understand her, really, any more than we understood Isobel. If the question had arisen in 1940, you might accuse us of a dash of selfishness. We did love having her here. But in 1941 she was stuck here, whether we liked it or not.'

'And you liked it very much.'

'Very much. Took our minds off the news, which in those days was terrible.'

'Didn't the other grandparents want her? She'd have been even safer in the Highlands than here.'

'They wanted her for a bit, and they got her for a bit. She spent a couple of school holidays there. She had a thing about the place, about the whole countryside up there, the people, her Raden grandmother, the old governess who was still about. A love-hate thing, as they say nowadays. She couldn't explain it to us. Not so that we could understand. When she went the second time, part of her was longing to go, and part was dreading it. I couldn't make out what she was dreading. Nothing physical. Nobody beat her.'

'Ghosts?'

'More like that.'

'All those fairies?'

'Yes, more like that.'

'You'd think she'd like them. Or was she afraid she'd like them too much?'

'At the age of ten? Maybe. It wasn't something she could put into words. She said – it comes back to me – she said she could explain it with a picture. She did a drawing. Imagine

20

that – a scrap like that doing a drawing to express her feelings. I couldn't make head or tail of it.'

'Do you have the drawing?'

'It's barely possible. My wife kept a lot of things like that, and I haven't thrown anything away. If so, it's in one of the drawers of the tallboy in the morning-room. She wrote her letters there. And she said she filed the letters she got. She didn't, of course, she just shoved them into any drawer. Piles of letters from Herbert at school and Ralph at school and Melissa at school. School reports. Probably Melissa's drawings. She drew very well. When she drew a tree you could tell what kind of tree it was. Not that time, though. Even if we found it, you wouldn't make anything of it.'

'I just might. I studied psychology for two years. You can learn a lot from drawings. They're not only therapy, they're diagnosis.'

'We'll have a look, but it's odds against.'

He was wrong: they found the drawing almost immediately, under a stack of school reports.

He was right: it was meaningless: a lot of hard diagonals crossing or crossed by soft curves, and heavy black shading. If it was a diagram of a feeling, it was not one Helen could recognize. It diagnosed nothing she could put a name to. It had no reference in nature.

'I'm sure Melissa's forgotten all about it,' said Lord Kendall. 'A scrawl done nearly twenty years ago.'

'I guess she would have. I won't remind her.'

'No. Don't remind her.'

'Are those other grandparents still around?'

'He's dead. She's in a bin. Mad as a bird. Another cause for worry.'

'Not necessarily. Senile dementia just means the machine has gotten too old to work.'

'A condition I imminently face.'

She was a bit bossy, that young Helen, thought Lord Kendall. A bit sure of herself. Knew all the answers and didn't hesitate to tell you.

All the same he was for her. She was attractive and quick on the uptake. She saw the point of Sterney. When Dick inherited, after his own death and Ralph's death, if Dick was still alive, and if Dick and Helen were still together (no better than an even-money bet, these days) the place would be in good hands.

Sterney would be safe in another sense, too – in a far from contemptible sense. His younger and surviving son Ralph, Dick's father, had married a great deal of money.

Old Lord Kendall died, suddenly and peacefully, in the middle of October. It was nice that he had lived long enough to know his first great-grandchildren; that he had been perfectly lucid to the last, and enjoying life to the last; that his terminal illness had gone on for hours rather than days or months or years; that he died knowing his beloved Sterney was safe from taxmen, mortgagers, developers or Arabs.

The obituary in *The Times* was not long; he had not been a national figure. It talked about his years on the County Council, his years as Lord Lieutenant, his Presidency of the County Agricultural Association, his moderate success on the turf, the fame and beauty of his house and garden, the death of his elder son and the scientific eminence of his younger.

There was a family funeral in Sterney Church, and one memorial service in Milchester Cathedral and one in St James's, Piccadilly. Ralph, now Lord Kendall de Sterney, came over from California with his wife Beth. He took three weeks in England, and they made all three services. Dick and Helen came over from New Hampshire. They could only take a long weekend, and they went only to the funeral. Dick's two sisters came, the elder with her husband.

To house and entertain all these people, Melissa and Simon moved temporarily into the big house. They brought the twins and their nurse.

The old lord's death left a large hole in the local world and in the family. But nobody was stunned by grief. He had been eighty-four, and there was so much to be thankful for.

Helen regretted that she had not heard more family reminiscence. She related more and more strongly to what Dick called *Kendallismus*.

Simon wondered where he stood. Ralph could keep him on or not.

Melissa looked other-worldly in black. Her uncle and

cousins found her an enchanting hostess, devising entertainments for them, or leaving them alone if they wanted. The twins were much in evidence. Simon was little in evidence. His work grew no less because he had no master. His guests saw him only in the evenings.

The weather changed and Beth felt the cold. She felt twinges of arthritis and neuralgia. A life spent almost entirely in California had not equipped her for an English autumn.

'Beth can't do it,' said Ralph.

They had come back from the memorial service in London to a late informal supper left on the table by the housekeeper. Ralph, Melissa and Simon were still up; the others had gone to bed. There was a fire in the small saloon, which Ralph's father had used as a study. Simon had taken off his black coat and put on a cardigan, but Ralph was still dressed for church. Melissa seemed exhausted and subdued. She crouched in front of the fire with a cup of Bovril.

'Beth. . . .?' said Simon, not knowing what Ralph was talking about.

'This climate. This house. Marble floors. I know the doors fit and the central heating is pretty good, but she can't do it. I can't do it to her. There's my work for NASA, too. I can't run out on that, not without notice.'

Like Dick, Ralph was American in England even though he was English in America. His clothes and glasses and hairstyle were American. Californian. He worked in San Diego. He was a research scientist, saying nothing whatever to anybody about what he did.

'I've consulted my conscience and I've consulted Dick,' said Ralph. 'I thought maybe he'd settle here at once, especially as Helen fell in love with the place. He says one day he probably will, but not yet. He says he has to achieve something on his own, before he sets up as a landowner. I think he's right. He inherited the American work-ethic, to my relief.'

Simon wondered what was coming. Melissa looked as though she knew. She sipped her Bovril by the fire. Her position would have been awkward in anybody else; for her it was graceful, catlike. She was a golden Persian cat. Four months after the birth of the twins she was climbing trees again.

'We want you to move in here and keep the house warm for Dick,' said Ralph. 'It has to be lived in and I don't want to let it. You'll continue to manage the estate, exactly as at present, and I ask you to keep me informed. I imagine Dick will come over when he can, and I certainly hope to. I would favour letting the Dower House, leaving the details to you.'

'No,' said Simon. 'Oh no.'

'Why not?'

'We couldn't possibly afford to live here.'

'I'm not asking rent, for God's sake.'

'Heating. Servants. The gardens. Maintenance.'

'Do you realise how much Beth would pay, just not to have to live here?'

'What about your daughters?'

'Andrea? That can't be a serious suggestion. Can you imagine Bob Ivens lord of this place?'

Andrea's husband. An advertising man. Simon saw Ralph's point. Bob was incongruous even as a guest at Sterney.

'And Stella's only twenty-two,' said Ralph. 'A year out of college and as wild as a wolverine. You must see the logic of our suggestion, Simon. I know an estate agent's salary doesn't heat a place the size of this. Since I require that it be kept heated, for the sake of preserving the structure and decorations and contents, I will cause it to be heated. Since I require the gardens to be maintained, I will cause gardeners' wages to be paid. Those are my clear duties as custodian of this inheritance, to set beside my duty to my wife and that to my colleagues. I know my father would have agreed with that. You have to admit so much.'

'Yes, but –'

'I think my father would have approved of this whole deal. Remembering that I will *not* take the hideous risk of letting the place to a stranger, what alternative is there? I'll consider any suggestion.'

Simon had no suggestion.

'What do you think, Melissa?' asked Ralph.

Melissa turned from her contemplation of the firelight. 'I liked being a child here,' she said. 'I should think the twins would, too.'

Simon continued to argue feebly against his installation in Sterney Court.

24

'Listen,' said Ralph. 'I've done more enquiring than you realise. I've been a deceitful old snooper, while enjoying your hospitality. I've talked to the lawyer and the bank and some people in your profession and some neighbours. Everybody's completely happy with the way you manage the estate, as I know my father was, and as *you* know he was nobody's fool. I know your family, your father and sister. I don't want anybody better taking care of my property. Another thing, equally necessary. We've watched Melissa being châtelaine of Sterney. She does it better than my mother did. You know *that's* true, Simon. This arrangement is inspired as much by faith in Melissa as by faith in you. For heaven's sake, what's your objection?'

Simon could think of no objection he could voice. The others won.

His objection was to the scale, the grandeur, occupation of the public eye, dressing and acting up to the role, being host to duchesses and circuit judges; his objection was to the falsity, the masquerade.

He liked having supper in his slippers.

He had been brought up in a vicarage, with paraffin heaters and threadbare, well-loved sofas.

After three weeks' living at Sterney Court, he felt like a fish out of water, a fish on a marble slab in the Harrods Food Hall, being inspected by dowagers.

He said this to Melissa.

She said, 'What kind of fish do you feel like? I won't have you feeling like a hake.'

Melissa had known for days what Ralph was going to say.

Eleanor thought: So the Fra Lippo Lippi angels will have their Palladian frame.

CHAPTER 2

Ralph meant everything he said, but he left one thing out. He did not want at all to live at Sterney. For him it was fortunate that Beth's health – or anyway her happiness – made it impossible.

Melissa said that she had enjoyed childhood at Sterney. Herbert had. Ralph had not. It was a protracted humiliation. In everything he did he was compared to Herbert, and compared himself to Herbert. Herbert was three years older, and everyone made allowances for that; but they compared Ralph at ten with memories of Herbert at ten, and Ralph came out badly. In all the Sterney things he came out badly – the active, sporting, physical things that gave a point to living in the countryside. Ralph overcame his infantile terror of riding, but he never became any good at it. He never got used to the bang of his four-ten; he never got the knack of casting a fly against the wind; he never got any excitement from killing things. He felt like a stranger at Sterney, an inferior outsider.

Thinking about it later, he did not blame his parents. They struggled to be fair. They were disappointed to have an unsporting, bookworm son. It deprived them of a king to their ace, of insurance in case anything happened to Herbert.

Ralph somehow acquired an obsession about aeroplanes. He was interested only in science, in science as it related to aeroplanes. His father thought that, in the strange uncomfortable post-war world, this might be another sort of insurance. Science meant authentic progress. Scientists were sane when everybody else was going mad. Cocktails, the Charleston, indecent short skirts, very rum people going to parties and making the headlines – it might be a comfort to have a scientist in the family. In any case, since Ralph's heart was set on it, there was nothing to be gained by being negative. So Ralph became a scientist; and after Cambridge he went in 1927 to MIT. He became something that had not existed before, a research aeronautical metallurgist.

He stayed on in America after his post-graduate course, because there were better jobs and better facilities for research. He went out to California. In 1929 he met and in 1930 he married Beth Seward. Her father was a lawyer by profession and a real-estate developer by trade. He had made a great deal of money, and he kept it through the financial earthquakes of October 1929. The wedding was lavish beyond anything Ralph had ever seen. He was shocked, comparing this orgy of ostentation with the bread-lines.

None of his own family could come so far. They sent cables and presents. They were sent little hunks of wedding-cake in silver boxes with silver bows.

Thereafter, until 1939, Ralph alternated between industry and Academe, more valuable in both spheres because of his experience in the other. He thought, almost without pomposity, that he brought the financial disciplines of the boardroom to the laboratory, and the intellectual adventurousness of the laboratory to the boardroom. When they were living on a campus, Beth had the tact to hide her wealth.

Because of his work, and because of the birth at two-year intervals of their three children, they only made two trips to Europe in those nine years. On the ocean, Beth did not think it necessary to hide her wealth.

Ralph found Sterney completely unchanged. He found his feelings about it unchanged. Beth found it dull. She wanted concerts, operas, tennis tournaments, polo, and a lot of good stores. These were the things of which her life was composed, and they were not available at Sterney. Other things were, to be sure. They were not to be despised. Beth saw, as well as Ralph, that if that was the kind of thing you liked, Sterney was a good place to find it all. Beth was deeply relieved that Herbert, not Ralph, was heir to Sterney.

Ralph met Isobel, Beth Herbert and Isobel, for the first time.

Beth found Isobel beautiful but baffling. She might have been talking a foreign language. Her jokes were meaningless and her references inscrutable. Nothing she said made any sense. She made the others laugh – even Ralph's parents, even Ralph himself; Beth, who had read a lot of popular anthropology, realised that as Isobel and she came from widely different cultural-ethical sources, it might be years before they communicated. Since they only had interrupted weeks, they never did communicate.

Isobel was expecting her first child. Beth found her attitude abnormal, almost unbalanced. She was riddled with ancient superstition, of a kind Beth thought had gone out with witch-burning. Stuff like seeing hares and counting magpies and not walking on lines in a marble floor.

Their second trip, after Beth had given Ralph their own second child, Isobel's baby was four years old. Spoilt and wilful, Beth thought. Idolised to an unhealthy extent. She seemed a darling, in spite of it all. Her mother Isobel still didn't make any sense to Beth, but Ralph still laughed at her jokes.

On those two visits, Ralph got to know Herbert, for the first time properly, as an adult. What he discovered surprised him. To Ralph, as a child, Herbert as a child had been exactly what Sterney called for. He was active, physical, sporting, brave, uncomplicated emotionally, not immune to art and beauty but gruff about his reactions to them. This was not an untrue picture of Herbert in his middle thirties, but it was an incomplete one. Herbert was odder than Ralph, three years his junior and (by Sterney standards) vastly his inferior, had ever had a chance to realise. He was better matched to Isobel, the child of Faërie, than people saw.

Herbert, as a child, had successfully pretended to be what Ralph had hardly dared to try to be.

Herbert was no more a mindless, hard-riding sportsman than Ralph was. He had pretended to be one, because it was expected of him and it made life easier. He told Ralph so, in

28

1936, when he was thirty-four and Ralph thirty-one. The conversation was possible because they were both grown-up, married, fathers. Probably it was possible because Ralph was almost a foreigner.

It made Ralph wonder if their father also had played a role all his life, because he had been born to it, because it was required of him. The conversation that would have enquired into this was not possible.

Ralph had neither the time nor the training to enquire into Herbert's idiosyncrasies. He did not greatly want to do so. He valued the privacy of his own psyche, and respected that of others. It was enough for him to know that Herbert had redeeming oddities. Beth would have dug, given the chance, but Beth never knew anything about any of this. It gladdened Ralph to know that Herbert varied in important respects from the archetype to which he seemed so totally to subscribe.

'D'you think people are what they seem, through and through, twenty-four hours a day?' said Herbert. 'The Regimental Sergeant Major of the First Battalion of the Grenadier Guards? The Bishop of Milchester? Isobel's dotty old governess? People are not loaves of bread, the same dough from crust to crust. They're not paper cut-outs. They've got dimensions. I'm surprised you're surprised I've got them.'

This gladdened Ralph. At the same time it worried him a little, in relation to little Melissa's future. One nutty parent was more than enough.

It consoled him to think that he and Beth were both massively normal, massively sane, but completely different. Their children would be sane, but their tastes and talents were unpredictable. Everything about Herbert and Isobel's little daughter was unpredictable, including her sanity. Probably she would be pretty sane, but probably not totally.

In 1939, just before war was declared, Ralph sailed to England. Beth obviously stayed in California with the children, now three with the youngest only a year. Ralph tried to enlist, but they sent him to the Royal Aircraft Establishment at Farnborough, and he was a desperately overworked boffin for five years.

His brother's death in 1941 made him heir to the title and to Sterney. These things seemed terribly unimportant at a time when Britain was on the point of being invaded, and only miracles in the air stopped the barges crossing the Channel. Ralph was working twenty hours a day, and sleeping on a camp-cot in his office. Beth's letters were full of the growth and beauty of the children. Until Pearl Harbour, the war was a long way from California. If she had taken in the implications of Herbert's death, she did not say so. Ralph hardly had time to read her letters. He hardly had time to get down to Sterney. When he did so, he found a beautiful, wayward child, approaching adolescence, whom he had difficulty recognizing as his niece.

Eleanor was sorry that Dick and Helen had had to leave so soon. Intellectually, they were far more stimulating than anyone she usually saw. Dick was a gentle and serious man, deeply informed about some of the things that most interested Eleanor, but also happy to learn about the local history in which she was expert. He was far from humourless. Helen was a little humourless, perhaps. She seemed very young to Eleanor.

Helen was not visibly, not crudely covetous of Sterney. But it was evident to Eleanor that she hugged to herself the thought that she would one day be mistress of it. In England she was the Honourable Mrs Richard Kendall, although that might be ridiculous and misleading in America; she was the wife of the heir to the Baron Kendall de Sterney. She liked all that very much. Eleanor wondered how clearly she had been aware of these implications, when she married Dick. Knowing her, fully aware. At least she had not known what Sterney looked like. Now she did. It changed her attitude to a lot of things, Eleanor thought.

It amused and annoyed Eleanor that she and Helen had versions of the same name. It meant 'bright' in Greek, according to an appendix to her dictionary. Well, they were both bright. Helen was brighter. She was certainly better educated. In some ways the two of them were quite alike. Their futures were as different as they could be.

Eleanor discovered in herself, with contempt, a strong twinge of envy.

Less keenly, she regretted Ralph and Beth's departure. She thought she dimly remembered the second of their pre-war visits, when she was twelve. Ralph said that he well remembered calling at the Vicarage, and of being handed biscuits by Eleanor. But she thought she remembered only an awkward afternoon at Sterney, with Isobel leaving the party to play Pooh-sticks with Melissa on the Chinese bridge. It was awkward because they were in full view of the others, who were having tea under the cedar-tree on the lawn. Isobel made no attempt to pretend that she was taking Melissa away for any good reason. She was simply declaring that she was bored with the lot of them. Ralph had pretended not to notice, but Beth had been offended. Her own manners were punctilious, and her children were being strictly brought up. That was what Eleanor thought she remembered – her own twelve-year-old embarrassment at Isobel's rudeness.

It must have been about that time – that year, or the next – that Simon began going so often to Sterney. Her parents, his, were dubious about the effect of this intimacy with greatness. They feared it would give him a taste for what were, to him, the waters of the moon – broad acres, butlers, a huge and magical garden, a prodigality of expensive toys – when his destiny was to work hard and live decently on a moderate salary. It was no good his starting life dissatisfied, yearning for the unattainable, despising his own lot and his own background. That was how their minds worked. They were overruled by Lord Kendall's entreaties. That was when Melissa had been left with her grandparents, when Herbert and Isobel went abroad, or to house-parties where children were not wanted; or when Isobel was having a rest-cure.

Simon would have been eight when he became what Eleanor sourly thought of as Melissa's assistant nanny. He would just have started at his first boarding school. Little boys did in those days, if they were intended to be gentlemen. It was possible because the sons of Church of England clergy had important discounts at certain schools founded and financed with just this objective. Eleanor went by bus to a girls' day school in Milchester. This was unfair but inevitable. It was unfair but inevitable that Simon, not herself, became an *habitué* at Sterney.

To the anxious eyes of his family, there was no sign that Simon was rendered dissatisfied with the Vicarage, with his small bedroom, the shabby furniture, the single cook-general; with a future at Marlborough rather than Eton, a remoter future with a job as a farm manager or estate agent rather than a seat in the House of Lords. He even seemed to come home with a certain relief. The Kendalls were endlessly kind to him, but some of their guests were evidently terrifying. He was afraid of dropping bricks, of making himself ridiculous, of getting lost in the big house when he was trying to find the lavatory.

He surprised Eleanor by saying that he was glad he did not have to live in a house so huge; that it was like a public place, like Marlborough College or Milchester Cathedral, not like a home. He came back to the secure and familiar.

By the time the war started, Melissa was still only seven and Simon ten. Their intimacy grew more surprising rather than less. An aspect of it, which no one had foreseen, was that Melissa could teach Simon so much. Even at that age, with that differences of ages. She taught him to ride a pony, to sail a boat, to swim and dive. She had been brought up to do all these things. They were part of life at Sterney, as they were unthinkable at the Vicarage. All the facilities were there for them – ponies, a boat, the lake; and grooms and gamekeepers and gardeners to teach and to oversee.

Simon and Melissa saw more of one another after the war began, when Melissa was always at Sterney. The first winter of the war was very cold; the lake froze, and Melissa taught Simon to skate.

One summer morning in 1941 Eleanor herself bicycled to Sterney, with a recipe for an eggless cake her mother had cut out of the newspaper. She was sixteen, romantic, fully informed about love in its spiritual and its physical aspects. She had had no actual experience, but she was ready for it when it came.

She went up the drive, then branched off to go round to the back of the house. Part of it was now a nurses' training college, in which Eleanor expected to enrol if the war went on that long. She passed the wing where the student nurses were, and the arch into the stable-block.

She was shocked to see, in the archway, Simon and Melissa passionately embracing. He was twelve. He was still a young boy, though his voice might be expected to break in a year or two. Melissa was nine. She looked exactly that, but she was very beautiful. There could be nothing specifically dangerous in these children hugging one another, but it was unseemly and unhealthy. They were clinging to one another. Scandalised, Eleanor jumped off her bicycle and pulled them apart. She saw that Melissa was weeping. Melissa dodged away from Eleanor and into Simon's arms. Nothing would keep her out of his arms. Eleanor tried to tug her away, but Melissa clamped her arms round Simon's neck, and Simon his round Melissa's back. Over Melissa's head, which was buried in his shoulder, Simon told Eleanor that Melissa's parents had been killed.

Eleanor bicycled away, herself in tears, without giving the recipe to the Sterney cook. She understood that Simon's was the comfort that Melissa needed. She thought she had learned a new thing about love, which had not been whispered by her school friends, or taught in biology classes. Melissa's little arms were locked round Simon's neck because it was there that she felt safe and there that she found comfort, and Simon knew it.

Melissa had a man in her life, who was a skinny little schoolboy with a piping treble voice; she turned to him rather than to her grandparents at this moment of shock and pain and loss.

Melissa was ahead of Eleanor in the direct experience of love.

For the old Lord's funeral the weather had been clear and warm. The leaves were turning but not falling. Then October wheeled into November, and the weather grew cold and clammy. There was no question of the twins lying about on the lawn, nor of Melissa sewing on buttons in the tree-house – her old, childhood tree-house, still sturdy after nearly twenty years, in a beech tree beyond the walled kitchen garden.

The twins might have missed the sunshine, and the autumn songs of the wrens and dunnocks; but they looked perfectly happy to Simon. They grew and developed before his eyes, miraculously, opening up like morning glories. They liked being bounced in a lap, if they were bounced together in the same lap. They slept in a double cot. Any other arrangement would have made them wail, and kept their nurse up all night. Unfamiliar with infant twins, she supposed this was normal.

In every other way, the nurse said, they were the loveliest

33

babies she had ever looked after – the cleanest, the sweetest-tempered, the most beautiful. Simon wondered if she said this to the parents of all babies. He thought not. He thought she meant it. Probably she often said it, but this time she meant it.

November wheeled into December. There was snow before Christmas. The old Lord had put in oil-fired central heating. The whole great house had to be heated, by Ralph's specific instructions, in order to keep the fabric dry, to preserve everything for the future. It was comfortable. Simon was appalled at the bills that went off, whenever the two-thousand-gallon tanks were filled, to Ralph's lawyers in Milchester.

The Dower House was offered for rent. A local estate-agent handled the letting, but Simon showed many of the enquirers round. It was too out of the way for most people; there was no industry nearer than Milchester, and not much there. The prospective tenants were surprised that so much of the house remained to be decorated. There was little general interest in the splendid new tree-house, although Simon tried to make it a selling point.

It upset Simon to go tramping with strangers through a place he had loved, where he had loved and been loved, where he had been happy beyond any imagining.

Christmas. The carol-singers (Eleanor among them) in the great hall at Sterney. The estate staff party, tractor-drivers, water-keepers, cowmen, secretaries, beer and mulled wine and whisky and presents for the children. Simon felt like a bad actor in a 1930 play, putting on a suit, making speeches of welcome, acting Squire Wardle of Dingley Dell or Lord Kendall de Sterney. Melissa made the people laugh. She led some of the children away to meet the twins. She was radiant. When she got people muddled, they forgave her. When everyone had gone she collapsed with fatigue on to Simon's lap, clinging to him as though to save herself from drowning in the waves of exhaustion.

He remembered the first time she threw her arms round his neck, when she ran out of the house to the stables with the news that had just come for her grandfather. Simon, aged twelve, had no words. She did not want words. When he tried to speak she silenced him. She wanted his arms round her. It was his narrow shoulder she wanted to sob into. Simon was startled, moved, to find himself needed.

Eleanor came, misunderstood, understood, and went.

She had not really misunderstood at first. She had not really understood afterwards.

For the rest of the morning, Melissa made a pilgrimage to the places her parents had loved. She held Simon's hand all the time. She would not have gone to those places without him, to the Chinese bridge where she and her mother had played Pooh-sticks, to the boat-house on the lake, to the box where her father's favourite mare had foaled, to the clearing in the beechwood where her mother's Pekinese was buried, to the dovecote, and the baby maze, and the wrought-iron seat beside the topiary yews.

The bodies, dug out of the rubble, were brought down to Sterney to be buried. Melissa stayed close to her grandparents. Over the open double grave, she raised her bowed head once, to stare at Simon. Her look said: they need me just now even more than I need you.

The next year, in the autumn, Simon went to Marlborough, again possible because of concessions to the sons of clergy. They put him in an in-college house. It was a different world from that of the churchy little preparatory school – a world of rugger boots, coal smoke, clothes drying on hot pipes, porridge and obscenities. Often in chapel a name would be read out – another Old Marlburian killed in North Africa or Burma.

Simon was not unhappy because he was sociable and good at games. He discovered beagling. He discovered serious music, unknown at home.

He did not write to Melissa. She had told him not to, because at her school all incoming and outgoing letters were read by the mistresses.

When he came back for the summer holidays at the end of his first year, his voice had broken and he had put on much bone and muscle. He was an adolescent. Melissa was a little girl of eleven.

She hugged him in greeting.

She said, 'I won't be able to do that much longer.'

He said, in his strange new baritone, 'I shall miss it horribly.'

'Yes. So shall I. But still I won't be able to do it when I'm your age, not again till I'm about eighteen.'

'Why?'

'Because. Don't you know about things? Must I teach you all that, as well as riding and sailing? Come and see my piglet. I smuggled him out of the sty. All the others are being fattened up until they're big enough to kill. Not this one. At awful risk I saved his life. I'm the Scarlet Pimper-Little-Nell.'

'Did you think of that?'

'Yes. Sort of. No.'

'What's your piglet called?'

'What *do* you think? Can't you guess?'

'How can I possibly guess?'

'He's called Simon. Because he's my favourite pig. I did think you'd guess that.'

Eleanor went off to learn how to be a nurse, in 1943, when she was eighteen. It was obvious that the war was going on for some time yet. She met Dermot Malcolm, just commissioned. She brought him home to the Vicarage when he had a forty-eight-hour leave. He was a little dark man, a Wykehamist with a place at New College after the war. Simon had never thought about his sister being in love; he had never wondered how she would look or act. She looked pink and acted secretive. She seemed not older but younger. She took Dermot for a long walk, and they came back engaged.

There was only cider at the Vicarage to drink healths in. Simon was fifteen; he was allowed cider. Dermot was killed eight months later. Eleanor thereafter hardly ever spoke about him. She hardly ever went out with men, although she was independent and living in London. She became a radiologist, X-raying some frightful casualties of doodlebugs and V-2 rockets.

Their mother was in the Royal Observer Corps. She wore battledress, and sat on top of the church tower spotting enemy aircraft. By that stage of the war there were no enemy aircraft. But there was another cold winter, and she caught pneumonia. It became pleurisy, and the weakness of her heart was discovered for the first time.

She died while the church bells were ringing on VE-Day.

Simon was brought home from school, and Eleanor from her hospital in London. Melissa, not quite thirteen, was still young enough to hug Simon. She hugged him fiercely, and brought him comfort.

Everyone was kind to them all, the village and the Kendalls and other clergy and their families. Melissa's loving childish hug was all that comforted Simon.

Simon finished his last year but one at Marlborough. He came home to find that Melissa had developed, changed, as suddenly as he had done three years earlier. Little breasts thrust out the front of her Aertex shirt. Simon wanted to touch them. He tried not to be seen looking at them. Melissa caught him looking at them. She blushed, and hunched her shoulders. The time for childish hugs had gone forever. Grown-up embraces were far in the future.

Probably the time for grown-up embraces would never come. Simon had the sense that the door had closed on the Garden of Eden.

For a gap yawned. It had always been there as a crack, a hairline fissure between Sterney and the Vicarage. Children could jump over it, heedless. Adolescents were bound to feel the chilly edge of the shadows of the 'hoary social curse'. Simon's road and Melissa's had run happily side by side; now they forked. Everything about them was beginning to be different, and everything would get more different as they both grew up.

There was no blinking it. At fourteen Melissa could pretend to blink it, though she could no longer unselfconsciously hug her old playmate. At seventeen Simon could not blink it, at seventeen Melissa would not.

Friends made a diagram of the process. Simon brought home the sons of solicitors and soldiers, one or two at a time. Melissa brought home the daughters of peers and politicians, a dozen at a time. The groups met but did not mix. Age was a problem, but only a bit of the problem.

It all ought to have disappeared, in the post-war world, under a Labour government. There were people on the euphoric back-benches at Westminster who could believe it had disappeared; in the real world there was a gulf between Sterney and the Vicarage.

'Wait till we're grown up,' said Melissa, after a grossly unsatisfactory tea-party at Sterney. Simon had brought two friends who were staying. Melissa had five friends staying. The boys thought the girls were toffee-nosed little snobs. The girls thought the boys were great clumsy hobbledehoys. The girls talked only to each other, all the time. Neither the boys nor the girls themselves realised that this was because the girls were shy.

'You seem to me grown up already,' said Simon.

'I know. Exactly half the time I feel grown up, and exactly half the time I feel a baby.'

'Which do you prefer?'

'Both equally. Neither. I weep for the past and I look forward to the future. The present is a dreadful crawling deadly bore.'

'It shouldn't be. This place. All your friends.'

'School is the most crippling bore. The only thing I like about it is the boilerman's kitten. There are boilers. So there's a boilerman. He has a kitten. It's called Boiler. Have you ever heard a better name for a kitten? Soon it will be a cat, and I shall lose interest. I shouldn't, but I will.'

'What became of your piglet?'

She looked at him blankly. 'I never in my life had a piglet.'

'Simon.'

'Oh, *Simon*. That piglet. He grew into a pig, and I lost interest. I shouldn't have, but I did.'

'Will you lose interest in me when I grow up?' asked Simon. There was a tremor in his voice; there was audacity in the question to this self-possessed little beauty, who was growing up, who was more worldly than himself, from whom a new gulf divided him.

'I should, but I won't,' she said. 'Since you're named after the only pig I ever loved.'

Simon left Marlborough with moderate Higher Certificate results and a place at Cirencester. He sat about at home, waiting to be called up. Eleanor was now living there, keeping house for her father and becoming immersed in local doings. She was only twenty-two. Nothing except doom, as far as Simon could see, doomed her to spinsterhood.

Melissa, at fifteen, startled Simon into silence. She had grown upwards and outwards. Her legs were lovely and her complexion flawless; pimples on those pink-gold cheeks were as unthinkable as molehills on the Sterney lawns. She moved in a series of sprints, forwards or sideways, or upwards; this staccato quality, this perilous suddenness, was the only thing about her that remained childish. The thought of hugging her now made Simon's mouth feel dry.

He wanted a photograph of her, for when he went away to join the Army. The words would not come. They played tennis. She hit the ball high over the stop-netting, or with vicious accuracy just inside the sidelines. She called 'Out' when his shot was in, and burst out laughing and retracted.

The brown envelope came. Simon had his hair cut very short, and reported to the barracks in Milchester. His hair was immediately cut much shorter. He shared a barrack-room with twenty others, lorry-drivers' mates and farm labourers and shop assistants. Some of the toughest by day wept by night because they had never been away from home before.

Simon was commissioned into the county regiment. He was posted to Egypt. He came home in uniform, pips bright on his epaulettes, on a week's embarkation leave. It was June. Melissa was away at school. This had been predictable, but the disappointment was almost more than he could bear.

Eleanor saw, and grieved. Simon was far too young to feel what he thought he was feeling; and feeling anything beyond friendship for Melissa would be certain heartbreak, then or later. To Eleanor – day-school girl, assistant radiologist, Vicarage housekeeper – the hairline fissure had always been a gulf, bridged in the old days only by Lord Kendall's kindness and by Melissa's loneliness as a child. She was not lonely any more. Going there, Simon was letting himself be patronised. Melissa was not for the likes of him. Probably, in all wisdom, she was not for the likes of anybody. What would Isobel have turned into, if Isobel had survived? What would Melissa turn into, out of her padded nursery into a sharp-cornered world?

It was schoolboy mooning, puppy love, self-indulgent and silly. She told him so, as kindly as she could. He looked at her as though she were talking a foreign language.

In Egypt, for the first time in his life, he tried writing poems.

He came home to be demobilised the following September, having been in the Army exactly two years. He was deeply tanned. There was a full moon over the troopship; even the Bay of Biscay was as calm as glass. They danced on the boat-deck, nurses and ATS and young officers. Simon had practically never danced in his life; there had been no teenage parties of that sort in Sterney village during the war. He was taught to waltz and quickstep by a bouncy little WRAF with freckles; he had a natural sense of rhythm and a natural elegance of movement, and he learned quickly. She taught him to dance cheek-to-cheek, when they turned the lights sentimentally low. She taught him to kiss her. It stopped there. It meant nothing. It was fun. She was the first of the girls who told him he was good-looking.

He reached home just in time; the Cirencester term began a few days later. Much back-slapping went on in the village, and he was stood drinks in the Star Ascending.

Eleanor told him Melissa was away, abroad, in Florence.

To his own astonishment, Simon found himself tugged between two emotions. He was bitterly disappointed not to see Melissa, intensely curious to do so; and at the same time, most unexpectedly, he felt a warm wind of relief. He was alarmed at the prospect of Melissa. Two years in the Army had left him almost exactly as he had entered it. The mess was a prefects' room; the men were small boys; peacetime regimental soldiering was public-school life in fancy dress. But the last two years of Melissa's life would have carried her far and fast. She was seventeen, practically adult, about to come out, awesomely sophisticated, with a whole new circle of resplendent friends among whom he would look like a navvy.

Eleanor had all the news. Everybody had it all. Melissa was going to a finishing school in Switzerland, and coming out in London the following season. Her grandmother was taking a house in Eaton Place from March until July. They would give a great many dinner parties; Melissa would go to one or two or more dances a night. In July, just after Goodwood week, there was to be a dance at Sterney.

Eleanor hoped Melissa would take pity on Simon, not by asking him to her dance, but by not asking him to it.

40

There were rich young men at Cirencester, learning how to manage the estates they were going to inherit. They were richer and grander than most products of Marlborough, than the officers of Simon's respectable but unglamorous infantry regiment, than anybody near Sterney except the Kendalls. Only briefly, at Eaton Hall as an officer cadet, had he been on intimate day-to-day terms with Etonians and Honourables. There denims and spit-and-polish and ironing battledress, and drill and lectures and weapon instruction, were great levellers. Not so at Cirencester. Simon became aware of sports cars and hunters at livery, and invitations to the great houses of Gloucestershire and Oxfordshire.

To his genuine astonishment, he found himself given lifts in the sports cars, hacking and occasionally hunting those horses, and included, at the request of his new friends, in some of the invitations. He supposed he had been well enough liked at school, where in any case he had been ridiculously idolised because he was good at rugby football. He had got on fine in the undemanding society of his mess in Egypt. He now found himself to be popular, in a something-like-adult world. Popular with all kinds of men, and with the girls he met with those men.

He was told he was a good dancer. He blessed his bouncy WRAF. He was told he was handsome.

One of the tricks, if you had to think in terms of tricks, was never to pretend to be what you were not.

At a dance in a country house, a girl said to him, 'I suppose you inherited your dinner-jacket? It can't be meant to be that colour. It's nice. My pa's got his grandpa's frock coat. He says it's a hundred years old. He wears it. He's proud of it. Is your d.j. a hundred years old?'

'I should think so,' said Simon. 'I bought it second-hand in Shaftesbury Avenue.'

This did him no harm with the girl, whose father was a Marquess. It did him no harm that he was the son of a country parson. She asked him to stay in the spring.

It seemed to Simon, a dozen years on, that he had been forced to forget that trick. Living at Sterney, he was manifestly pretending to be what he was not. He had to. Slippers and cardigan at dinner were not fair on the staff; and the master of Sterney was expected to entertain.

41

He was ill at ease, comparing his visible circumstances with what he was, comparing his accommodation with his father's and sister's; he was ill at ease when he rose to greet his guests, in a new dinner-jacket, in the great saloon.

Melissa was at ease. The twins were at ease.

Spring came, and the twins once again lay about on the lawn. Now they sat about on the lawn, sharing a spread rug, sharing toys, sometimes chewing opposite ends of the same toy.

People expected them to develop visible differences, being non-identical, being of different sexes; people expected Peter to assert his masculinity by snatching toys from Pandora, or she her femininity by snatching toys from him. But they remained almost impossible to tell apart, in appearance or personality or development.

They did not snatch toys from one another. They rattled the same rattle, four-handed. They both had Melissa's thick fair hair.

It was the Sterney lawn they sat on, between the topiary yews and the lake, in the sun or in the shade of the cedar tree. They were framed by the lake and the Chinese bridge, by the lawn and the yews and the dovecote and the lovely Palladian facade of Sterney. They were at ease there.

Simon came home for the Christmas of 1949; Melissa came home from Lausanne. He had the sense of seeing her only at a distance. This was ridiculous. They met and talked, naturally. He went with his family to a small party at Sterney. He met and talked to Melissa, and it seemed to him that they were calling to one another across miles of country, or telephoning on a bad line. She was not being snobbish. Her friends were cheerful.

He was asked to several dances in London in the summer, because of people he had met at parties in the country. He was several times asked to dinner in London by Melissa's grandmother. Most of these invitations he refused; it was too far, and he was too busy. It was entirely necessary that he should justify the money his father was spending on his professional training. He accepted a few invitations, and roared or puttered to London in the cars of his friends. A tail-coat became necessary; he bought one second-hand in the shop he knew in Shaftesbury Avenue.

The first person he saw, at the first dance he went to, was Melissa. She was dancing. She wore a strapless dress with a skin-tight bodice and a full, romantic skirt. Most girls at that time had their hair cut short. Hers was long. It shone like a lamp, and swung across her bare shoulders as she spun in an old-fashioned waltz. He had never before seen her wearing either lipstick or jewellery. Dress, make-up, necklace and earrings did not change her. They intensified her. She was singing as she danced. She still looked capable of a sudden sprint forward, sideways or upwards.

He never got nearer to her than that. He did not speak to her, or wave. People clamoured round her. He thought she did not see him. He had to leave the dance early, to go back to Gloucestershire.

She was much talked about, among his friends and in the country houses where he played cricket and tennis. She was much photographed, and often in the gossip columns. She was tipped as Deb of the Year. It was all far out of Simon's reach. He was on the outermost fringe of a world in which she had taken her rightful central place.

Other girls continued to compliment him on his dancing, and to say that he was good-looking.

Of course he was asked to the dance at Sterney. Eleanor and their father were asked also, which put Simon's invitation in a realistic context.

'I haven't seen you once, all summer,' said Melissa.

'I've hardly been in London.'

'You've practically lived in London. I've seen you constantly. In the distance. Twirling round. Drooling over frightful tarts. Over all my friends. No wonder you borrowed your name from a pig. I was going to invite you to have a drink in my tree-house, but now I won't.'

'You couldn't climb a tree in those clothes.'

'No, of course not. I wasn't proposing to. Naturally not. I was going to invite you to.'

They were standing on the Chinese bridge. It was two in the morning. The night was fine and warm; a young moon had set. Light from the doors and windows of the house spread bands of gold over the black acres of the lawn. *Thump-thump* went the rhythm section of Tommy Kinsman's band, of which Melissa had weeks before autographed the big drum, at a dance at Londonderry House.

'Years ago,' said Simon, 'you said, "Wait till we're grown up."'

'Yes. Wait. There's no hurry. I'm grown up but you're not. We've changed places.'

'That's what I was thinking.'

'You're still in the middle of your education. Two more years of learning about muck. I've finished my education. I don't actually know anything, but that doesn't matter because I don't need to know anything. I can't actually do anything, but that doesn't matter because I don't want to do anything. Everything I've just been saying is completely wrong. Your education is almost finished, and mine hasn't begun. What I'm talking about is whether I play safe. Probably in the end I will. I shall see it's the right thing to do, and I shall do it. But I must look about first. I'm going to America.'

'To look about?'

'I shall do it better in America.'

'I didn't know. When was this decided?'

'I didn't know either. It was decided one second ago.'

'I'm sorry talking to me has the effect of sending you off to America.'

'It does. That's just the effect it has. I must put off playing safe for a bit. America will be a good place for putting off playing safe, I think.'

'Will you find a tree-house in America?'

'I shall scour it till I do. It's one of the things I shall look about for. The challenge of a new tree-house.'

They played Pooh-sticks for a short time. Melissa claimed victory. Their sticks were completely invisible in the black water under the bridge.

'I don't understand,' said Simon.

'Yes you do. You do if you think. My mother played safe. As safe as she knew how. Not so very safe, as it turned out, not as safe as she thought. But still she had the right idea. She looked about a bit in London, then played safe. Probably she didn't look about long enough. Or perhaps it was quite long enough, and she just wanted to stop. You understand, don't you? If I didn't look about I'd never know if I was right. I'd never know what I might be missing. I'd never know if I needed to worry. At the moment I don't feel I need ever worry ever again about anything, but that's your bad influence. You're aspirin. I must try brandy. Try it, and note the effect. Probably I won't like it very much, but I ought to try it.'

'For how many years,' said Simon, 'will you need to try brandy?'

'I shan't know till I've tried, shall I?'

They had slipped back into the lifelong habit of intimacy. It was as far from romantic as it could be. The warm darkness, the light washing out over the lawn, the distant thump of the band, the bridge over the black water – it was all a copybook context for romance. Simon would have felt more or less romantic, with almost any pretty girl, in such a place, at such a time. But these friendly confidences were a different kind of conversation, and created an atmosphere in which romance was stillborn.

Probably it was just as well. He had a lot more time to put in at Cirencester. And then he had to get a job. It would not be, straight away, a job he could marry on.

He had seen a lot of farm managers' cottages, visiting estates as a student. Girls could live in them, nice girls. He must resign himself to setting his sights a fathom lower. Eleanor was right. He was entitled to be on this bridge, at this moment, as an old friend, a childhood playmate, a confidant, the local parson's just-presentable son.

'Playing safe' might mean himself; it might mean a lot of other things too. It might mean himself, but it was not how he wanted to be seen, he who had been told so often that he was handsome and a good dancer, he who now cut a respectable figure on horseback, and looked well in his second-hand evening tail-coat.

Melissa took his arm as they strolled back to the house. Time was, she would have taken his hand.

CHAPTER 3

Ralph was pleased that his little niece wanted to come to them, as a kick-off point for looking around America. Beth was dubious. She remembered Isobel before the war, moody, unpredictable, sometimes outrageous, making people laugh in what to Beth was a foreign language. She remembered Ralph's account of his brother's confidences – Herbert an altogether odder and more complex man than his tweedy and sporty exterior would ever have suggested. Most of all she remembered Melissa herself as a spoiled brat.

Ralph had seen Melissa fleetingly during the war, after her parents had been killed. She was growing up just as beautiful as her childhood had promised; just as sweet; and apparently just as kookie.

To Beth, it all added up to the house-guest she least wanted to entertain. She pictured the ladies' charity lunches with which she was often involved, the concerts and recitals, the club meetings and university activities. Melissa would have to be asked along. Beth's own friends would think it weird if she were not. If she were anything like her mother, she might commit all kinds of unthinking, irresponsible atrocities, giving offence to terribly influential people. Her being British, her being aristocratic, her being beautiful, made the whole risk worse. Publicity. 'Limey Lord's Granddaughter Dances on Table. The bi-annual lunch of Today's Women For Yesterday's

Values was treated to an unrehearsed exhibition of Flamenco dancing yesterday, when . . .'

Dick, far away in his senior year at Phillips Andover, was keenly curious to see his glamorous cousin, only a year older than himself. His younger sisters were also curious, but alarmed. Melissa might do them a lot of good with their friends, or a lot of harm.

In the event, Melissa stayed so short a time in California that she did nobody any good or any harm. Dick never even got to see her, and Ralph hardly did. She arrived looking lovely and behaving rationally. Beth gave a party in her honour, of carefully screened kids of her own age. A folk-singer gave a pretty successful imitation of Burl Ives. There was a wine cup. Nobody got drunk. It was an excellent party. Everybody said so. Melissa was found at midnight, in a little room upstairs, reading a Dick Tracy comic book. She said the party was too exciting for her.

It reminded Beth of Isobel, going off in the middle of a party to drop pieces of wood off a bridge.

Next day Melissa made a lot of calls, to people whose names she had been given. The day after that, Beth took her to the Greyhound depot.

If there was one thing Beth hated, it was an anticlimax.

People in England received a lot of postcards from Melissa, haphazardly stamped.

One to Simon was postmarked Acapulco. It said, 'Fallen in love. His name is Pogo.'

Simon was depressed, until somebody showed him the comic strips in the *International Herald Tribune*.

She was back in May, after eight months.

'No good?' said Simon.

'No tree-houses,' said Melissa.

She took his arm but not his hand. She was feeling larger waters with her toe.

She got a job at a shop in London staffed by a shifting population of barely employable ex-debs. She was installed by her grandmother in the top floor of a friend's house in Bayswater, and two other girls were recruited to share it. Rugs, pictures, and a few bits of furniture were expensively ferried up from Sterney. Before Melissa started work, she and the other girls devised an elaborate rota of duties for the housework and cooking. They planned bright little dinner parties, and one of the girls planted up the window boxes.

Melissa left the job after one morning.

'They said I had to work in the basement,' she explained. 'I said I couldn't, but they said I had to. So that's the end of London.'

'There are other jobs,' said Simon, at home for the summer vacation.

'Not for me,' said Melissa. 'The whole of London is a basement.'

This remark was overheard, and gravely quoted as confirming everybody's worst fears. It was quoted to Simon by Eleanor, who did not realise that it was to him that the words had been said. Eleanor was as grave as everybody else. Simon was angry. He understood the absolute sanity and rightness of anybody who said that any city was one vast airless gloomy basement.

He was worried, because he saw what Eleanor meant.

Melissa went to Italy for six months. She was handed on, it seemed, from one princely family to the next. Piecing together her adventures from her postcards, as her grandparents tried to do, you could get the impression that her successive hosts were transferrng one to another, as a gigantic favour, the temporary glory of such a guest; or that they were passing a ticking bomb from hand to hand as fast as possible.

Melissa was home for Christmas, still with a golden tan from the Sicilian autumn. She had no sense of direction whatever.

To different groups she told a long and intensely exciting story, which varied in the telling, about the time she was kidnapped for ransom by a gang of Sardinian bandits.

To Simon she said, 'I haven't been quite truthful about those bandits. Actually it was me that kidnapped them. And actually there was only one of them. It was a puppy, a hungry stray puppy. I don't know what it was a mixture of. St Bernard and Pekinese. I expect you can guess what I called it.'

Simon guessed correctly.

Simon graduated in the summer of 1952. He had a great many friends, an old motorbike, and respectable qualifications.

He was offered a job as Assistant Resident Manager of the Sterney estate.

He was dubious. He suspected a kind of nepotism, paternalism by Lord Kendall on behalf of the parson's son, remembered gratitude for Simon's patience with Melissa when they were children.

Not so, said the old Lord. He had confidential reports, requested and delivered quite improperly; he had the benefit of years of observation, more searching and objective than Simon would have realised, and, in sum . . . the present agent George Martin was to retire in three years. The succession had to be assured. If one regarded the first year as probationary, at a commensurate salary – since, after all, Simon could live at home . . .

Simon allowed himself to be convinced that he was offered the job on his merits.

That winter Melissa's grandmother died. Melissa flew back from somewhere. Simon hugged her for comfort, she him, for the first time since his own mother's death.

Melissa was still only twenty.

It was a kind of love: a kind that had to do with comfort and ancient friendship, and not with anything else at all. In a moment of misery, Simon's was a shoulder Melissa was accustomed to crying on.

He had been Melissa's assistant nanny, according to Eleanor. He wondered drably if he had now become her uncle.

In the next three years Simon worked hard, determined to succeed Edgar Martin, determined to be, and to be seen to be, fully competent to do so.

Melissa sped in and out of their lives like a dragonfly with a full engagement book. She was still looking round, in Sydney and Mexico City and Tokyo. She was putting more than a toe into these exotic waters. Simon thought she had not tried drugs, but he thought she had tried everything else.

He tried a few things himself. He met girls at hunt balls and country dinner parties. Some said no and some said yes, and the ones who said yes seemed glad they had done so. One girl was really serious about him. She started by saying no, fell in love with him, said yes, and had her heart broken. Simon kissed her, and saw Melissa's face. His own heart was wrung. He felt deeply guilty about this episode, the disastrous course of which took him utterly by surprise. He had not supposed himself capable of arousing such storms of feelings. He had not supposed himself obsessed by Melissa.

He caught her looking at him searchingly, when she settled briefly at Sterney. He heard that she asked questions about him, ever so casually, of Eleanor and of neighbours, and in Milchester and London. Had he a girl? Heavy? Steady? What did he get up to?

He was still in her pending tray.

In 1955 there were two significant retirements, at Sterney and in the village. Edgar Martin retired, to be succeeded by Simon Collis. The Reverend Jonathan Collis retired, to be succeeded by the Reverent George Martin. There was only a partial general post of houses, since the Revd Collis and his daughter stayed where they were.

Eleanor could not understand Simon's need to have his own establishment. A poky little place, too. His sheets would be damp and his saucepans dirty. She kept a sisterly eye on his domestic improvisations. She frowned when she discovered hairpins.

Dick Kendall arrived in the autumn, on a Rhodes scholarship, to do his PhD at Oxford. To Ralph's astonishment, and Beth's relief, he had reverted from science to the arts. He came to Sterney for Christmas.

He was not like anything any of them had met before, though they knew his parents: a solemn, horn-rimmed Anglo-American scholar. Even Melissa, who had met an awful lot of Americans, had never met one quite like this one. She had done her looking round in circles far from his; she knew New York better than he did. He talked to his grandfather about family history and the architecture of Sterney; to Melissa about her travels; to the Reverend Jonathan Collis about patristic studies and perpendicular architecture; to Eleanor about the prehistoric tumuli on the nearby hills; to everybody with any intellectual interests about their subjects. To Simon he had nothing to say at all. They might have got away on music, but somehow it never came up. Dick struggled to be interested in basic slag and calf-pens, but he could not simulate a fascination he did not feel.

Simon remembered with a shock that this boring, decent man would one day be lord of Sterney.

'My ear is bent,' said Melissa. 'Also my vocal chords. On a diet of Dick. A big dose of little Dick.'

'Hardly little,' said Simon. 'He's taller than me.'

'He's wet behind the ears. Have you noticed how big his shoes are? Great things like galoshes, with squeaky soles. Only children wear shoes like that. People ask me if I've learned anything on my travels. I have, I have. Only children wear shoes like galoshes with squeaky soles.'

'I'm sure I'd like him, if we could find anything to talk about.'

'I do like him, and we find far too much to talk about. You don't know how lucky you are.'

'No, I don't.' said Simon. 'Not yet.'

She knew exactly what he meant.

Dick was offered a horse, but he did not ride; a gun, but he did not shoot. Melissa found girls, younger than herself, his age; and he wanted to know what they were majoring in, and described his own studies.

He smoked a pipe. Doing so, he was already posing for the photograph on the back flap of his first book.

Melissa drove him to Oxford for the start of the Hilary term. She reported that she kissed him goodbye, as a good cousin should, but that all she made contact with was his pipe.

When people had asked Simon that Christmas what he wanted to be given, he had asked for record tokens. He always did. He was building a decent collection expanding outwards from Bach and Mozart, and beginning to include complete operas. He bought carefully, critically, trying different recordings in the shop in Milchester, and guided by the critics in the serious Sundays. He could not afford to buy the wrong records. He could not really afford to buy the right ones.

He did not need to buy the *Observer* and the *Sunday Times*. His father subscribed to them, principally for the crosswords. Simon lunched at the Vicarage after church nearly every Sunday. Then his father would sit with the Ximenes crossword and his Chambers Dictionary in his lap, and Simon would make careful notes of new recordings critically compared.

Eleanor did not know which was the greater waste of time.

Music had been difficult at the Vicarage. Played at a proper volume, it disturbed the others. And Vivaldi would be competing with *Songs of Praise* or religious programmes on the radio. This was one of the reasons for Simon to set up on his own, as soon as the cottage became vacant.

The hairpins pointed to a second and sufficiently compelling reason.

The strongest reason of all was no reason. Simply, at twenty-six, Simon had outgrown living at home. He learned to his amazement from Melissa that an Italian son, placed as he was placed, would never have left home until he married, and often not then. If young Italians wanted flats of their own, they had to take jobs in distant cities. Simon was thankful not to be Italian. Eleanor meant infinitely well, and he loved her dearly; but he had outgrown being mothered by a sister only four years older than himself.

Simon thought his father perfectly understood, though probably not about the hairpins. Simon had a sense of exchanging winks with his father behind Eleanor's back.

Dick came again for a fortnight in the spring. He was pleased with the progress of his thesis. Eleanor was his best listener on the subject.

Simon thought there was something appraising, something proprietorial in Dick's eye, when he contemplated Sterney and its acres. Dick was entitled to feel like that. But it was a bit premature. The old Lord was still vigorous, and Dick's own father was not much over fifty.

Melissa missed this second visit. Friends had asked her to Kenya, Mau Mau having been contained and peace restored. Simon received a card from Samburu with a picture of a warthog. Melissa wrote, 'Guess what he's called?'

Melissa had, naturally, kept in a kind of contact with her Raden grandparents in Sutherland. They got postcards like everybody else, and she telephoned at Christmas and on their birthdays. They never came south. After those two school holidays during the war, they never asked Melissa north. They could no longer cope with people, any people, even their single grandchild. Their letters were affectionate but garbled, incomprehensible. Colonel Raden's writing became faint and wavery.

Their doctor reported to Melissa that Isobel's death had given them both a shock from which neither had ever fully recovered. They were excellently looked after, and he saw them regularly. He did not advise a visit; indeed, he advised against one.

Colonel Raden died in May 1956, just after Melissa's return from Kenya. She was his only close relative; if he had had more distant kin, she did not know about them.

Melissa did a lot of telephoning. She took a train as far as possible, then a Godfrey Davis car. She saw the doctor, the day and night nurses who had been living in the house, the lawyer, the undertaker, and the Registrar of Births and Deaths. She impressed all these people by her calmness and competence. There were no other relatives. The decisions that had to be made she had to make. She made them.

She arranged, with the doctor's help, to move her grandmother into a private nursing home. Her grandmother was scarcely aware of the move. When she opened her mouth to speak, meaningless sounds came out. Melissa got the permission of the nursing home to move in some things of her grandmother's – pictures, rugs, a few small pieces of furniture from her bedroom. This was sensible, humane and normal. It was completely purposeless. Her grandmother looked inwards with stricken eyes, and spoke gibberish in a high, keening voice.

Melissa arranged, with the lawyer's help, to put the old house on the market. She met the estate agent from Lochinver; he was not optimistic. Damp; remoteness; large expenditure to make it habitable by the standards which purchasers nowadays required; perhaps a summer retreat for people who craved solitude, who wanted to get right away from it all.

The estate agent, going over the ancient place with his new client, saw her shivering. It was late May, lovely weather. Even in those dark and clammy rooms it was not cold enough to make a body shiver.

Melissa was taciturn about her ten days in Scotland. It was all business, she said, transacted by the professionals, with her looking on and asking silly questions. The fields had been covered with wild orchids, and there were cormorants on the seashore.

A week after Melissa's return, Simon came home late to the agent's cottage where he lived. He was bottomlessly tired, after a day in the office and on the farms that seemed to have lasted for forty-eight hours. To his astonishment he saw lights on; as he let himself in he heard the Mozart clarinet concerto – his own record, on his own hi-fi.

Only one person in the world would think it was all right to burgle his house and put his record on his record-player.

Melissa was almost horizontal in the one big chair in the sitting-room. She looked drained, utterly exhausted. Coming back from Scotland, she had looked no more tired than the journey warranted. Now it had hit her, as a blow on the head knocks a man out, days later, with delayed concussion.

She looked ill and old, somehow shrunken.

The music was loud, too loud.

Simon turned it down to a tolerable level. He extended both hands to Melissa. She took them.

Melissa said, 'This was the sanest music I could think of.'

Sanest?

Simon said, 'Did you borrow Eleanor's key?'

'I found a ladder. I went in through your bedroom window. How tidy your bedroom is. You don't need anybody.'

She sat up. As soon as she had done so she dropped his hands. She dropped, or covered, the exhausted mask of her face. She became bright, friendly and remote. She apologised for gate-crashing. She said she had been very careful with the records. She said she had not had a drink, or stolen his tie-pin.

She jumped to her feet (sprinting upwards). A piece of paper fell to the floor, from somewhere among the pleats of her skirt. It looked to Simon like a drawing, some kind of abstract drawing. Melissa swooped to retrieve it. She crumpled it into a ball, and threw it into the waste-paper basket.

'What's that?' said Simon.

'Nothing. A doodle. I wanted to see if your Biro worked. Waste of paper. Only it wasn't wasted, because there was something on the other side. Heavens, I've mucked up a vital letter. The ranch is lost. The ranch is saved. I think it was a bill. Now you won't be able to pay it. Aren't I a useful friend, saving you money by destroying your bills?'

She refused a drink. She would not stay. She did not touch him again.

Simon lay back with a deep sigh, in Melissa's chair and in Melissa's position. He listened to the rest of the concerto. Serene, autumnal, beautiful, sad because it was Mozart's last major work.

Sanest?

Simon wondered what letter it was that Melissa had doodled on the back of. It would not be important. Important correspondence went to the office. Simon put it out of his mind. At the end of the concerto he dragged himself out of the deep chair, made himself a whisky and soda, and set about getting his dinner.

Revived, he remembered. He fished the crumpled paper out of the basket, and spread it flat on the arm of his chair.

On one side was a receipted bill from the wine merchant in Milchester.

On the other was her drawing. She was right. It was a doodle, meaningless, a way of seeing if his Biro worked. Diagonals, crossing or crossed by curves, dark shading.

Somehow Sutherland had done it.

Nearly six years of bumming around the world – bumming pretty luxuriously, as a rule, cushioned by Marquesses and money – had not done it. It took ten days in Sutherland.

Whether attending alone the cremation of her grandfather. Whether seeing her grandmother mewing and incontinent, needing no help from her, herself powerless to help. Whether prowling through that gloomy castellated ruin. Whether reliving childhood, or not reliving it. Whether the orchids or the cormorants. Whether something altogether odder and more ancient, Sutherland had done it.

On five successive evenings Simon came home to find Melissa in his cottage. On four nights, listening to his records. On the fifth in silence. On four nights, in the warm, adequate glow of the lamps in his sitting-room. On the fifth in semi-darkness.

Her voice came out of the deep chair. All Simon could see of her was a gleam of bright hair.

She said, 'Now I know. I waited till I was sure, and now I am.'

He stood motionless in the door. He felt shy and frightened.

She said, 'I knew I was taking a chance, waiting so long. Have I waited too long? You didn't have to wait. I didn't ask you to. I couldn't. It turns out I was right from the beginning, from when I was six or something. It turns out I needn't have waited, but I didn't know that, not for certain, not till now. I may have mucked things up, hanging about for so long. Tell me if so, and I won't babble on any more. I hate monograms, I mean monologues. Can't you say anything, you desperate clod?'

'No,' said Simon.

He could not. He dropped to his knees beside her chair, and Melissa's arms folded like pythons round his neck.

He was astonished by her passion. He felt knighted, ennobled, beatified. It was the first time he had made love to someone he was in love with. It was the first time anyone had cried out, long, soft, wordless, a long lovely note on a Mozartian clarinet.

She lay on her back on his bed, a slim pale miracle barely visible, moving lazily, holding his hand to her breast.

She said, 'You know what I've just done?'

He said, 'I know several words for it.'

'Crude lout. Darling love. I've proposed marriage to you. Wedlock.'

'I'm supposed to do that to you.'

'You can do something else to me, in just a minute, as soon as you're ready. Perhaps after dinner. I'll cook your dinner. I'll start as I mean to go on. I'll ring up grandpapa and tell him I'll be out for dinner. I must do that. Being engaged to be

56

married is no excuse for thoughtlessness. I'm engaged to be married, you know. I find I like it. I wasn't sure I would, but I find I do. It gives me a thirst.'

They drew the curtains, and turned on a few lights. Melissa telephoned. It was warm, the beginning of warm June. There was a bottle of Vouvray on ice. Melissa cooked dinner wearing only an apron. She took off the apron for dinner; she said it was common to sit having dinner in an apron. They started by sitting opposite one another, across the small table in Simon's kitchen. Melissa moved her chair so that they were sitting side by side. There was hardly room; they were squeezed together. Simon could not believe any of this was happening to him. They did not finish the excellent light dinner Melissa had cooked.

'You left half your dinner,' said Melissa. 'How rude.'

She had resumed her apron, but nothing else. She looked marvellous. She looked more provocative with the apron than without it.

'Your fault,' said Simon. 'If you'd stayed put I could have managed a bit more.'

'But I couldn't stay put. That's your fault. You made me acquire a taste for you. An addiction. I've never had an addiction before, except for crystallised apricots. That *was* an addiction. It nearly destroyed me. You're lucky I kicked it. You wouldn't have had a look-in. I went to a psychiatrist in Los Angeles. He cost me six million dollars, but he helped me kick my addiction. He said I could do it if I really wanted to. Of course it was agony. I couldn't tell you about the withdrawal symptoms. I chewed gum, everything. Now when I see a crystallised apricot I can take it or leave it alone. I can't leave you alone. Would you say I seduced you? But I'm going to make an honest man of you. Have you ever made love to music? I don't mean to a girl called Music, I mean while music's going on.'

'Hum,' said Simon, who had.

'What's best? *Tristan?* I don't want to hear about it. Storms of passion. I like them, but I don't need outside help. Except yours, and I'd call that inside help. Police suspect an inside job. Don't look shocked. It's silly to look shocked when you've got nothing on. It suggests insincerity. You're a hypocrite, pretending to look shocked when you're sitting there with nothing on. You do look nice. I knew you would. Ribs and things. Oh darling, I love you.'

Simon said, 'I must go and form up to your grandfather.'

'All old-fashioned. He'd like that. One young man said, "Sir, may I have your permission to press my suit?" and the girl's father said, "Yes, it's high time, I should have it cleaned too." I remember laughing at that, but I can't think why.'

Simon did laugh. Melissa, sitting in his lap with the apron discarded, was bounced up and down by his laughter.

'This is the way the lady rides,' she said. 'Do "Rockabye Baby".'

Simon did 'Rockabye Baby'. He spread his knees when he came to 'Down will come baby, cradle and all'. Melissa screamed when she subsided on to the floor between his feet.

'This is the beginning,' Melissa said, 'of a new and glorious era in Anglo-English relations.'

Reactions were mixed. Wide variations showed on scales measuring surprise, understanding and approval.

Surprise. At one extreme Dick Kendall was utterly astonished, incredulous, that a beautiful, aristocratic nut, and his own first cousin, should be hooping herself to a cultureless nothing like that hired hand. At the other extreme, Melissa's grandfather had been expecting this outcome for nearly twenty years. In between, Eleanor and her father were surprised not at Simon's question but at Melissa's answer, supposing that a conventional proposal had been made. Old Mr Collis got used to the idea quicker than Eleanor did. On the surprise graph, Simon's family occupied an approximately central position. The estate staff were on the whole less surprised, having got to know Simon intimately in his professional capacity; some of the stiffer neighbours were more surprised, having seen Melissa at dances.

Understanding. Melissa herself was the only person who understood completely. Simon thought he understood almost completely; he was aware that there were things he never would understand. Eleanor and Lord Kendall both thought they understood completely, but they were both wrong. Many girls understood Melissa falling for Simon; many men understood Simon falling for Melissa; both groups were right as far as they went, but superficial. Dick Kendall found it incomprehensible, unimaginable. He had supposed a class system – however reprehensible – to have survived in England. He knew from his Oxford days that this was so. He knew from Sterney, and life as viewed from Sterney. Dick's mother Beth shared his shocked incomprehension. His father Ralph, born to the world they were talking about, saw clearer.

Approval. Widespread but qualified. Envy entered some attitudes. Instant, unqualified approval only from Lord Kendall. Some doubts and fears from Simon's father and sister, expressed by him only to her, by her to a larger audience.

An immediate marriage was impossible. The parties most concerned had to accept this.

The bridegroom's father was not immediately convinced that his son's happiness lay in such a union; marriage in the middle of the twentieth century was under unprecedented stresses even in the most perfect circumstances – couples with identical backgrounds, with shared interests, neither used to irresponsible globe-trotting or a bottomless chequebook – and to add to the problems endemic to the times this imbalance of birth and money was to compound the risk of misery. The Reverend Jonathan Collis besought them to take time, to ponder well, to pray for certainty. Simon had to agree. Melissa had to agree because, as Simon saw, the last thing she wanted to do was to start her married life with the hostility of her father-in-law.

The 'Americans', as they were half-accurately called, had to come; they were Melissa's only close relatives; it was necessary to fix a date possible for Ralph, Beth, and their children.

The couple had to have somewhere to live, and Simon's job meant that it had to be on the spot. His cottage would not do. Melissa said that it would, but hers was a lone voice. The Dower House would do, but the existing tenants had to find somewhere else, and much had to be done to the house.

And so forth. No one objection to an autumn wedding was overwhelming, but put them all together and the earliest feasible date was the following July. This placed a strain on Simon which he thought would drive him mad. He wanted

Melissa badly, all the time; but they could very seldom have each other. If they had been living in London flats, they could effectively have been living together without anybody knowing about it. But Melissa was Caesar's granddaughter, and Simon was the High Priest's son. And he had to keep the respect of the estate employees, of the whole inquisitive, sharp-eyed and highly communicative countryside.

There was this about it: when they did contrive a clandestine lunchtime, it had the magic of suspense and rarity.

Melissa, showing unpredicted executive competence, took charge of the modernisation of the Dower House. The wiring and plumbing had to be complete before redecoration could be attempted. Simon was thankful he did not have to pay the bills. He could not possibly have done so. He was aware that he was already, in those yards of copper tubing and those miles of electric flex, getting the benefits of marrying above himself. It made him uneasy; it made him fanatically conscientious in his job; it made him admit that Eleanor and his father had a point.

In the weeks running up to the wedding, Simon and Melissa passed up one or two opportunities they could have manufactured to be together under nobody's eye. Previously, they would have grabbed them. All that winter and spring they would have grabbed them. Now old-fashioned morality overtook them, as the sacrament of marriage approached.

Simon said he was surprised to find this feeling in himself. Melissa said nothing could be less surprising that that, but in herself it was astonishing.

It seemed a good omen. It was obscurely comforting. It was nice not to feel raffish and sly.

To Beth Kendall, the wedding compared miserably with her own. The men in neckties instead of Ascots. All of them crowded into a church, instead of being graciously disposed about the great rooms of Sterney. Only the ordinary little church choir, instead of a disciplined glee-club singing spirituals. The bride attended only by children – no maids or matrons of honour. Did she have no college girlfriends, no room-mates? At the reception afterwards no sit-down banquet, no orchestra for dancing, just a kind of champagne party with nowhere to sit down and all finished by five o'clock.

Melissa did look beautiful, it was true. Her veil was antique lace, her delicate tiara an heirloom. She looked radiantly happy. She looked a different creature from the neurotic, ungrateful oddball Beth had tried to entertain seven years before. Beth was not fooled by appearances.

Beth's daughters Andrea and Stella said the bridegroom was a joy, a living doll, a strawberry lollipop.

Ralph did not know if his new nephew-in-law was a living doll or a lollipop. He did know that he was a personable and well-mannered young man who was holding down an exacting job with great professionalism. He thought the Kendall family was lucky to have Simon aboard.

He told Beth the wedding was exactly correct, exactly conventional. It was how the British did it. Beth thought a rich Lord might have done a little better than obey the local rules, especially when people had come seven thousand miles for the party.

The honeymoon was limited to a fortnight. It had to be. Simon had to be back for the harvest. They came back brown from Spain.

Eleanor caught them smiling at one another. They might be divided by half a dozen people, by the length of a room or a dinner-table, and they would catch one another's eyes and smile.

Eleanor thought Melissa was certain to be restless. In seven years she had hardly spent a single month on end at Sterney. A card would come from somewhere saying 'Wish you were here,' and Melissa would wish she was there, and turn thought into deed, and go. Surely she would miss that. She was committing herself, with apparent cheerfulness, to painting and papering, to cooking Simon's meals and darning his socks, to bringing chaos to the order of the Dower House garden. It was too good to last. Her feet would get itchy. Simon, tied to the estate for fifty weeks of the year, would not be able to go. He would not be able to stop her going. Roads which had come together would diverge again. It was inevitable.

It might be inevitable, but it did not seem to happen, not all at once. It was impossible to doubt that Melissa was happy. The novelty had not worn off. Her life, for the moment, kept her absorbed. It was a new experience; she was not yet tired of it. Simon kept her absorbed. They went to parties and gave parties, but not often. To Eleanor, as close to them as anybody, it seemed that their evenings alone together were the things they both most liked. They listened to a lot of music.

After a year, Eleanor was obliged to admit to herself that Melissa had dropped anchor. She was tied up safe in harbour, out of the rip, out of the broken water, and she liked it. Obviously she had liked her adventurous years (her well-padded first-class-travel adventures) but she had left them behind without regret.

Simon had a tree-house made. It was a waste of money, but not a waste of Melissa's time. Eleanor would find her climbing down the ladder with a basket of finished darning.

They gave a first anniversary party – Buck's Fizz on the Dower House lawn, round which was a garden in a state of transition.

Eleanor put her thoughts to Melissa, knowing she would not be misunderstood.

Melissa said, 'I always knew this is where I'd finish up, working my fingers to the bone. Look at them. Worked to the bone. You can't see the bones because I've got these gloves on that imitate hands. Sewing buttons on shirts, that's the worst bit. Luckily I found some nice stuffing for the shirts.'

'Don't you miss zooming about?'

'Oh *yes*. I miss a few things. Not the zooming. Airport lounges are the world of the future. Airline meals are the food of the future. Plastic on plastic. I miss being able to buy little propellors on sticks, on street corners, like you can in New York. Never a street corner, at certain seasons, without a man selling little propellors on sticks. I miss that.'

'Venice? Florence? Rome?' said Eleanor, who would get to none of these places.

'Venice, oh yes. I miss the garbage-barges. I bet you can't say that quickly eighteen times. You can understand a whole civilization by studying its garbage. You knew that, of course. Probably it was you who told me. Never mind pictures and cathedrals, look at the dustbins. Here they tip them straight into a lorry. You could sit inside the lorry, if you were a serious student. I've often thought of doing that. But it would be too dark to see. Obscurantism. Is that a word? The government's behind it. Official garbage secrets act. In Venice it's all spread out for inspection, in a barge. You stand on a little bridge and feast your eyes. Then you go to Harry's Bar and feast the rest of you. And so the long Venetian day wears on.'

'Everybody who goes to Venice wants to go back there, I'm told.'

'A taste for garbage, once acquired, is not easily lost.'

'May I have orange-juice without the champagne?' said Eleanor, as jugs approached them across the grass.

'Yes, of course,' said Melissa. 'That's what I'm having. I don't need booze. I find I don't need anything, really. My needs are nil, except for one thing.'

'My brother, I hope.'

'No. I don't need *him*. Just his dressing-gown. I've appropriated it. I couldn't do without it. I believe it's one you gave him. If you give him another I'll have that too.'

Eleanor pictured Melissa, her little lithe body enveloped in the enormous dressing-gown.

She said, 'What does poor Simon wear?'

'My dressing-gown. He looks sweet all among the frills, like a lamb cutlet in a French restaurant.'

Nobody could deny that Melissa had settled down, that the marriage was going well, that Simon was extravagantly happy.

Melissa was nearly twenty-six. It was time they started a family.

There was no sign of one, that year or the next.

Eleanor delicately asked if this was intentional. They were waiting, perhaps, until more of the house was redecorated?

'I really want a mouse,' said Melissa. 'Like *Stuart Little*. Have you read it? My favourite book. I'm asking about to see if we can arrange it. I've been to the Royal Hospital for Mothers and Mice, and the Great Ormonde Street Hospital for Sick Mice . . .'

'Try the British Mouse-eum,' said Eleanor, who never, ever made remarks of this kind except when talking to Melissa.

If Melissa didn't want to tell you anything, she didn't. She never said, 'Mind your own business' or 'I don't want to discuss it.' She had never been heard to snub anybody. She just diverted you, in all senses. There was often method in her conversational madness. Not always, but often.

Eleanor wondered, not for the first time, how much of Melissa's dottiness was camouflage. Camouflage hiding what? Aware that her thought was banal, Eleanor remarked to herself that one knew nobody as well as one thought one did.

Nearly two years after Melissa's wedding, Lord Kendall had a long letter from his son in America. The news was that Dick was getting married. Ralph hoped his father would feel up to the journey; in any case they expected Melissa and Simon. The wedding was to be in Cambridge, Massachusetts, where the bride's family lived. Helen's father was Professor Frank Denniston, an orientalist of international reputation. She herself had just completed her PhD at Harvard. She was a beautiful and cultured girl, and in every way a perfect match for Dick. Distance must not be allowed to deter the people at Sterney. Cambridge was as big a trip from California, for Ralph and Beth and their daughters, as it was from England. A warm welcome in Cambridge was promised to Dick's English family, in the houses of friends.

Ralph wrote to Melissa in the same terms. Dick wrote to his grandfather and to Melissa. The wedding was to be at the beginning of September.

It was difficult to picture Dick married – Gregory Peck, with stoop and horn-rims. He was so very serious. It was difficult to imagine him dancing, courting, kissing, but, to become betrothed, he must presumably have done these things. Melissa said his proposal was probably in Latin.

Eleanor knew what they meant. But she thought that, if she had been ten years younger, Dick might have done very well for her.

It was out of the question that Simon should go. A tenant farm was being taken in hand, and all sort of problems arose. The tenant was retiring. He was moving with his wife to a cottage on the coast. His sons were far away and otherwise engaged.

After long discussions with the accountants, and with lawyers expert in predicting changes in landlord-tenant legislation, Lord Kendall and his agent agreed to bring the farm under central management. Staff had to be engaged, stock bought, buildings and fences patched, drains cleared. Simon could perhaps get away for a long weekend, but it made no sense to fly to Boston for seventy-two hours.

Lord Kendall was tempted. He had never been to America. The fall in New England was said to be very beautiful. Ralph was his heir and Dick his grandson, and he regretted losing any chance of contact with them. But the doctor shook his head. A grandfather in a state of collapse would not add gaiety to Dick's wedding feast.

Somebody had to go, and it had to be Melissa.

She utterly refused to go without Simon. They had not spent one night apart since the wedding. Travelling alone was horrible, and she had done too much of it. The people at the wedding would all be the way Dick was and Helen sounded. She could stand it, but not without support.

It was confirmed to Eleanor that Melissa really had dropped anchor. She was deeply reluctant to head out into the open sea again. Although she had spent so long there, it was as though she was now frightened.

She was unusually serious, piling up reasons, barricading herself behind excuses.

Eleanor would have liked to suggest herself as the family representative at the wedding, if somebody would pay her fare. She could not do so. She could not colourably represent the Kendalls. Beth, in particular, would not be flattered by such an arrangement. Eleanor saw that it was impossible, and kept silent; she saw that she was losing her one faint chance of ever seeing America.

They all had a go at Melissa. It took Simon, of course, to persuade her in the end. The decision taken, she was efficient and economical about the bookings and her necessary shopping. Just before she went, she spent the whole day in the tree-house and the whole night in Simon's arms.

Simon met Melissa at Heathrow. She ran to him, dropping her bags, and embraced him passionately.

She said, 'I've missed you unbearably. I never would have

gone if I'd known how much I'd miss you. I reached out in the middle of the night and you weren't there. I nearly died. Never again.'

She hugged him again, twining round him, childlike. Simon was suddenly and unnervingly reminded of her desperate hugs when the news of her parents' death came to Sterney.

'It's just as well you weren't there,' she said in the car. 'You wouldn't have been amused. I was only a little bit amused, and only when things went wrong. I don't mean to sound snide or ungrateful. They were terribly welcoming. It was embarrassing, actually. I was made to feel like a VIP, like the queen. They have these formidable formal manners. I quite like it, actually, it's old-fashioned and stately, like a minuet. What's the very slow one? A pavane. Their manners are like a pavane. But it all goes on too long. "Will you sit here, Mrs Collis?" That's all you need to say, when you're dotting people round a dinner table. But they make it into *Gone with the Wind*. Exhausting. I've never been exhausted by courtesy before. Everything was immoderate, except the drinking. That was *very* moderate. The conversation was immoderate. They're nice people. The people I stayed with were nice. They wanted to know what I did. They really wanted to know. I said I looked after you. They said *what else*? Was I *realising my potential*? I said that was exactly what I was doing. Potentially, I said, I was very good at looking after you, and I was doing my best to realise my potential. They thought it was a joke. They laughed in a grown-up way. They thought I was a card. There's a word I've never used before. I didn't know I knew it. Oh darling, what joy to see you and touch you.'

'Careful about touching me,' said Simon, 'when I'm overtaking a lorry.'

'Foul clod. Have you missed me?'

'I can't tell you how much.'

'Try.'

'I reached out in the middle of the night,' quoted Simon, 'and you weren't there, and I nearly died. The dogs reached out too, and you weren't there, and *they* nearly died. That was almost the worst bit.'

'There is much in your reply that is original, M'sieur,' said Melissa, 'and much that is good. But that which is good is not original, and that which is original is not good.'

66

'I've never heard you quote Voltaire before.'

'I wasn't quoting Voltaire. I've never quoted Voltaire. I've never read Voltaire. That's a lie. Forgive me for lying to you, darling. There is much of any epigram which is good, and none which is original. Shall I tell you about the wedding?'

'Start at the beginning, and move very slowly towards the end.'

'Yes. And while I'm doing so, move very quickly towards Sterney. The beginning. What was the beginning?'

'Your flight.'

'Best forgotten. Dick met me. I didn't recognize him. He was utterly disguised. He was wearing a baseball cap. Incongruous. Like Bertrand Russell in a skid-lid. Like me in a bowler.'

'I've often seen you in a bowler.'

'Hunting, yes. As incongruous as that. So eventually we made contact, when everybody else had left the airport. So he took me to the residence of Professor and Mrs Clumps.'

'Impossible.'

'I swear. Tumps. Tombs. *Graves.* Professor and Mrs Graves. They were sweet. They had a gracious guest-room. There's a sampler over the bed. You won't believe the next bit.'

Simon grinned, waiting for the next bit. He was driving as fast as he dared, because he wanted to make love to his wife.

'The sampler,' said Melissa, 'says "East West, Home's Best".'

'Telegraphic sampler.'

'Just what I said to myself. At least, I would have, if I'd thought of it. It was worked by Mrs Graves's great-grand-mother, when she was a slip of a girl. So we went out to dinner with Dick's bride's family. More professors than you could shake a stick at. Uncle Ralph's a professor, some of the time. What's the collective word for professors? Same like a charm of goldfinches?'

Simon pondered, smiling as he drove. He would get the full story in the end. Meanwhile these byways were fun.

'A colloquy of professors,' he suggested.

'They did colloque. They were very polite. They laughed at each other's jokes. That could only have been out of polite-ness. A cackle of professors. So I met Helen.'

'So?'

'Young. Pretty. Dark. Learned. Priggish. Votes the straight Democratic ticket.'

'I wouldn't know what that implied.'

'Nor did I. The others explained. It means priggish. The ones who explained said that what they did was vote the straight Republican ticket, so I daresay they're prejudiced. She's the kind of girl who only laughs at in-jokes. You know. You have to understand fluent Neapolitan in order to understand the joke. Or you have to know your Sophocles. Or you have to know why Doctor Thing was suddenly dismissed as President of Whoosis College. She laughed like anything at all those jokes. I managed a sort of tolerant smile.'

'I wouldn't have managed even that.'

'Nor did I, after a bit. So Helen thought I was an ignorant degenerate. But there. We can't be all things to all brides.'

'She sounds just the job for Dick.'

'Badly put, but true. I tremble to think of their children. I tremble to think of their efforts to conceive children. The mind boggles.'

'Did he propose in Latin?'

'No,' said Melissa with certainty. 'She proposed. She proposed in medieval Portuguese. So then there was the wedding. It was more what I expected than I expected. They're Episcopalians, like in Scotland. The reception started off like a reception, but it turned into quite a different party. I sat on the bride's father's right hand, only I wasn't supposed to, so I had to move. It was lucky, because I was hurting his hand. They all went on being very nice. They went out of their way to be nice to me. They went *miles* out of their way. So I didn't mind it during the day. But I hated it during the night. Darling love, don't let me leave you again.'

They reached home, and locked the door, and their clothes fell off them like autumn leaves. Simon was moved as never before. Familiarity had bred unity, ever-deepening need. A ten-day separation recreated honeymoon. Melissa wept long and happily on Simon's shoulder. She kept touching and clutching him, as though to be sure he was really there, that she had really come home to him.

She said, 'I bet that's done it.'

'Done what?'

'Started something. I feel it. It was absolutely special. Extra magic. I'm sure of it. What a good beginning for a new life, a moment of such bliss. Kindled in absolute happiness. Tomorrow I shall suffer from morning sickness.'

She did not, then or later; but as to the rest she was absolutely right.

CHAPTER 4

It was no great coincidence that, almost simultaneously with the conception of the twins, things came right for Helen and Dick for the first time. They had been married five days. They were between the lavendar-scented sheets of a small, excellent hotel in rural Ontario. The five days had seen a dozen attempts, during which the husband had cursed his inexperience, and the wife had made a sincere and conscious effort to rise above, or sink below, her virginal modesty. It took her five days to start feeling unselfconscious; it took him five days to get the hang of timing things.

Their lives were immediately richer, their affection stronger, their honeymoon enjoyable. Helen had begun to feel that an awful lot of fuss was made about these undignified callisthenics. She changed her mind about that.

They talked about it, analysed it. Where they had gone wrong, where they had at last gone so beautifully right. Lessons for the future. Possible experiments. Helen was pleased to find herself sexy, to be marvellously normal. Dick was happy at her happiness and at his own. They told each other so. Between them there were no forbidden areas. They might strike some people as an old-fashioned couple in some ways, but they were pretty modern in others. They were modern in their decision to postpone starting a family for at least two years, so that Helen could continue undisturbed the studies which would qualify her to collaborate with Dick on his first book.

They were both glad, Helen as glad as Dick, that Melissa had made it to the wedding. Professor and Mrs Graves had loved having her – they found her original, enchanting, a delight. She had put Professor Graves in mind of Lovelace and Herrick, Mrs Graves in mind of Watteau and Fragonard. They had looked at pictures of Sterney, in one of their big books on architecture, and seen how Melissa matched her context. They said all this to Helen, there at the wedding party. It made Helen want to know Melissa better, to understand the product of an environment which shared a common culture with her own but practically nothing else. Helen wanted to see the pictures of Sterney, but they were in the Graves's house at the other end of Cambridge. Helen was intellectually curious, as a student of the history of civilization, as a student of the effect of environment on psychology.

She was curious because she knew very well where Dick stood in the Sterney succession.

Helen was able to indulge some of her curiosity when they came over for the Christening of the twins.

She met Melissa's husband and his family. She saw that Ralph was right, Beth wrong, about that marriage. Her own background – the household of an under-rewarded academic – was a lot closer to Sterney Vicarage than to Beth's family's Californian ranch-style palace. She felt perfectly at ease in the Vicarage, at ease with Eleanor and her father. She got Dick to see things her way. He seemed pretty nearly convinced.

She was stunned by Sterney. She never had got to see the pictures in the Graves's book, and nothing had prepared her for such beauty. The very incongruity of a Palladian villa in an English landscape lent an extra dimension of magic.

She was fascinated by old Lord Kendall's account of Herbert, Isobel, Melissa. It stimulated reconsideration of the old heredity-environment debate. She was fascinated by Melissa's childish attempt at non-verbal communication, having seen similar attempts, by seriously disturbed people, in the psychology textbooks. She was pretty fascinated by Lord Kendall. She had never met an old-style English aristocrat on his own ground – only her father-in-law, who was *déraciné* and even *déclassé*, and Melissa, who was *sui generis*. Helen kept being surprised by her own surprise that she was married to the grandson of this *grand seigneur*.

The flying visit for the old Lord's funeral would have been impossibly extravagant; but Dick's parents paid for the tickets. It was a good thing to have done, for all sorts of reasons. Renewing friendships. Showing sympathy, concern. Lightening grief by sharing it. Observing another untouched, antique English ritual. Observing how a person born to it managed being mistress of Sterney.

Brief as the visit was, Helen took a lot of valuable lessons home with her to New Hampshire.

Ralph, Lord Kendall de Sterney, did not use his title in America. He was sufficiently known, in the world that mattered to him, by the name he had used all his life. Beth sometimes used the title. She had a perfect right to. A lot of people said 'Kendall *dee* Sterney.'

It was still possible to dress the twins identically: especially as, on the brilliant June afternoon of their first birthday party, they wore very little.

The party took place on the Sterney lawn, half in the shade of the cedar tree and half in the sun. Idle fish were making rings in the lake, over which hung gently revolving clouds of small insects. The fantail pigeons cooed continually from the dovecote; on its roof a succession of male birds, chests thrust out and broad tails trailing, stalked after a succession of the slenderer females, who felt or feigned reluctance. Melissa's silky bantams, recently introduced, skirted the edge of the birthday party, hoping for bits of cake. When a cock crowed, Peter crowed. When a hen clucked, Pandora clucked. Melissa's dogs, labrador and lurcher and Peke, sniffed the tails of the bantams as though they thought the bantams were dogs. The bantams ignored them. Above, at the tip of one of the drooping branches of the cedar, a pair of goldfinches had built; they went to and fro feeding their clamorous chicks.

There were two guests of the twins' generation, all the babies that could be locally recruited. One was Charles Watkins, firstborn of Tommy and Barbara in the village, nine months old and fretful. The other was Nicholas Montgomery, nearly two and perilously mobile. Charles had been brought by his mother, who sprawled on the grass with Melissa and the children. Nicholas had been brought by his nanny, for whom a chair had been carried out.

The Montgomerys had taken the Dower House, after it had stood empty most of the winter. It could have been sold, for a fair price, many times over, but Ralph Kendall was not about to break up an estate of which he regarded himself trustee. It was difficult to let because Ralph at first refused to consider more than a one-year renewable lease. Simon saw the point of this, but he also saw that nobody was going to finish redecorating the house with the risk of being out after a twelvemonth. Ralph and his lawyers were finally persuaded to cede this point, and Gregor and Rosie Montgomery had signed a thirty-year lease. Gregor was himself a solicitor, junior partner of a firm in Milchester. He had no wish to buy because he was due to inherit. Unlike the proverbial lawyer who dies intestate with his affairs in a muddle, Gregor looked after himself with anxious care. There was nothing wrong with that. There was nothing wrong with him, except that he dismantled the tree-house on the grounds of danger to his children. There was nothing wrong with Rosie except for what she had done to the inside of the Dower House, redoing even the rooms which Melissa had finished. Their two other children were too old for the twins' party. Rosie kept them at home, trying all the time to get them out into the sun.

The twins' cake had been designed by Melissa. It was two cakes, joined together and then iced as though they were one cake – a figure-of-eight cake, such as nobody had ever seen before. Melissa and the Sterney cook had together done the icing, Melissa making the cook laugh so much that some of the piping round the sides was a mess.

The twins seemed agreeable to having guests. They stared at Charles Watkins when he cried, as though the sound were strange to them. They sat on the ground side by side, their chubby legs stretched out in front of them. It had become automatic for Melissa and the nurse to place them so. It was natural; it was what they liked. They were pretty stable. They pushed one another, but so gently that neither keeled over. They made various noises, addressed to the bantams and dogs and people. It was often possible to interpret the noises – they wanted things they were not being offered, or did not want things they were being offered. They were not strident when demanding things, nor shrill when rejecting them. Perhaps this was because they were used to being given everything they wanted, and having nothing forced on them they did not want. They seemed to communicate with one another, as the dogs and bantams did. Melissa claimed they called up to the goldfinches, who called back; Barbara Watkins and Nanny Montgomery thought this was fanciful.

Barbara would have liked to believe that her own Charles was more beautiful than the twins. Even her besotted eye could not send her brain this message. Nanny Montgomery thought the twins were too beautiful. Peter would end up a popinjay, Pandora a vain little madam. There was no danger of that with Nicholas.

Simon came home early, to catch the end of the party. He threw himself on the ground, kissed Melissa, and prodded each of the twins by way of greeting. The twins gurgled. Peter reached out a hand, and after a moment of groping grabbed Simon's left ear. At the same moment – as though they had planned it – Pandora grabbed his right ear. They thought this was the best game ever invented. Simon howled, in pretended agony. The twins howled back, in purest joy.

Nanny Montgomery frowned. Already the twins were being petted and indulged. Nanny knew what that led to. It was not doing a favour to a child to spoil it. It was like giving it too much rich food – it did harm for life.

Dick's and Helen's secret life, once fairly launched between those lavender-scented sheets, continued satisfactorily. Helen's studies also continued satisfactorily. She was able to believe, and to say to Dick, that each enriched the other: by studying she earned her joy; by understanding the essence of physical love, by participating fully in its ancient rituals, she could better appreciate the great corpus of art which had love as its referrent.

She was awarded her doctorate in the summer of 1961; after debating the matter with Dick, she abandoned the pill. She felt ready for the fulfilment of motherhood. Ralph needed a grandson. She conceived within days of the distant twins' first birthday party. As soon as she knew she went on a careful diet, and Dick gave up smoking his pipe around the house.

In private, Helen stroked her stomach and said, 'The seventh Baron Kendall de Sterney.'

The twins had two methods of locomotion. They crawled, or they crossed the ground on their behinds. Both were normal. Most children, said the nurse, preferred one or the other, but the twins liked both. They could achieve remarkable speeds by either method. It was assumed that they imitated one another – took cues from one another. At any rate, it was noticed that although they were both equally adroit at both means of getting along, when one crawled the other always crawled. And usually they started at the same moment.

Eleanor said that, since they were subjected to the identical stimuli, they naturally responded in the same way. Anything that triggered Peter into wanting to crawl across a room would have exactly the same effect on Pandora. It would have been surprising, said Eleanor, if they had not done the same things at the same time.

Melissa thought there was more to it than that.

The saloons at Sterney were full of fragile objects. Melissa and Simon, caretaking for Ralph, had as much responsibility for them as for the roof of the house. The twins were not debarred from these rooms. On the contrary, they were frequent and welcome invaders. They would, there as else-where, suddenly explode into high-speed movement. Had they gone in opposite directions – one towards the rosewood table with the collection of patch-boxes on it, one towards the glass-topped case containing the scarabs – then anyone alone with them would have had the greatest difficulty fielding both before calamities occurred. But they went in the same direction; they went together. They were after the same objective – cushion, dog-basket, stuffed toy. Having reached it they shared it.

Eleanor explained it all with great commonsense.

Eleanor herself was alone with them, one dark afternoon in October, in their day-nursery. Melissa had taken the nurse to the dentist in Milchester, and Eleanor had gladly agreed to sit with the twins. There was a nice little fire behind the heavy nursery fireguard in the grate; somebody would bring tea. These were both unaccustomed luxuries to Eleanor: at the Vicarage they only had open fires when they entertained, and when tea was produced Eleanor produced it. And it was still a delight, always a delight, to be with the twins. They were sunny-tempered beyond any children Eleanor had known, and her social work brought her into contact with hundreds. They were no trouble that afternoon. They sat quietly, side by side on the floor by the sofa, sharing a rag-book with an air – two identical airs – of understanding the pictures. Eleanor glanced up often from her own book.

She glanced up, and saw that for the first time the twins were on their feet. Both of them. They had pulled themsleves up, simultaneously, by the flounce of the nursery sofa, and turned away from it to face her. They took a few experimental steps towards her, and collapsed in a pile together.

It was startling, until Eleanor thought about it sensibly. They had been born within seconds of one another; they had had an identical diet for the sixteen months of their lives; they were at exactly the same stage of physical and mental development; they were seeing the same objects, which had the same message for them. What more natural than that their first steps should be taken at the same time?

Melissa was sad to have missed this great leap forward. The next few weeks made up for it.

In April Helen had a son, called Ralph Francis after his grandfathers. Melissa sent a telegram, and followed that with a silver cream-jug which she had had engraved with the initials R.F.K. under the coronet and crest which the first Kendall of Sterney had bought from the College of Arms.

From Ralph a photograph arrived – cabinet-sized, suitable for framing – of mother and baby. Helen stared dreamily at her baby, and the baby looked like a baby.

'There's no reason he shouldn't be very handsome,' said Melissa. 'By Gregory Peck out of that solemn little bird.'

'Having a baby might make her less solemn,' said Simon. 'Having babies has made you much less solemn.'

'I know. It's awful. My studies abandoned. I hardly ever read Schoppenhauer any more. I will *not* go to the Christening, unless you come, and probably not even then. I want to be here when the twins start talking. From the way they've been gargling recently, I should think that'd be pretty soon.

Very educated gargles. Actually I think they gargle in French.'

'Dada,' said Simon.

'That's not French. That's Russian. Russian for "Yes yes". Also a silly lot of painters.'

'It's what all babies say first. It's well known.'

'I bet ours don't. I bet they say something light but penetrating.'

Peter's first words, a month before his second birthday, was 'Pa'. He was not talking to his father. He was talking to his sister. He was aiming at 'Pandora'.

Pandora's first word came back at him, in immediate reply. It was 'Pee'. This was not a rude and precocious reference to a natural function. She was trying to say 'Peter'.

They learned fast after that. They were undoubtedly precocious. They speeded one another up. This was not apparently rivalry, but because they passed to each other whatever they learned. It was almost as though they shared the task of collecting new words, and pooled the result.

They began to sing. From birth they had been surrounded by music, because their parents listened to so much. It had gone in through their pores. Now it came out again, songs with and without words, solos and duets.

Melissa introduced them to the piano, and encouraged them to strum. They loved it. Neither ever wanted to do it alone. They sat side by side on the piano stool, sometimes playing antiphonally, as though having a musical conversation. They would start lessons as soon as they were old enough.

They were still amazingly alike, and amazingly like Melissa. They had her eyes, her hair, her heart-shaped face with the broad brow tapering to the little pointed chin. There was a photograph of Melissa, taken at Sterney when she was about two, sitting under the cedar-tree where the twins so often were. Either of the twins could have been the subject of that picture. Nobody could see anything of Simon in them. Nobody could tell their voices apart, when they talked or laughed or sang. Strangers did not know which was boy and which girl, and even people who knew them well found it easy to confuse them.

They had accepted the need for occasional, brief, necessary separations. They had to be brief, and they had to be necessary, or the twins would not accept them. Had separation been forced on them, they would have shown an ill temper and a misery of which they were normally miraculously free. Everybody understood this; everybody was touched. The twins were together for practically every minute of their waking and sleeping hours. Even the Montgomerys' nanny said it was sweet to see two little people so attached to one another.

Eleanor showed Melissa a magazine article about twins. Somebody had been researching them. It seemed there were identical twins, separated at birth, brought up by different families at a great distance, who in middle age had the same jobs and interests and had given their children and dogs the same names.

The twins were listening too, with close attention. Eleanor took it that the conversation was over their heads.

'But my twins aren't identical,' said Melissa.

'Yes we are,' said Peter.

Pandora nodded vehement agreement.

Eleanor did not think they knew what 'identical' meant.

Christmas; the twins two and a half. In the nursery and in the garden they could still wear the same clothes – the classless, unisex children's clothes of the time – but for a Sterney Christmas they had to be quite different, for the parties that had to be given, for the show that had to be put on. Melissa had expected problems about this, but there were none. Pandora liked her party frock, Peter his trousers and ruffled shirt. Each had been present when the clothes had been chosen for the other; each had approved. It was as important, at least to the twins, that Peter liked Pandora's frock as that she liked it; that she liked his frilly shirt. Nor did Peter make a fuss when his hair was cut. The twins' abundant corn-coloured hair – Melissa's hair – was almost to their shoulders. Peter was therefore moderately shorn, to what the hairdresser called a 'Mick Jagger'. Beyond insisting that Pandora came with them to the hairdresser, Peter made no objection. He knew he was a man. Pandora knew she was a woman. They knew they were different. It was as though they had discussed the matter, and accepted that they were different. They no longer claimed to be identical.

Clothes apart, Peter's haircut apart, they were identical.

Simon still found the Christmas party for the estate staff an ordeal. They had to have it. The families expected it and enjoyed it. It was a tradition which could on no account be allowed to lapse. Simon knew from Christmas parties in the Army – from parties in sergeants' messes and corporals' clubs and cookhouses – that it was perfectly possible for an officer to be relaxed and casual with his men, without losing authority. It ought to have been no more difficult at Sterney. It was more difficult. In the Army his position had been legitimate. It might be because of luck, of the accident of birth and education and accent, but his rank was gazetted, official, unquestionable. Not so at Sterney. All the staff knew that he was no less a salaried servant than themselves. And he was Melissa's consort.

You had to forget you were the boss without ever forgetting it. You had to pretend you were not an imposter in Sterney Court, when it was impossible to forget that you were one. You had to impersonate a much-loved man who was dead, or a man nobody knew very well who was six thousand miles away.

The twins were no more bothered by any of this than Melissa was. They had belonged to Sterney, and Sterney to them, since they were five months old. Many of the older estate staff called them 'Master Peter' and 'Miss Pandora'. (Melissa, married five and a half years, was still often called 'Miss Melissa'.) This was the first Christmas party to which they could make a real contribution, and they made one. They said hullo to everybody, getting names hilariously muddled. There was competition for their attention – adults made funny faces, and little boys shouted and showed off. The twins smiled at these efforts to impress them. They did not shriek with laughter, as the comics hoped. They were not aloof, or kept in cotton-wool. They joined in the games; they rushed round with the other children, becoming as scarlet and tousled as the rest. There were guessing games, conducted as for the last half-dozen years by Eleanor. It was expected that the twins would be outstanding in their age-group, being so bright and precocious, having such parents. They did unexpectedly badly.

Eleanor was startled to realise – to be suddenly and almost totally convinced – that the twins did badly on purpose. She knew very well that the twins were cleverer than they were letting themselves seem. Were they bashful about being quicker, about having larger vocabularies? They were not bashful about anything else, as far as Eleanor knew. They were not afraid of the limelight – they were used to it, they liked it; they had always had, perhaps, too much of it. It could only be generosity. They needed the little prizes less than the estate children did. And, loved as they were, they did not need to prove anything to anybody. It was extremely difficult to believe, of children of that age; but Eleanor was forced to believe it.

There was one unfortunate moment, observed, luckily, by few. A child of three, a noisy, clumsy but not ill-natured little boy, kicked Pandora on the ankle as he was rushing past. It was not intentional. Pandora was hurt. Her face went pinched; pink, then pale. She did not cry but she came very near it. Peter, without any hesitation, kicked the boy as hard as he could, also on the ankle. The little boy roared and rushed to his mother. It was understood that Peter was avenging his sister. Probably he had kicked harder than he meant. It was right that he should defend his sister – plucky and sporting of him – but he overdid the kick in the heat of the moment. You could not be cross with a toddler of that age kicking a bit harder than he should have.

Neither Simon nor Melissa saw the little flare-up. Probably they would never hear about it.

All the children were tired by now. Families were beginning to collect their things and leave. Peter and Pandora said goodbye to them all, with their parents. They said goodbye to the boy Peter had kicked, with a comic little air of grave politeness.

Spring. At Sterney the far side of the lake was frothed with daffodils, and the wild cherries with blossom. Eleanor made time to go often to the Court, to take the twins for walks. She taught them the names of flowers and trees and birds; she taught them to recognize birds by their songs. Perhaps because they were musical, they were particularly quick at that, very soon distinguishing birds with similar songs – willow warblers and chaffinches, chiff-chaffs and great tits, blackbirds and song-thrushes.

Eleanor wanted them to start collections of pressed wild flowers; she would give them an album each, and sheets of blotting-paper; they could press the flowers under piles of books on the nursery table. At the end of the year, Eleanor said, she would give a prize to the one with the best book.

'One book for flowers, Aunt Eleanor,' said Peter.

Pandora nodded. 'We'll do it together.'

'Not pick so many flowers,' said Peter.

'We both get the prize,' said Pandora.

They were interested in wildflowers; but they were not at all interested in rivalry.

Pandora could not quite get her tongue round the 'ch' sound. She talked about 'taffintes' and 'tiff-taffs'. Peter took to doing so too, though he could if he wanted say 'cheese' and 'choose' quite normally. It was as though, having accepted differences between themselves in some regards, they would not accept differences in others; or as though Peter did not want Pandora to suffer in comparison with himself, even in so tiny a matter.

They were growing fast.

Their nurse, who still adored them, reported freely and frequently to Melissa. This was almost unnecessary, as Melissa saw a great deal of her children. The nurse also confided in Eleanor, for whose good sense she had a high regard; anyway, it gave her a change to talk about her favourite subject. The nurse told Eleanor that, when the twins were dressing up for anything special, they scrutinised one another like sergeant-majors before a ceremonial parade. As though they were so passionately proud of one another, as Eleanor understood it, that neither could bear to see any inadvertent lowering of standards in the other; as though they were committed to upholding a joint standard, impeccable, before the world. Neither, said the nurse, would go downstairs before staring at the other; neither would go before being stared at by the other, and, it seemed, passed fit.

They asked a great many questions. They absorbed

knowledge like sponges. They looked at pictures in books. Sometimes they shared a book; more often they looked at separate books. They constantly asked to be read to, almost any books, on any subjects. Very often, what they heard must have gone clean over their heads. Often things made them laugh inexplicably. Always if one laughed, both did. To see the two of them bursting with laughter was moving and delightful. They preferred their mother to read them stories, because she put on so many different funny voices. They preferred Eleanor to read to them about facts. They did not so much like being read to by their nurse, who had a flat voice with a Midlands accent. Eleanor thought that, being so musical, they found the nurse's voice monotonous and ugly. Neither Eleanor nor the twins ever said this.

They grew up surrounded by music. Melissa still took the Radio Three concerts with her wherever she went, and Simon usually put something on the record player the moment he got home. The twins asked for, and got, their own record player in the nursery. They were given nursery-rhyme records. They listened to them attentively, and asked for records like Daddy's. The nurse did her ironing to Schubert, which was not what she would have chosen. This was one aspect of the twins' development which was outside Eleanor's understanding.

Like most children who have newly discovered speech, they were very talkative, to all other people and to one another. But their nurse told Eleanor that they never seemed to speak to each other when they were alone together. The nurse could not be sure about this, obviously, but it was the way it struck her.

Eleanor, interested in everything about the twins, asked them about this.

'We talk a lot,' said Peter. 'Pandora talks too much.'

Pandora laughed. 'Peter's a tatterbox,' she said.

Already they had learned Melissa's trick of evading questions.

Photographs arrived of Ralph Francis Kendall's first birthday party. A letter from Helen, enclosing them, said what a pity it was that the twins could not have been there.

It seemed that Melissa was right – Ralph was a beautiful child.

'Fancy,' said the twins' nurse, who knew exactly who was who in the family. 'One day that scrap will be Lord Kendall de Sterney. Every stick and stone and every blade of grass will belong to him.'

The twins studied the photographs of little Ralph.

The weather was once again glorious for the twins' own birthday party, which was therefore held part in the shade of the cedar tree, part in the sunshine. There were a dozen children. Melissa had organized a treasure-hunt. Eleanor, whom nothing would have kept away, was startled once again by the oddity she had seen at Christmas. The twins deliberately let another child win the treasure-hunt. They could certainly have done so themselves. They could run faster and think quicker than any of the others, and they had local knowledge. It seemed that the awareness that they could have won was enough for them.

It was now obvious to Eleanor that the twins were 'gifted children', in the specialised educational sense. She wondered where the money would come from to educate them to their full tremendous potential. The elder Ralph still paid all the basic bills at Sterney, but it was not reasonable to expect him to pay school fees too.

Melissa collapsed in happy exhaustion after the twins' guests had all been taken away. The twins, who had covered miles, were not exhausted at all. They talked at high speed about the games, the tea, their presents, the other children. Melissa said excitement would keep them chattering all night. Their nurse was sure that, though they were awake all night, they would not talk to one another.

The success of the little party, and perhaps a glass of wine two hours earlier than usual, had Melissa in holiday spirits. She sang to Simon from her dressing table; he was having a bath before dressing for dinner in the sea-green bathroom off the bedroom and his dressing-room. Melissa came in to talk to him. Suddenly she peeled off all her own clothes and joined him in the bath. She screamed when she leaned back against the hot tap. At thirty her figure was perfect and her skin flawless.

'I don't know which is worse,' she said, lathering Simon's

toes. 'The hot tap being so hot or the cold tap being so cold. Like Christopher Robin saying his prayers. If I was any happier I'd explode.'

Half an hour later they were lying on their bathtowels on top of the great bed. Their hair was still wet but the rest of them was dry. Melissa snuggled up against Simon.

She said into his neck, 'Watch it. Countdown. I'm going to explode. Miracles keep happening. How did you come to be so clever? I believe it's happened again. I feel just like when I came back from America. I've been waiting for that for the past year. I want a daughter called Sarsaparilla. Have you ever drunk it? I never have. I never heard of it until today. I read about it. It's made out of a plant called Smilax. I'm going to have a daughter called Smilax.'

Simon never knew how Melissa knew. Nobody did. She did not know herself. But once again she was right. They were overjoyed.

The baby, its reality once confirmed, was referred to as Smilax, even by the twins.

Smilax gave no trouble. Melissa felt great, all that autumn and winter. She was glad that when she was vast the weather would still be cold; but sorry that Smilax would not all at once be able to lie about on the lawn.

Melissa found a first pony for the twins. Simon said it was absurdly soon, but Melissa showed him a photograph of herself, completely naked except for a hat, at the age of two, sitting on a Shetland pony and holding the reins. Somebody else was holding the reins too, but Melissa in the photograph radiated confidence.

'I didn't know you'd been a nude model,' said Simon.

'Only an equestrian nude model. I'm not nude. My head is decently covered.'

The new pony was another Shetland, a tubby, hairy skewbald gelding called Pooter. Pooter was a huge and immediate success; after a week it was hard to believe that the twins had only been riding for a week. But after six weeks it was clear that the twins had already outgrown him. Melissa found a sturdy New Forest, a dark bay called Daisy. At the same time she found a miniature trap and a second-hand set of harness (the harness somewhat more expensive than the trap). Pooter was harnessed and put to the trap. His sharp, bouncy, indefatigable trot was far better suited to pulling something than to the saddle. The twins learned to drive as quickly as they had learned to ride. They went out together, one in the trap and one on Daisy, changing places constantly, while Melissa wobbled behind them on an elderly bicycle.

Melissa herself often drove the trap into the village, the twins squeezed beside her. The turn-out became a familiar and popular sight. Pooter was well up to pulling Melissa and the twins. The saving on petrol, said Melissa, would more than make up for the cost of ponies, trap and harness.

The twins cleaned Daisy's tack and Pooter's harness, covering themselves with saddle soap and brass polish. In February they helped Melissa repaint the trap – green, with yellow wheels picked out in red. Together they took over feeding Melissa's bantams, who scuttled across the stable-yard when they heard the corn rattling in the scoop. They fed the fantails, who descended in a white cloud when they heard the same noise under the dovecote, and settled on the twins' heads and shoulders. It was nice to see how amicably the twins shared these enjoyable chores – shared the fun, the labour, and the credit for their labour. They chattered continuously to Melissa and to one another. Nobody knew for sure whether they still chattered when they were alone together.

The baby was born in March. Mysteriously, immediately, he was given the name William. But the prenatal code-name stuck. He was Smilax, and then Smiler.

Simon took the twins to see Melissa and Smiler, in the same room in the same hospital. There was no doubting their excitement and delight.

In June Smiler was christened, by his grandfather, a few days before the twins' fourth birthday. People said how beautifully the twins behaved, and – though their clothes and hairstyles were completely different – how uncannily alike they still were. The leftovers from the Christening party were more than adequate for the twins' birthday tea.

Much use was made, all that summer, of Daisy and Pooter.

Sylvia the girl groom went with the twins, exercising Melissa's horse, because Melissa was more inclined in the hot weather to lie about on the lawn with Smiler. Of course the ridden animals could go where the trap could not. Whichever twin was in the trap was content to see the other disappear over fields or into coverts, far out of sight. Sylvia was surprised at the eagerness with which either, riding, left the driver road-bound. They really seemed to welcome a half-hour's separation. It was not because they got on one another's nerves, or for any reason of that kind. It was as though it was necessary to them – an almost daily necessity, a duty: it was as though, young as they were, they were preparing themselves for the much longer and more distant separations of the future, as a person who knows he is going blind will walk about with eyes closed to prepare himself for a permanent darkness.

When the weather was good, Smiler had his afternoon sleep in his pram on the lawn. The twins had to be quiet when they went near the cedar tree or the Chinese bridge, because if Smiler was woken up he never went to sleep again. When the weather was bad, Smiler had a cot in the day-nursery, where the nurse could keep an eye on his necessary slumbers. This barred music, even played softly. It barred strumming on the grand piano in the hall. It barred the twins from doing anything except sitting very quietly with picture books.

Melissa rarely read to the twins now. Since Smiler's birth she was more easily tired; she nearly always had a nap in the early evening, so as to be fresh and bright for Simon at dinner-time. Her nap coincided with the twins' bed-time, which was when she had usually read to them. Their nurse was busier, with another set of clothes to wash and mend, and presently another mouth to feed. Eleanor, aware of all this, came as often as she could; but it was not as often as she would have liked: not as often as the twins would have liked.

They were avid to learn to read for themselves. But they were very young; and nobody had time to teach them until they went to school.

News came that Dick and Helen Kendall had had another child: a daughter, Cathy, born in August. The predictable sheaf of gigantic photographs arrived in a stiffened envelope. The twins scrutinised the pictures of Cathy, without comment.

Smiler smiled at the pictures. He smiled at everything. He wanted to tear them up. He wanted to tear everything up. He tore up, smiling, a drawing Pandora had done of a bantam hen and her chicks. There was no ill will in his destruction of the drawing, and Pandora showed no ill will. She did a drawing of Smiler, smiling, and pinned it to the wall in the nursery. The nurse was mildly surprised that she had pinned it not at the top, but through the middle: through Smiler's middle in the drawing.

That autumn the twins did start at nursery school. They had poster-paints, percussion instruments, wooden alphabets. They were avid for everything that was put in front of them. They distinguished letters; they learned their sounds; they understood, faster than any of the other children of their age, how letters in combination made words. When they began to write the letters they had learned, their writing was identical. They showed a competitiveness in lessons which they had not shown in party games or treasure hunts.

They were immediately joint leaders of a gang, by dint of being tall, strong and clever. Perhaps their leadership was the more automatic because they were the children of the Sterney Court family. It was an amiable gang, given to singing. There was never any doubt about who should choose the gang's songs, lead its games, or decide what recruits should be admitted to membership. The twins did these things jointly. As between themselves, there was no visible leadership. It appeared that they reached every tiny decision jointly.

A tubby little boy called Timothy Haslam teased Pandora for saying 'teese' instead of 'cheese'. He went on and on about it, as small children will who have invented a joke or discovered a weakness. He had a fall during break from the climbing frame in the playground. Falling among the clamped tubes of the frame, he broke an arm and his jaw. It was never clear how the accident happened. One little girl said that Peter was by when Timothy fell, but it was proved that this was impossible. The teachers went into the matter most anxiously. Peter was with Pandora, listening to a story at the other end of the playground. He must have been, because –

before he could have had a chance to talk to Pandora – he correctly reported the story. He must have been there, listening to it. Nobody could remember which children were there and which elsewhere, but Peter could remember the impromptu story more accurately than any other child, more accurately than Pandora.

A research project of Dick Kendall's brought himself, Helen and their children to England. They expected to be over for several months. They came to Sterney as soon as they could. Dick had to be all over the country, looking at things and taking photographs; Helen was nearly all the time at Sterney, with little Ralph and baby Cathy.

In some respects the position was odd. The Kendalls were guests in their own house. Simon took Dick on tours of inspection, displaying his stewardship; Dick struggled to be interested.

It was predictable that Helen would have unfamiliar ideas about children's diet. It was predictable that Ralph would be coddled and over-protected. The first of these forecasts turned out to be right, the second quite wrong. Ralph was an active, extrovert and adventurous child. He was left to himself quite a lot, because of his baby sister, and he amused himself with energy and imagination. He seemed to Eleanor quite as precocious as the twins had been, at the same age, two years earlier. When the twins came home from school he wanted to do what they did; especially he wanted to ride and drive their ponies. It was the clear duty of the twins to share their animals with the smaller cousin, to whom these English country delights were all new. Eleanor marvelled at the uncomplaining generosity with which they did so; but Melissa showed no surprise.

Helen strongly encouraged Ralph's introduction to saddle and box-seat. Given his ultimate destiny, it was obviously good that he should know how to be a country gentleman.

Ralph enhanced life at Sterney. Cathy, teething, did not. She increased the no-go areas for the older children far more than Smiler had done.

Helen observed the twins narrowly, seeming as fascinated by them as Eleanor herself was. She revealed a specialised and academic interest.

One day Helen said to Eleanor, à *propos* of nothing, 'It would be easy to set up. A pilot, then some fuller tests.'

Eleanor had no idea what she was talking about.

'I'm sorry,' said Helen. 'I was talking out of the middle of a thought instead of the start. Has it ever occurred to you that the twins might be telepathic?'

'I thought American research had cast an awful lot of cold water on that,' said Eleanor.

'Yes, but maybe they simply didn't find a telepath.'

'They tried identical twins.'

'Maybe that was wrong. Let me hypothesise. Identical twins have this extraordinary similarity of taste, choice, thought-process. Not always, but often enough for the phenomenon to be observed and analysed. They don't *need* telepathy. They turn the same corners at the same moment without it. Those two here are not identical, by definition, but they do seem to show aspects of identicality. Is anything you've observed consistent with extra-sensory perception?'

'I don't know,' said Eleanor slowly. 'I think the answer might be yes. Do you sit them in different rooms, looking at different colours and shapes?'

'Yes. Effectively, that's exactly what you do. Ideally you'd have a computer produce a completely random sequence of objects or images. One subject examines them in succession, to a time-scale. It has to be monitored so the synchronisation is exact. The other subject is observed by somebody who is equally ignorant of the computer's list, in case the observer influences the subject. Maybe subliminally, maybe negatively as well as positively. That observer notes what the receiving subject picks. Then you just compare lists. If you have a sequence of straight right-wrong forced choice situations, like whether a card is red or blue, then over a reasonable length of test, chance would give you a fifty-fifty success rate. The longer the sequence, the nearer to fifty-fifty, if only chance is operating. But if you have a statistically significant swing from the norm, then you're in the presence of something.'

Eleanor felt a certain exhaustion, following this donnish exposition; but it seemed to make perfect sense.

'For practical purposes here,' said Helen, 'my idea would be to start with that straight blue-red choice. Get two packs of cards, shuffle them thoroughly together. Sit the kids where

89

they can both be seen, but where they can't see each other. Make them keep absolutely quiet. Somebody watches both, maybe sitting in the door between two rooms. One subject picks up a card, stares at the back. The other points to the colour he thinks it is. The observer notes right or wrong. That's how I'd start. A positive result would be pretty conclusive, even in that simple structure. A negative result wouldn't.'

'Why?'

'Because I'd hypothesise that some telepaths – if there actually are any – might both give and receive communications with a widely varying degree of sensitivity, depending on the type of communication. It seems to me possible that the colour on the back of a card might be just not interesting enough to beam. It's also possible that a telepathic image is monochrome. An unspoken verbal communication might be more effectively transmitted and received just because it was more complex and therefore more interesting. Maybe still more so if it had an emotional charge – if it was a warning, or a message of love or hatred. And I know some researchers in this field have formed the view that some telepaths can send but not receive, and vice versa.'

'Visual images might do better than words,' suggested Eleanor.

'With naturally non-verbal individuals, yes. I wouldn't describe the twins as non-verbal, but we definitely might try, like, a picture of a sailboat against a picture of a car. And of course we could try a more elaborately structured test, such as a choice between five images.'

'Harder to score.'

'Not at all. If it comes up random, the receiver has a one-in-five chance of guessing right. Twenty percent. All you have to look for is a significant improvement on twenty.'

'This is going to take a long time.'

'We'll wait for some bad weather.'

'What do you think, yourself?'

'I am completely open-minded,' said Helen. 'And I don't think I'll ever have a better chance of coming to a conclusion one way or the other.'

Eleanor and Helen between them devised a series of tests,

Helen contributing her college psychology studies, Eleanor her knowledge of the twins' awareness and experience. It was no good Peter trying to communicate to Pandora the image of an American doughnut, when neither of them had ever seen one.

Simon felt obscurely dubious about the project. He did not forbid it – could not have, when it could do the twins no possible harm. It was not as though they were being hypnotised or drugged; and his profoundly sensible sister was fully involved in it all.

Melissa seemed oddly uninterested. It was as though she knew the test would fail, or that it would succeed.

The twins were full of enthusiasm. 'Telepathy' was a new word to them; they used it importantly, though Pandora was apt to say 'peletathy'. They promised to try very hard to beam the colour blue or the shape of a triangle from the small saloon to the large one.

They drew lots as to who would start in each role. Pandora was to send, Peter to receive. The playing cards were in fact respectively green and black. Peter was given one of each, face down on the table in front of him. Pandora turned her first card. She stared at the green back of the card. Peter shut his eyes. There was a long silence.

Peter opened his eyes. He said, 'I can't see anything. No green, no black.'

They tried with other things – shapes, pictures, numbers. Peter could see nothing. They exchanged roles. Pandora could see nothing.

'Try just guessing,' said Helen.

Peter tried guessing. He guessed right a little under half the time. Pandora did a little better, but only marginally better than fifty-fifty. The twins were visibly, acutely disappointed. It was as though they had been promised the discovery of magical powers, and the promise had been broken.

Simon was secretly relieved that his children were normal and their senses earthbound.

CHAPTER 5

Helen and the children's nurse were thrown a good deal together while the Kendalls were at Sterney. They were oddly matched in conversational terms, but their continual contact was inevitable, since they had the care of the two babies. Helen could not unload responsibility for Cathy on to a nurse who had her hands full with Smiler, and who also had charge, some of the time, of the twins and their clothes and meals. She would not have wanted to. She had clear ideas about every aspect of child care; before having Ralph she had characteristically made herself expert in every aspect of the subject. This was long past the days of the gigantic influence of Spock, with his emphasis on freedom. The best opinion had swung the other way. Helen had been delighted to find that her own puritan New England instinct was exactly in tune with modern child psychology. Security, stability, derived from discipline as well as from love. Permanent damage could be done as much by laxity as by indifference or cruelty.

Without precisely criticising Melissa to Melissa's own employee, Helen made it evident that the twins ran far too wild. They were often indulged and often ignored. Simon was very busy; Melissa was still easily tired; both were besotted with Smiler. The twins still seemed entirely sweet-tempered and biddable, but Helen was uneasy; she thought it was being unconsciously implanted into their brains that, when it came to the point, they could get away with anything.

She could not discover that the twins had ever been punished. Melissa said they had never done anything to be punished for. Helen found this blankly incredible.

Helen told the nurse about life in America, when they were sharing the messy ritual of the babies' meals. The nurse heard about the wages and conditions for a trained person like herself. She had never been abroad. She wanted to go while she was young enough to enjoy it. Helen offered to look and ask around for her, when she got home. Helen and the nurse both reported these conversations to Melissa; there was nothing treacherous or secretive about it. Melissa quite understood that the nurse might double her salary, and see the world. She was a little aghast; but she could hardly grudge the nurse seeing a bit of the world when she herself had seen so much of it.

If the nurse ever did go, she would have to be replaced. Neither Simon nor the doctor would allow Melissa to try coping on her own.

As the twins had done, Ralph took to feeding the bantams and fantails. He did this when the twins were at school; when they came home it had been done. They could not at first understand how it was that all the birds ignored the rattling of the corn in the scoop. It was from Ralph's palm, on the flagstones of the stable-yard, that the chicks gobbled their crumbs, and on to Ralph's shoulders that the fantails descended from the dovecote. Helen took a lot of photographs of this charming sight. She thought one of the pictures might do as a Christmas card.

At the same time she noted that the free-range bantams, who roosted where they chose, made a considerable mess wherever they did roost, in the mangers or hayracks of empty loose-boxes; and that when the fantails got into the garages they made a lot of mess on the cars.

Whenever she had time, Helen explored the house, garden and park. She became familiar with every inch of the Sterney domain. She explored tactfully: she was being a student of architecture, interior decoration, and landscape gardening;

she was not being the wife of the heir presumptive. If she made notes and drawings on a pad, she did not do so obtrusively; she appeared to be sketching and learning, rather than planning changes.

Ralph himself – riding one pony, driving the other, feeding the birds – was not only adventurous. He was also beautiful. He had fulfilled the promise of his parentage; everybody said he would combine the craggy handsomeness of his father with the good bones and neat features of his mother.

He explored as his mother did, but with different objectives and in different places. He crawled into the secret centres of shrubberies, and climbed into the remotest corners of unused hay-lofts. He made many surprising discoveries. In the middle of a thicket of rhododendrons and azalea he found a small hut, with coloured pictures of wild animals tacked to the walls inside. In a corner of the kitchen garden, in a half-hidden shed no longer used for anything, he found a small table, perhaps a stool, with a bright embroidered cloth spread over it, and tacked above it a picture of a dreadful creature with lion head and dragon wings. On the table was a shrivelled bunch of grapes, and a bar of chocolate. Ralph inspected the chocolate. It was perfectly fresh. He ate it.

He reported this amazing event to the twins, when they came back from school. They listened politely, without comment.

After tea, in the semi-darkness of the autumn evening, the twins ran out, as they often did. Their errand was urgent. It was some new game. Helen and the nurse were busy with the babies; Melissa was asleep; Simon had not yet come back.

After she had put Smiler to bed, the nurse looked for the local paper. She thought she had left it on the nursery table. It was nowhere to be seen. She asked the twins, returning, if they had seen it. They shook their heads. They were not yet interested in newspapers, though they looked at the colour supplements.

On her way to bed, at eleven, the nurse passed the door of the twins' bedroom. She heard them talking. It was unusual – they slept like logs. She opened the door a crack.

'Sorry,' said a voice the nurse thought was Peter's.

There was a muffled giggle, which the nurse thought was Pandora.

'You'll be good for nothing tomorrow if you don't sleep now,' she said.

'You're still up,' said one of them. It was still impossible to tell their voices apart.

'Grown-ups don't need so much sleep.'

'Goodnight, nurse.'

'Goodnight, my pets.'

A moment later – it seemed only a moment – the nurse saw Peter, in his dressing-gown, coming along the passage towards their room.

'And where have you been, may I ask?'

'To the loo.'

The passage window looked out over the kitchen garden. Peter looked out into the darkness. Following his eye, the nurse looked too. Something was on fire.

'Where have you really been?'

'Just to the loo. I was in bed when you talked to us just now.'

'What did I say?'

'You said we won't be able to do anything tomorrow if we don't go to sleep. Something like that. You said grown-ups don't need much sleep.'

'Well, children do, so scuttle back and get your head down.'

The nurse ran downstairs and out, not wishing to rouse the household if the fire was only garden rubbish, and threatened nothing. She saw that it was the old unused shed. To all intents and purposes it was garden rubbish, and the fire did threaten nothing. How could it have started? Village children? Teenage vandals? They were sometimes a trouble, even in a quiet place like Sterney.

The nurse ran back and fetched Simon, who was on his way to bed. He decided immediately that the effort of getting hoses and fire-extinguishers to the place was out of proportion to the value of the old shed, and it was certainly not a thing to bother the Fire Brigade with. He stayed with the fire to make sure it did not spread. No harm to speak of was done.

It was hardly surprising that no teenage vandal came forward to admit starting the fire. But nobody could think of a better explanation.

Ralph revisited, after a day or two, the hut in the middle of the tangle of shrubbery. To his dismay, there was no hut. It had been completely destroyed. Fragments of planks, plywood and hardboard were strewn under the whippy, interlocking branches of the rhododendrons; shreds of roofing felt; little bits of coloured paper which might have been the pictures of animals, torn out of magazines, which had adorned the hut.

This seemed less the work of teenagers than of destructive young children. No young children from the village had been seen in the park, and none admitted to the destruction of the hut.

Nobody had known about the twins' hideaway in the rhododendrons. But it came as no particular surprise. Simon, Eleanor, Helen and the nurse all recognised that imaginative, precocious country children would play private games with secret headquarters. Melissa was even less surprised. She had had a secret hut, twenty-five years previously, in the same place. Hers was not really secret, because a kindly gardener had helped her build it. The twins had found and patched up her hut. That really was secret, until Ralph found it and told everybody about it.

The coincidence was extraordinary, but what else could it be? So said Simon, Melissa, the nurse.

The twins would surely not have destroyed their innocent secret hut in the shrubbery, for any reason; they had for a year been playing cavemen and Red Indians and such from that base. It was only secret because it was more fun if it was secret; all the grown-ups could remember their childhood well enough to understand that. And even if, for some inscrutable reason, they had taken it into their funny little heads to destroy the old garden shed, it was completely certain that they were both in bed at the moment the fire was started.

But Eleanor and Helen, discussing it all at anxious length as the intellectuals of the family, disliked coincidence – any explanation that rested on so gross a coincidence.

It was Eleanor who produced the explanation, so obvious that they could not imagine why they had been so slow to arrive at it. Of course there was no coincidence. A village child – perhaps the child of a gipsy or vagabond – had crept into the park, and had watched Ralph both when he explored the shrubbery and when he explored the shed. What followed was pure childish wickedness. This theory explained, as nothing else could explain, the destruction of both secret places immediately after Ralph had found them. It might have been envy, that children should have such magical places for their games; more likely it was wanton vandalism.

Helen was upset at the thought of prying, hostile eyes observing Ralph's solitary games. She kept her own eye much more closely on him. Since her movements were often restricted by Cathy, his movements were restricted. The reason was explained to him. He understood. He did not like it.

The nurse never did find her copy of that week's local paper. Nobody ever explained the bar of fresh chocolate.

Helen told Melissa that the twins, too, should be more supervised, for their own safety. Melissa thought not.

Dick, coming and going briskly between public galleries and private collections, could not understand what the fuss was about. His mind was full of Holbein, Van Dyke, Lely. He was developing theories about the manifestations of national character in art: about the continuity of Englishness in English painting even when the painters were foreign. Beside these large matters, the tumbling of a children's hut in some bushes, a little fire in a little shed in the garden, were trivial.

Dick accepted that Simon's stewardship of Sterney, estate and house, continued entirely satisfactory. He would report as much to his father. It was unlikely that his parents would make the trip in the foreseeable future. Beth remembered with horror the weeping skies and marble floors of Sterney. The older Ralph's health had been none too good. He was sixty. He was approaching retirement but by no means retired. There was a worry about his heart. Almost certainly this was a legacy of his sustained overwork at Farnborough during the war. He would see Sterney through Dick's eyes.

Dick did not make detailed examinations of either the books or the turnips. He had no time for a proper inspection of either, nor training to deduce much from figures in a balance-sheet or roots in a field. His father had made the decision to put full trust in Simon; he had gone along with that decision, and still did so.

He put full trust in Helen, too, in the matter of the

97

supervision of their son, where he should go, what he should do. He did not abdicate responsibility in the matter, but, while he was so much away and she on the spot, he thought it right to delegate it.

The twins disappeared when Eleanor, as she sometimes did, brought them back from school: just vanished into garden or park. Ralph, waiting for them, waited in vain. Under Helen's new rules he had to go indoors. It was not obvious to Eleanor that the twins had deliberately avoided Ralph.

Ralph stumped indoors, disappointed and moody. Obviously he felt left out. It was something, Eleanor knew, children could feel keenly, even violently. People made a very great mistake who forgot that children had feelings quite as sensitive as an adult's, could be hurt quite as easily and react quite as strongly. Eleanor wondered how often this had happened – Ralph being made to feel an outsider, a stranger, a nuisance, even though the twins would never have hurt him deliberately.

Eleanor suddenly had a new explanation for the destruction of the hut in the rhododendrons. Not for the garden shed, perhaps, but for the harmless, ramshackle hut. Even the nicest child sometimes, provoked, pushed over a playmate's house of cards. The twins had never done it to one another, but the twins were special and their relationship was special.

It was supremely obvious to Eleanor that Ralph had destroyed the hut in a fit of temper at having been left out of something by the twins. No purpose was served by mentioning this to anybody, least of all Helen. Except Ralph himself; Eleanor hoped Ralph would own up. He passionately denied destroying the hut. Eleanor sadly concluded that almost any child would lie under such circumstances, even a normally truthful little boy like Ralph. Not the twins. The twins, as far as Eleanor knew, had never told a lie in their lives. As they had never done anything to be punished for, so they had never done anything to lie about. If they wanted to keep you in the dark about something, they simply avoided your questions, by the trick their mother used.

They came in late and muddy for tea in the nursery, full of apologies, full of charm. Eleanor, who had stayed for nursery tea, asked if they had a new secret hide-out.

'We saw a red squirrel,' said Peter. 'At least I thought so.'

'I thought it was a grey squirrel looking red in the sun,' said Pandora. 'Everything was looking red in the sun. I saw a pigeon looking red in the sun. It was a red, red, red sun, because it was going down.'

'That was how we knew we were late for tea,' said Peter.

'It would be wonderful to see a red squirrel,' said Eleanor, 'but I'm afraid Pandora's probably right.'

Helen told them about the red squirrels of New England, and American red and grey foxes. Her manner was a little teachy, incongruous in somebody who was spooning food into a fretful baby.

Eleanor afterwards realised that the twins were not going to say anything to anybody about any new hide-out, but they were not going to be rude about it.

The Kendalls went back to America, Dick's sabbatical semesters having run their course. He had a trunk full of photographs and another full of notes. Helen would help him get the book in shape when they were home, as much as Cathy let her.

There was a small, clear, unstated and unmistakable sense of relief at Sterney.

Helen's long letter of thanks enclosed big prints of the best pictures she had taken – those of Ralph feeding the fantails and bantams, of Ralph driving the miniature pony-trap, of Ralph on the sixth rung of the ladder to the tree-house, the highest he had been allowed to go.

The twins asked for one of the photographs for themselves. They did not mind which one. Any one which showed Ralph clearly. The grown-ups were pleased at this evidence of cousinly affection. The twins never said what they did with their picture. It was presumably tacked up in one of their hide-outs, their new secret places. They avoided questions about it by talking quickly, antiphonally, about birds or wildflowers or something that had happened at school.

The twins started piano lessons. They urged it, and the teachers at their school urged it. Simon was alarmed that the tedium of beginners' exercises would turn them against it, perhaps against music. But they loved it. They practised long and hard, when they could. They understood musical notation with remarkable speed. They liked duets best.

It was difficult for them to practise at home. The grand piano in the hall disturbed the nap which Melissa needed after tea. The twins understood this. They understood that their mother was slow to recover her full health and energy after Smiler's birth. She had made a much quicker recovery after their birth, although there were two of them; the nurse told them how strange this was.

'You must blame Smiler that you can't practise now,' said the nurse, looking indulgently at the cheerful, destructive toddler on the nursery hearthrug, not thinking deeply about what she was saying.

Two letters came from Helen, arriving by the same post. One was for Melissa, one for the nurse. Helen was behaving with the scrupulous correctness that everybody who knew her expected of her. She was telling Melissa exactly what she was telling the nurse, that in six months' time there would be a vacancy for a trained nursery nurse in an academic family whom Helen knew well and esteemed highly. As in Dick's case, the family were a good deal richer than the husband's assistant professorship would indicate. They would pay tremendous wages, by British standards; the nurse would have her own car; the family vacationed in the Caribbean in the winter and Colorado in the summer, and the nurse would go along.

The nurse went to see Melissa, holding her letter. Melissa was holding her letter. The longing in the nurse's eyes shone like a fog-lamp. Melissa did the only thing she could; she strongly advised the nurse to take this marvellous chance.

There would have to be a replacement; there was never a moment's doubt in anyone's mind about that. Melissa began advertising. She had an attractive post to offer – only one toddler, two children at school all day, own room with TV, other staff kept. She began picking through replies, checking references, interviewing candidates. It was lucky that she had six months for the business.

'It won't make much difference to you,' Melissa said to the twins. 'You're outgrowing the nursery. The new one will be Smiler's keeper. I'll be your keeper.'

100

'We don't need a keeper,' said the twins.
It was almost true. They kept one another.

Smiler was walking. Smiler was talking, or thought he was.
Smiler blundered cheerfully after the twins. When they did
manage to practise the piano together at home, Smiler
pounded the keyboard too, delighted at his contribution. He
brought the keyboard cover down on Pandora's fingers. Her
fingers were hurt. She just stopped herself from crying. Smiler
was reproved but not punished because he had meant no
harm – he was simply discovering about the world. He would
not do it again. But he thought it was a good game, and he did
it again, to both twins together. He was smacked, and the
noise he made was deafening.

It rained on the day of the twins' sixth birthday. Melissa
exhausted herself organizing games indoors. Eleanor had not
been able to give her usual support, because she was attending
a social workers' course in Milchester; and Simon could not
get away from his office until late. Smiler – about whom the
word 'hyperactive' had been loosely but understandably used
– greatly enjoyed the party. He was made a great fuss of by the
twins' friends. He was even, by a general conspiracy, allowed
to win a race.

The nurse began to pack her bags. It was a wrench, after more
than six years. She was weepy. She was excited; she was
frightened of the new world she was about to be dropped into.
She drooped, sniffing, over Smiler's cot after she had put him
to bed.

The twins that summer discovered the tree-house. Melissa
had hardly used it, because they would have followed her
example when they were dangerously young. Now they could
be trusted to be sensible and safe. (Eleanor thought this
lunacy, but Eleanor had never understood about tree-houses.)
Simon inspected it. He had a few rungs of the ladder replaced;
otherwise it was perfectly sound. The twins adored it
immediately. It became, as it were, their public private place.
It was strange to Simon to hear them talking about it exactly
as Melissa had done, all her life until recently – there were

certain things that could only be done in a tree-house. A god-parent had given the twins recorders – wood, not plastic, and with the warm woody tone of good recorders. They would only play their recorders in the tree-house. It was magic, even for the unmusical Eleanor, to hear their little duets coming down from out of the luxurious late-summer foliage of the beech tree.

Most of Melissa's hopefuls were unthinkable. The agencies ignored her requirements, and submitted absurd candidates. Many were far too old. Many would have been miserable in so deeply rural a place. Some she reacted against instinctively, with an instinct Simon had learned to trust. Some, for various reasons, would simply not have fitted in with the life of Sterney.

A short list at last produced a single name. Her qualifications were fine. She had a glowing testimonial from her one previous employer, whom she had only left because the family was emigrating. A long telephone call, delicately conducted, confirmed to Melissa that the testimonial was sincere. She was twenty-seven years old, neat in appearance without either flash or frumpery, speaking grammatically with a pleasant country burr. She came, in fact, from Sussex. She was a farmer's daughter. She had been brought up with animals, including ponies; she was well used to harness, and as a child had often driven a pony to her father's milk-float at local shows. She fell immediately and visibly in love with Sterney, and with Smiler.

Her name was Joy Martin. For some reason she was known immediately by her name. Her predecessor might not have had a name, being 'Nurse' in the village as well as in the house. This was assumed to accord with the wishes of both girls. Joy was just as much of a nurse as 'Nurse', and wore the same uniform.

It worked out pretty much as Melissa and the twins had said – Joy's main concern was with Smiler, and she saw comparatively little of the twins. Arriving after the autumn term had started, she had only to feed them in the evening and get them up in the morning. They had breakfast with their father, and he or one of the estate staff drove them to school. Melissa usually brought them back; sometimes another parent; sometimes Eleanor. Their homework needed no supervising; they did it conscientiously, together. Then they disappeared out of doors, or into the tree-house or the hay-lofts or the attics of the house. They had watches now, birthday presents from another godparent, and they could tell the time. They were often back on the dot, for their baths and hot drinks and bed. When they were late they had apologies and reasons.

It was inevitable that their relationship with Joy should be quite different from their relationship with their other nurse: not because the other would nowadays have seen any more of them, but because she had known them since birth. There was no reason for them to become intimate with Joy, and they did not do so. But they got on perfectly well with her, and, when she had to give them orders, they accepted the orders equably. As in the past, the orders were apt to concern not waking up Smiler when he was asleep, or not waking up their mother when she was asleep.

They finished their homework together, quiet as mice, not talking even to one another. They got their recorders out of the drawer, and ran out before Joy could say anything.

She would have said something, to save them disappointment.

Because when they got to the beech tree, the ladder had gone. It was impossible for them to climb that great grey trunk without it. They ran to look for it, searching in different directions. Pandora found it in the stable-yard. Peter immediately joined her. They picked it up, and tried to carry it. They could carry it a few feet, but it was too heavy for them.

They ran to find their father, who was in his study. He was very sorry about the ladder. He said that Joy had taken her eye off Smiler for a second, and had found him almost at the top of the ladder. She had said that she could not keep an eye on him twenty-four hours a day; he had seen the twins going up and down the ladder, and of course he wanted to do it too; he would kill himself. Joy could not accept responsibility. It was hard on the twins, but it was better that they should do without the tree-house for a year or two than that Smiler should fall thirty feet.

103

They put their recorders back in the drawer, saying nothing about them then or later.

Helen's Christmas card, sure enough, was one of the photographs of little Ralph that she had taken at Sterney in the early spring. By an odd coincidence, it was a smaller print of the picture the twins had been given, the one that they avoided answering questions about.

Joy admired it. She thought the little boy was beautiful. She heard for the first time about the American cousins. It made her wonder how long she would have the job at Sterney.

There were still a lot of Christmas cards in those days. Drifts arrived in Simon's office, from suppliers of feed and fuel and machinery, from contractors of all kinds who kept the estate drained and fenced, and the buildings roofed, wired, plumbed. Drifts arrived in the nursery, from the twins' schoolfriends, from Joy's friends from childhood and college. Heavier drifts arrived in the great saloon, from all over the world, and Melissa had to spread them into other rooms.

None, not one, was more attractive than the small colour photograph of Ralph Kendall with the silky bantams. Somebody put it all by itself on a ledge in the hall. Little Ralph, on his solitary eminence, had an air of being king of all he surveyed.

In the coldest weather, Pooter the Shetland pony was not put to the trap. He would have liked it, but the driver would have got intolerably cold, especially as to the fingers. But at the beginning of March the trap was pulled out of the coach-house, and repainted all one weekend by Melissa and the twins; and the harness was unhooked from its brackets in the tack-room, soaped and polished, and buckled together.

Joy helped the twins with the harness. Melissa saw that they did not want to be helped. She was pleased that they had the good manners to hide this from Joy.

The twins came back from school on the first really fine afternoon of March. They went to the stables, to harness Pooter for the first drive of the year. The trap was not here, nor the harness, nor Pooter. Quite late, Joy came back, driving with Smiler. Smiler had adored it. He had held the reins for a time. It was too late for the twins to take the trap out.

Most fine afternoons, after that, Joy took Smiler out in the trap.

Joy mentioned 'Smiler's pony-trap' in a telephone conversation to someone in the village. She was overheard by the twins.

Joy's day off. Usually Melissa got one of the servants, or Eleanor, or someone from the village, to help look after Smiler. This time it happened that the cook was in bed with flu, the housemaid away on holiday, Eleanor laid up with a sprained ankle, and the available village ladies for various reasons unavailable. Melissa undertook to look after Smiler. It was only for a day. She had, without any trouble, looked after the twins whenever their nurse was away. Smiler might be naughtier, more active, potentially destructive, but there was only one of him, and his cheerfulness was as infectious as ever. Other mothers looked after whole clutches of young children, all by themselves, every day of their lives.

Melissa overrated her own unreturned strength, and underrated Smiler's capacity for mayhem.

When the twins were brought back from school, by another parent, they found their mother in a state of collapse, sobbing with fatigue and helplessness, and Smiler sitting chuckling among the ruins of the eighteenth-century tapestry screen in the saloon.

The twins helped their mother to bed, stopping at last tears which would not stop. They put Smiler to bed. He went placidly, having enjoyed his day.

The events of Sunday morning were established afterwards with complete precision. The timing of everything was known, by an unusual series of chances, with exactness, and the movements of all the people in and anywhere near the house. Painful as it was, this meticulous investigation had to be done.

Fortunately, few questions had to be asked of Melissa. She was still in bed with the newspapers when it all happened.

Joy found Smiler sneezing and snuffling. It seemed a nasty spring cold. She decided to keep him in bed, for the morning anyway. She went to tell Melissa so. Melissa was sitting up in bed, waiting for breakfast and newspapers. She agreed with Joy about keeping Smiler in bed. As Joy went back to Smiler's night-nursery she met the twins, on their way to say good morning to their mother. She thought they were going to be late for breakfast, and for this reason looked at her watch. It was two minutes past nine, so they were only going to be a very little late.

The twins kissed Melissa. They said they were sorry about Smiler's cold; they promised to keep away from the sickroom so as not to catch the cold. They ran down to breakfast. Simon was already there.

Joy came downstairs three minutes later; she put her own breakfast and Smiler's on a tray, and carried it up to the nursery.

Peter finished his breakfast before the others. Simon said he could get down. The time was 9.20. Peter had some business of his own in the stables. Simon imagined some new game, hiding-place, make-believe adventure. Pandora would share it, of course. Meanwhile she wanted another piece of toast and honey. Normally, Simon thought, she would have gone when Peter went; or, if she wanted the toast very badly, Peter would have waited for her. They still did nearly everything together. Simon reminded Peter to be ready for church by twenty to eleven.

The papers came, much later, as usual, than on weekdays. Simon took some of them up to Melissa. It was just before 9.40. Melissa had finished her breakfast; Simon took the tray down with him.

With the papers came *Horse and Hound*, to which Sylvia the girl groom subscribed. It was supposed to come on Friday, but for some reason was late. Pandora said she would take the magazine to Sylvia, who would either be somewhere in the stable-yard, or in her bed-sitter over the coach-house.

Sylvia was in fact in a loose-box, nailing new wooden slats to a hay-rack to replace ones that had rotted. It was the sort of odd job she used Sunday mornings for. Just outside the loose-box, and visible from it, was the ladder into the hay-loft. Pandora climbed the ladder. She told Sylvia she wanted to show Peter the cover of the new *Horse and Hound* – a colour photograph of the Duke of Edinburgh driving a coach in a competition.

'How do you know he's up there?' said Sylvia.

'You must have seen him go up,' said Pandora.

'No, I've only just got here.'

'I think he's there. We're Eskimos, hunting seals.'

Pandora disappeared through the trap at the top of the ladder. Sylvia heard her laugh. There was a rustle of hay and an answering laugh. There were murmurs. Sylvia did not hear what the twins were saying. She was struck once again by the impossibility of distinguishing their voices.

Pandora dropped the *Horse and Hound* into the hay-rack Sylvia was repairing, through the trap by which hay was dropped into the rack. This happened just after 9.45. Sylvia noted the time, aware that the twins would have to go indoors soon, to get clean and tidy for church.

Sylvia heard the twins above her, busy about something at the far end of the hay-loft. She heard Peter say 'Pandora' in what sounded like mock reproach; she heard Pandora's answering laugh.

Simon had another cup of coffee. The maid came in to clear the breakfast table. They chatted for a minute about a headline on one of the papers. Simon took his paper into his study, to get out of the maid's way. He looked at his watch as he went, because of the deadline for getting to church: it was 9.50.

Having cleared away the breakfast things, the maid could relax in the big, sunny kitchen until it was time to lay lunch. She and the cook sat in amicable silence with their own Sunday papers, which had arrived with the rest. They noted the time on the electric wall clock, because the cook had to get the roast into the oven at 10.15.

Just after ten, Joy came into the kitchen with her tray. It was a mess, because Smiler had upset his milk. They talked about children's colds, and how amazing it was that the twins had never had anything wrong with them at all. There was still coffee in the pot; the cook gave Joy a cup.

Sylvia banged the last nail into the last slat of the hay-rack. She saw that it was 10.17 – nearly time for the twins to go indoors to tidy up for church.

'Stop hunting those poor seals,' she called up to them.

Pandora's head appeared in the trap at the top of the ladder. She said, 'Have you finished? Let me see.'

Pandora came down the ladder like a monkey. She inspected the hay-rack. She nodded vigorously.

She called up, 'Peter! I'm going in. Don't be long.'

Peter presumably made some reply, but Sylvia did not hear it because Pandora immediately said, 'He's inventing a new game but it's not properly invented yet. He'll come in a minute. Don't forget *Horse and Hound*.'

Sylvia picked up the magazine, and her hammer and pliers and paper bag of nails. Pandora went with her to the end loose-box which was used as a work-shop. They went into the workshop to put the tools away. Pandora was even chattier than usual, and kept Sylvia talking in the workshop. Sylvia kept an eye on the time; it was 10.22.

Simon looked at his watch, put down his newspaper, and went to get the car. It was 10.23.

At 10.25 Joy left the kitchen and started the climb up to the nursery.

The cars were in a converted barn behind the stables. Simon met Peter coming out of the stable-yard. There was hay sticking to his sweater.

Simon said, 'Where's Pandora?'

'With Sylvia. Did you see the *Horse and Hound*? There's a super picture of Prince Philip on the front. Daddy, could we get a proper coach? Have you ever driven a coach and four?'

'No to both questions, I'm afraid,' said Simon. He called out, 'Pandora! Time to get decent!'

Pandora came out of the workshop with Sylvia; she trotted across the stable-yard towards her father and brother. Simon looked yet again at his watch. It was 10.28. He hurried the twins indoors.

They were met by Joy, running out. She looked terrible. She ran up to Simon and tried to speak. She could not speak for shock and for rasping, hysterical sobs. She pointed wordlessly upwards, up towards the nursery. A terrible premonition came to Simon. He ran indoors and upstairs, Joy following. The twins watched them go, with astonished faces.

Smiler's pillow was over his face.

The doctor said Smiler had been asphyxiated. He was far too old, sturdy and active to suffer a normal cot-death, the accidental and tragic stifling which sometimes kills very young babies. His cold was not severe enough to have asphyxiated him. He was fairly cheerful, considering he was being kept in bed, when Joy left him with the tray.

He must have put the pillow over his own face; but the doctor had never seen or heard of a death so caused. It was not in nature; it was incredible. There would have to be police and there would have to be an inquest.

Circumstantially, there were two horrible possibilities. Joy could have stifled Smiler either before she took the tray down or after she came upstairs again. Or Melissa could have come along the passage to the nursery. A third explanation, equally horrible, had seemed possible until the putting together of the place-time jigsaw had made it impossible. The point was that Sylvia could not remember whether she had actually seen Peter in the hay-loft. She had heard what she was sure was his voice, but that was inconclusive unless she had heard the twins talking simultaneously; she could not remember whether she had done so. But he must have been up there. Sylvia could swear that the twins had no contact between the moment when Pandora came down the ladder and the moment when Joy ran out of the house. But Peter had seen the new *Horse and Hound*, and described the cover to his father. He had left the house before its arrival; he could only have seen it in the hay-loft. He could not have left the hay-loft and returned to it except by the ladder which was in full view of Sylvia. The police came to this inescapable conclusion with gigantic relief.

There was never any serious suspicion of Melissa or Joy. There was never the least possibility of charges being brought.

Simon, Joy and Sylvia were called to give evidence at the Coroner's inquest. It was not felt necessary to subject Melissa or the twins to this ordeal; the effect on all of them could have been devastating. The court was able to get a picture of an energetic, unpredictable, destructive child who was, just barely possibly, capable of an idiocy like putting a pillow over his own face and holding it there.

The inquest found that death was accidental, and that nobody was to be blamed in any way. The Coroner remarked that it was a million-to-one chance, and that Miss Joy Martin should not reproach herself, nor be reproached, for leaving her charge unattended.

CHAPTER 6

The worst thing about Smiler's death was the effect on
Melissa. The best was the behaviour of the twins.

Melissa did not obviously break down. She was perfectly
rational, on the day of Smiler's death and thereafter. As spring
turned into summer, she stood or sat in the garden, under the
cedar or by the dovecote or on the Chinese bridge, and tears
rolled quietly and interminably down her cheeks. She
suddenly began to weep in the middle of dinner, alone with
Simon, or sitting in the nursery with the twins. She did not
want to see anybody outside her immediate family – Simon,
the twins, Eleanor, old Mr Collis. The long letter from Helen
she left unread.

One day a week, sometimes two, Melissa spent in bed. She
was not physically ill, though undernourished and still more
easily tired. She simply had no taste for getting up and taking
part in life. She lay staring at the ceiling. She did not read.
Radio and record-player were silent.

Simon tried to get her to eat. Obediently, for the sake of his
feelings, she tried to eat.

A psychiatrist came, at the village doctor's suggestion.
Melissa was willing to see him, willing to do something about
the wreck of herself. He made obvious, sensible, predictable,
kindly suggestions about trips abroad and new interests.
He was a great waste of money.

111

Joy left. Everybody understood that she could not bear to stay. She was not replaced. The twins, as they had said, were one another's keepers; and the cook and housemaid, and Sylvia, and Eleanor, helped when help was needed. The whole estate and the whole neighbourhood helped when the twins needed help. They seemed to manage pretty well without help from anybody except one another.

Melissa was the one who needed help; and Simon, labouring to help, was in despair.

And then the twins took charge. They told Eleanor they were going to do so, and they did so.

In May, without telling anybody, they persuaded two of Simon's tractor-drivers to re-erect the ladder to the tree-house. They began to work on their mother to climb it. She was too weak. They cajoled and wheedled and bullied her into eating, giving always the reason that she must have strength to climb to her tree-house.

They got their recorders out of the nursery drawer, and their duets came down once again out of the foliage. Melissa was drawn out on to the grass by the sweet, uncertain music; and one day she climbed the ladder to the tree-house.

The twins snipped buttons off some of their father's shirts. They took the shirts, the buttons, a needle-case and a reel of cotton up into the tree-house. Melissa sewed the buttons onto Simon's shirts in the tree-house.

The twins harnessed Pooter to the trap, and brought him round to the door. Pooter was groomed as far as a shaggy Shetland can be; his hoofs were oiled and his mane plaited; his harness gleamed and the wheels of the trap had been washed. Melissa allowed herself to be half-pushed, half-pulled into the trap. They were out for an hour, under the May sun. There was more colour in her cheeks that evening, Simon thought, than he had seen there for a year.

The twins put music on the downstairs record-player. They were careful with records and stylus. They did not put on records which their mother had much played since Smiler's birth, but her favourites of three and four years before. They asked Simon which those were, and found them in the racks and put them on, so that music filled the saloons and library and hall.

112

The one confidante to whom Simon could bear to talk, in those weeks of despair and recovery, was Eleanor. Eleanor had never seen a grown man weep; but in the privacy of her room at the Old Vicarage Simon broke down and wept. Eleanor did what she could to help Melissa, but she saw that she could do nothing like as much as the twins. She was amazed at their strength, and at the strength they were beginning to give their mother.

Melissa, to Eleanor's anxious eye, was making a heartrendingly visible effort to put the past behind her: to live in the present and the future: to live with and for Simon and the twins.

On the Friday evening of the first week in June, the twins were very busy in the nursery with poster-paints and large sheets of stiff paper. Nobody was allowed to see what they were doing.

On Saturday morning they rushed out to the stables immediately after breakfast, their pieces of paper rolled up under their arms. They shut themselves in the coach-house. Sylvia was politely commanded to keep out.

After an hour they came in again, and went upstairs. They were still mysterious about their game. They got a suitcase out of a box-room, and packed it with various things from various parts of the house. They staggered out to the stables with the suitcase. They said none of the things they had borrowed would come to any harm.

They were off again to the stables immediately after lunch; and at last they reappeared. They were driving Pooter with the trap. They, the trap and Pooter were all transformed. They had blackened faces; they were smothered in Simon's oldest and most disreputable clothes, which he kept for the dirtiest jobs; their heads were almost invisible under old tweed caps. To the sides of the trap were tacked bold posters advertising pots and pans; and pots and pans swung and clanked from the sides and back of the trap. Pooter himself was a walking hoarding, with posters pinned to his girth, and a plume of peacock feathers tucked into his browband.

Melissa came out into the portico, brought by the clanking of metal.

113

'Pots and pans,' shouted the twins. 'Very best pots and pans.'

Melissa laughed, for the very first time since Smiler's death. It had worked.

The twins were adamant that they did not want a birthday party: just themselves, their parents, and Eleanor. The dogs and bantams would join them on the lawn, and after they had gone indoors the fantails would peck about under the cedar tree for crumbs.

The twins explained to Eleanor: their mother would be reminded of that other party, the big party on the lawn when their friends all made such a fuss of Smiler, and let him win a game.

And Smiler had died just before his own third birthday; and his presents had gone to the children's hospital in Milchester. The twins had saved up their pocket-money, and bought him a foot-high Shetland pony, with silky nylon hair the same bright skewbald as Pooter. The pony had gone to the children's hospital.

'I've just understood something. And I don't think I can live with it.'

Eleanor looked in terror at Melissa. They were in Melissa's bedroom. Eleanor had come to help Melissa sort out old clothes for a jumble sale. Melissa was sitting on the side of her bed; Eleanor was knee-deep in dresses. Melissa looked shrunken, broken. All the magical recovery of May and June was gone; she was as pale and huddled as in the days after Smiler's death.

'Tell me,' said Eleanor.

'No. I can't tell you or even Simon. Simon least of all. It was something that happened yesterday. I understood for the first time. Probably I understood before, but I didn't think about it. I didn't think it mattered. We've all been fooled. We've all been deliberately fooled. I've thought and thought, and I understand how it was done. I thought and thought – why? I understand that, too. It was done for me, partly. I don't know if that makes it better or worse.'

'I'm terribly sorry, Melissa,' said Eleanor, 'but I don't know what you're talking about.'

'I hope you never do,' said Melissa.

Melissa began to weep, sitting silent and huddled on the side of her bed, as she had after Smiler's death.

Eleanor came away aghast, completely puzzled. She had tried to comfort Melissa; she had tried to put her to bed. Melissa would not be comforted. She would not go to bed, but sat like a beggar, like a cripple, weeping silently.

Eleanor found out from the servants and from Sylvia what Melissa had done the day before. Something which had undone all the twins' healing magic. A letter? There had been letters. The telephone? There had been calls. Something in a newspaper? Eleanor looked at the previous day's papers, and found nothing. Her day: breakfast in bed. Downstairs by 10.30. Some letters. A conference with the head gardener about cutting back the Black Hamburg grapevine in the conservatory. Lunch, alone in the breakfast room, with a book. What book? The maid had noticed – a recent republication of early P. G. Wodehouse stories. Melissa ate not enough, but more than she would have eaten even two weeks before. A walk, with the labrador and lurcher, the Peke coming with them for the first two hundred yards, then turning back and going home on his own, as he always did. The gardeners, as always, amused by this laziness and independence. A rest after the walk, not to sleep but with music. The servants unfamiliar with the music, with any of the music played by the family. Music, anyway, not chosen by the twins; music, perhaps, that sang of Smiler. The twins brought home from school by somebody. Nursery tea, Melissa and the twins. Melissa laughing with the twins: a joyful report carried by the maid to the cook that their mistress was laughing.

It was after that, then. What, after that? The twins' homework, three quarters of an hour. Then Pandora riding, Peter and Melissa in the pony trap. The evenings very long now, midsummer approaching. A golden midsummer evening. Melissa laughing as Pooter rattled away pulling the trap; Sylvia thanking God to hear the sound of Melissa's laughter.

Sylvia was out when they got back; her boyfriend had come for her in his car. Melissa and the twins unharnessed Pooter, rubbed him down, and put him out in a paddock; they untacked Daisy and put her out.

Melissa indoors with the twins. The twins to their supper in the breakfast room, Melissa straight to bed. Too tired to eat, too tired to talk. Concern below stairs; the servants seeing concern on the faces of the twins.

The cook made bold to telephone Simon, kept late in his office. Simon home at once. No knowledge, on the part of the servants, of what passed between Simon and Melissa. Simon tucked up the twins. He dined alone. Rich soup taken up to Melissa; soup brought down again untasted.

Melissa 'thought and thought'. She lay in bed thinking. Now she was sitting on the side of the bed, huddled like a beggar, weeping.

Something happened when they were out, she and the twins. She heard something, saw something, understood something; and then thought and thought about it, with this unendurable result.

Eleanor brought the twins back from school. They were as worried as she was, and as puzzled as she was. They had no idea why their mother was suddenly so sad. It had been a perfect evening when the three of them were out. Both twins had driven, both ridden; both had adored it; but suddenly their mother was crying.

Melissa said she would sleep alone. She had occasionally done so, since Smiler's death. Simon had a cot in his dressing room. He left the door open between the rooms, but Melissa shut it. She was to take two Mogadons.

Simon went to bed feeling ill with worry. He hated leaving Melissa to her lonely misery, but he could not force his company on her if she wanted to be alone. He supposed Smiler's death had suddenly come at her out of the sky, and knocked her back into despair. It might have been because of the pony-trap, which the child had loved so much; it might have been birdsong, or the pink evening sky, or a remark from one of the twins in a voice that sounded like Smiler's. Simon could make nothing of the conversation Eleanor had reported, if only because Eleanor could make nothing of it either.

Simon prayed for Melissa. He prayed most urgently that she would have a good night's sleep. In despair he lay in the dark, wakeful, picturing her lying wakeful. He could not imagine that he would sleep himself; but he had had a long and exhausting day, and soon after midnight he fell deeply asleep.

The under-gardener found Melissa at eight in the morning. She was floating face down, in her night-dress, two yards from the bank of the lake, in eighteen inches of water.

They said they thought she had been dead since three in the morning.

She had not taken the sleeping pills. She had been very quiet, opening and closing her bedroom door without waking Simon, opening and closing whichever outside door she used.

It was Smiler's death.

She had suffered a black night of the soul, mourning Smiler. The pain of her grief was past her bearing. She had always been sensitive beyond other people's understanding, feeling more, pitying more, grieving more. Her laughter, her electric and unpredictable sense of humour, were the other side of the same coin.

It was delayed shock. For all her tears, she had been too sane, too rational, on the day of Smiler's death, and all the days since. A breakdown would have been better, cleansed her soul, equipped her after she recovered to face life without her baby.

That was what everybody said. But Eleanor remembered, and wondered. Something new had come to Melissa's eyes, ears, brain. Not Smiler's death, of itself, but a new discovery. Made while out with the twins. Nothing the twins were aware of. If learned from them, then something they taught her unconsciously.

Something about herself, Eleanor thought.

'I don't think I can live with it.'

She was blaming herself, in a new way, for Smiler's death? She was accusing herself of sleepwalking from her bedroom to the nursery, of putting a pillow over Smiler's face? Why should she have such a horrible delusion? Why should she have it suddenly, out in the pony-trap with the twins on the most beautiful evening of the year?

Melissa, as wife and mother and neighbour, as housewife and hostess, had been perfectly competent and sane – far more so than Eleanor and her father had expected. Liable to act on absurd and sudden whim, as in the matter of dinner in the tree-house, but not crazy.

Suddenly crazy, at three o'clock in the morning. Driven to the side of the lake by something she could not live with. Wide awake, undrugged. Driven by a misery she could not bear, by a discovery which was new.

About herself. It must be about herself. She imagined she had cancer? That caused suicides, sometimes completely needless. How should a drive with the twins give her the idea she was dying?

Round and round and round went Eleanor's helpless, horrible thoughts; and Simon went about like a man in a dream, shattered, dumb; and the twins sat silently, side by side, close together.

The twins' seventh birthday was more than any of them could bear.

To go on living at Sterney was, Simon thought, more than he could bear. Every corner of house, garden, park screamed of Melissa. The house had never been haunted. Melissa haunted it.

A letter came from Ralph the elder, Melissa's uncle, in California. The expressions of condolence were conventional, but Simon knew they were meant. Ralph begged Simon to stay at Sterney Court. Dick and Helen had reported in glowing terms about the condition of everything; Simon was, please, to continue in his stewardship of the house and its contents as well as of the estate. There was just no acceptable alternative. Everything Ralph had said after his father's death still held. The maintenance, heating, rating and wages bills would continue to be paid, exactly as heretofore. Ralph's own health, to say nothing of Beth's, made a move as impossible as ever; and Dick was now deep in his book, and could not be parted for a day from the library and his filing cabinets.

There was a hint, graciously worded, that whatever his personal feelings Simon owed it to the Kendalls to carry on looking after Sterney, after the years he had been subsidised to live there.

Simon had to accept this. He did owe Ralph a gigantic debt of gratitude. He had to accept Eleanor's point that to uproot the twins, at this moment, would be monstrous.

He moved into a different bedroom.

Eleanor moved temporarily into the big house, arranging for friends in the village, in relays, to look after her father. She suspected that her father rather looked forward to being fussed over by a succession of ladies, many of whom were excellent cooks.

Eleanor supposed Simon would find a housekeeper, or possibly promote the cook. Meanwhile somebody had to be specifically responsible for the twins, at least morning and evening.

Simon and Eleanor went through Melissa's clothes. Riding things, classic suits, shoes were stored in case they should one day be useful to Pandora. The rest went to Oxfam. There was no need to have anything cleaned; there was nothing that merited being thrown away. Neither the servants nor Sylvia could fit into anything of Melissa's. Eleanor could; Simon offered her anything she chose. But she did not want that kind of souvenir of Melissa.

Melissa's few jewels went to the bank. Eleanor did accept a seed-pearl brooch.

Simon himself went through the papers in Melissa's desk. There was not much – she was not a magpie as her grandmother had been. A few letters from her parents and grandparents; all his own letters; photographs which had not been stuck into the album; only current household bills and receipts.

There was a drawing – a scrawl – which aroused a flicker of recognition in Simon. It was extremely recent, from its position on top of a recent bill from the fishmonger. It meant nothing to Simon, except that he was certain he had seen something like it before. It was simply a lot of diagonals crossed by curves, with heavy shading.

Simon continued to do his work. He felt himself an automaton, unconsciously going through well-drilled motions. Everyone was kind to him, tactful, low-voiced, on the farm and in the office. Sometimes he wanted to scream at them. He did not scream at anybody; he knew they meant well. He was aware that they were conspiring to ease his work-load. He did not want it eased. A practical problem which commanded his full attention was the only pain-killer which worked; it did not always work, and it never worked for long.

Eleanor saw them in the distance, across the park. Simon with the twins each side of him, bright blond heads in the evening sun, Simon with a child's hand in each hand, strolling. They were not talking, Eleanor thought. They were comforting one another, Simon the twins, the twins Simon. They were leaning on one another, the twins on Simon, Simon on the twins. The twins were as strong as Simon. His need was as great as theirs.

Of course he had not been as close to them as Melissa. He was now, and would be.

Something woke Eleanor up – a cry, a bellow. Simon. She struggled out of bed. She hurried along the passage from the room which had been Joy's, pulling on her dressing-gown as she went. She passed the open door of the twins' room. It was full of moonlight. The twins were not in bed.

The twins were in Simon's room, the new bedroom he had moved to. One stood each side of the bed. Simon seemed to be asleep. He had cried out, in misery, in his sleep. He was quiet. Each of the twins had one hand, palm down, on his brow. Pandora, facing the door, raised the finger of her free hand to her lips when Eleanor came in.

Dizzily, Eleanor wondered whether the twins were pulling weakness out of Simon or pushing strength in. She was not needed there. She tiptoed away.

As little as two years earlier, Simon's father would have been a massive help. His faith was then as strong as ever in his life, and in private he could powerfully communicate it. But he did not take in what had happened. He had not taken in Smiler's death. He took in very little outside the walls of his study and bedroom. It might have been possible to face him with the double tragedy, but no good purpose would have been served.

Two years earlier he would have helped Simon. Two years earlier the twins would hardly have been able to do so. Now that he could not, they could. It was odd to think of two young children successfully replacing an elderly parson in the function of bringing spiritual comfort; but so it was.

The twins stayed away from school for the brief remainder of the summer term. They would go back in September.

For the moment – for another three or four years – they could go on at their local private day school. Then they would be ready for Common Entrance and the next step. Simon and Eleanor argued about that. Eleanor thought they should go to different schools; they could be together every minute of the holidays, if they still wanted that; it might be healthier and more helpful to divide them in the term-time. They could not live their adult lives in each others' pockets. Pandora could go by day to the Milchester school where Eleanor herself had been pretty well taught; Peter, if Simon could afford it, might follow his father to Marlborough.

Simon took what to Eleanor was the bizarre step of consulting the twins. They said they must be together, when they were twelve and fifteen and eighteen as much as now. This decided Simon. He made enquiries about co-educational schools which were not so absurdly progressive that nobody passed any examinations. Eleanor thought it grotesque, irresponsible, to allow seven-year-old children to decide their own educational futures. Simon listened to her with his invariable politeness, and wrote to Bedales and Bryanston.

To Eleanor, this became dangerously the pattern of Simon's attitude to bringing up the twins. All that summer she looked for, and saw, signs of Simon buying the love and support of the twins by giving in to them about everything.

No one example could be held up as really gross indulgence, on its own. No one concession, on its own, was sinfully weak-minded. But there were an awful lot of mickles, Eleanor thought, making a formidable muckle.

There was, first and most woundingly, the matter of herself. In July she started dividing her time about equally between the Court and the Vicarage. What brought her so much to the big house was the twins – their need for structured and disciplined lives. Helen Kendall, with all her slightly absurd American reverence for theory and pronouncements of sages, had been sound about that. Eleanor got the twins up at breakfast time and in bed at bed-time. If they were late for meals they went without, however charmingly they apologised. When they lolled about reading or listening to music, they did it in their own part of the house, in their nursery, not in the saloons or the library.

The twins chafed under these moderate and normal rules. There was no doubt in Eleanor's mind that they got at their father about it, behind her back; and behind her back he made the arrangement the twins wanted.

The cook had been at Sterney long enough to know how to manage it. She knew all the tradesmen Melissa had used. She would keep Simon fully informed. She would be housekeeper. She had been teaching the maid how to cook, and she could still supervise that and help with it. The bulk of the cleaning – all the 'heavy' – could be done, as before but to a larger extent, by daily women from the village or from cottages on the estate. There was no longer any need for Eleanor to neglect her father, her garden, her social work, her bird-watching and botanising and bell-ringing.

Eleanor had the sense of being given the sack by her own brother; and she knew very well the twins were behind it.

She had a long talk with the cook – now housekeeper, and so solemnly called Mrs Hawkins – who was an old ally. At least, Eleanor supposed she would still be an ally. But Mrs Hawkins did not react as Eleanor expected.

'We must give them a bit o' latitude, poor motherless mites,' said Mrs Hawkins.

The twins had Mrs Hawkins exactly where they wanted her.

From this derived the matter of supper. Children of the twins' age had nursery tea, and a biscuit and a hot drink at bedtime. That was invariable, as far as Eleanor knew, and it was right and necessary. Simon dined later. The twins got at Simon and at Mrs Hawkins; and they began having supper with Simon. Eleanor expostulated with Simon. Simon as good as told her to mind her own business.

There was the matter of the dogs. The household still had three, Melissa's labrador and lurcher and Peke. The twins wanted dogs of their own. They had a schoolfriend whose mother bred cocker spaniels. The dogs they had already were nice dogs, but they wanted personal puppies of their very own. They would feed them and train them; the dogs would sleep in baskets in the twins' bedroom.

Eleanor knew she was wasting her time, telling Simon that for a man who was out all of every day he already had too many dogs.

The dogs, both bitches, cost £120 each. The twins called them Brenda and Begonia. They said they knew themselves which twin owned which dog, but they never told anybody else. The puppies were very messy, until Simon and Mrs Hawkins together house-trained them. They were inclined to chase the silky bantams, until Simon and Mrs Hawkins cured them of that. At meals they begged, and the twins fed them scraps. Simon seemed not to mind; if he minded he said nothing. Eleanor, coming to lunch, was shocked by this; she hated fawning, begging dogs. Charley, her own ageing Norwich terrier, would have been sent straight out of the room. The twins said that Brenda and Begonia had been taken away from their mother, and they must be loved and even a bit spoiled because of that. Eleanor was silenced.

Eleanor thought Simon was showing a kind of moral cowardice. She agreed with what Helen had said in the winter: it was doing the twins no favour in the long run.

In spite of all this, Eleanor had to admit to herself that you could not fault the twins' manners. Or, she thought, their common sense. They were young to be practical, realistic, aware of the limits of the possible; but they were. The things they got from their father were things he could give them, would give them. They never asked for the impossible – the impossibly expensive, or the dangerous, or the silly. Dogs could be got; meal-times could be changed. They did not ask for the moon, or a paddle-steamer on the lake, or a pair of helicopters.

When it came time for the autumn term, Eleanor thought it possible they might make a fuss about going back to school. They had run so completely wild and free since the middle of June. Then Simon, of course, would have to be firm, at whatever cost in rage, tears, mulishness. But none of that ever arose. The twins accepted that they had to go to school; since they had to, they made a virtue of necessity; they were determined to enjoy it, as they had in the past; they did enjoy it. They resumed their position of being joint leaders of their very peaceable gang; they enjoyed that; they enjoyed learning, and being joint top of their form.

Beth Kendall died in February. She was only sixty-three – the same age as Ralph – but she had been in poor health for two years.

Simon remembered liking Beth, but being a little alarmed by her. He wrote to Ralph with condolences which, he was aware, were as conventional as those Ralph had written to himself. He found it impossible to find fresh words. Melissa would have found them. This thought brought Simon's sense of loss back in a dark flood over his head. The pain was more than he could bear. He did what he had come to do whenever he felt that knife turning in his guts – he went to find the twins, and sat with them, and he was comforted.

Beth had been the sole heiress of her father's real-estate fortune. The money had been prudently administered by bankers and brokers and attorneys. It had grown substantially, in spite of Beth's generosity and life-style. Beth left a number of moderate legacies to friends, godchildren, and various artistic and charitable foundations. The whole of the rest went to Ralph.

Ralph was now completely retired. His own health was poor. His brain was as clear as ever. He considered the future, made plans, dictated letters, had long talks to his son Dick, and at last signed portentous documents.

In April Simon had a letter from Ralph. Unusually, it was dictated and typed.

My Dear Simon,

Let me first thank you for your kind letter about Beth. I ought to have done this moons ago, but as you can imagine there has been a great deal to sort out, and I find nowadays that I can only concentrate, as these matters require concentration, for short spells.

You are personally affected in some degree by the dispositions I have made. It is in order that you should be in no doubt about the future that I am committing the discourtesy of sending you a typewritten communication.

In brief, I have set up the Sterney Trust, suitably financed, with the object of insuring that the house and estate will be maintained in perpetuity as a family home as

124

well as a national treasure. It was built to be lived in, like its Italian original. I do not want it to become a museum with a curator – although there is a sense in which you have been fulfilling, admirably, just that role.

There are two Trustees. I thought it right – and secured the ready agreement of my advisers here and of Dick – that the Trustees should be English and in England, in touch with affairs there and able to visit Sterney without crossing the ocean. Both are *ex officio*. One is Senior Partner of the firm of solicitors who handled my father's affairs; the other is the Curator of the Milchester Museum and Art Gallery. People of experience, ability and probity are certain to occupy both these positions, and the necessary expertise and sympathy is assured. The Trustees are bound by the terms of the Trust to disburse such periodic sums as are required for the maintenance of the property in all particulars. In plain terms, they will pay the bills that I have been paying; they will also pay your salary. This arrangement will continue regardless of who is occupying Sterney Court.

I take it that the occupant will, in the fullness of time, be Dick my son, and after him Ralph his son. In the event of either of them not inheriting by reason of predecease, or of being unable or unwilling to accept the inheritance and its concommitent responsibilities, the Trustees will have discretion to install a tenant, giving priority in their choice to members of the family. I have specifically excluded my daughters and their families from consideration in this regard, since – this is in the strictest confidence – they are not feasible occupants of Sterney. That point need not be laboured. They will be compensated financially on the event of my death, as they already know.

On a completely different subject, I note that your twin children will be embarking on the secondary stage of their education in three or four years. I have been making enquiries about the cost of the best English schools, and was frankly appalled. It would seem a little patronising, I think, for me to offer to pay, so I am causing your salary to be adjusted to take school fees into account.

I dearly wish I could see Sterney again, since I have long outgrown the ambiguous memories I have of childhood there. But it cannot be. They won't even let me fly.

With kindest possible regards to yourself, and a grand-avuncular salute to the twins,
Yours affectionately,
Ralph Kendall

'What actually does it all add up to?' asked Eleanor.

'I keep my job. I'm paid more. And if Dick's children don't want Sterney, the twins get it.'

'Oh,' said Eleanor. 'Oh.'

The Trustees came out to Sterney. They both knew the house: the lawyer, though not then Senior Partner, had many times come to see old Lord Kendall; the Curator was a friend of Eleanor's, and she had taken him round. Neither had met Simon, the rather solemn young widower who seemed to fit extremely well, in dress and manner and ability and commitment, into his role as stop-gap lord of Sterney.

Sterney was to be preserved as a family home. What of family life in this motherless household? The Trustees saw the nursery; the horses and pony-trap; the tree-house; the bantams and fantails and the five dogs; they saw the twins who were in the middle of their Easter holidays.

They came away confident that Lord Kendall – who called himself Mr Ralph Kendall over there in California – had made the optimum choice of caretaker.

The twins were looking at albums full of small black-and-white photographs of their mother's childhood. Melissa at eight had looked exactly like Pandora at almost eight.

The twins found a page of photographs of their mother in her miniature sailing dinghy on the lake. They looked from the pictures to their father, smiling, raising their eyebrows identically.

He laughed. (He had been re-taught to laugh, by the twins.)

He said, 'I'll see what a boat costs.'

The boat had to hold two, to be made of fibreglass, to be unsinkable; the twins had to have life-jackets, even though they could swim very well. It was all rather expensive.

Simon (taught so long ago by their mother) began to teach the children to sail as soon as it was warm enough.

Eleanor pursed her lips. It was an insane extravagance. What with dogs and ponies and the trap, the twins had more than enough expensive toys. To the Trustees, it was a proper, valid use of what Sterney offered a family suited to living there – it was what the Trust was about. They would have liked to have paid for the boat, but their discretion did not extend so far.

Dick's book was published in September, by the University of Yale. Copies came to the Sterney library and to Eleanor personally. Eleanor read it conscientiously. Simon, very tired, turned over the pages and fell asleep.

A photograph of the south front of Sterney illustrated a passage about the assimilation, by the *genius loci* of the English countryside, of the totally exotic. A picture of Mereworth made the same point: as did, by way of ingenious and thought-provoking juxtaposition, eucalyptus and mimosa and peacocks looking very much at home in an English garden; oriental porcelain and Persian carpets in an English drawing room; and – audacious touch – Virginia tobacco in that most English object, an old man's clay churchwarden pipe.

Eleanor thought the whole book was a piece of solid scholarship, and a labour of love, which solemnly and interminably stated the obvious.

Her friend the Curator of the Milchester Museum had also received a copy for his library. He was shocked at Eleanor's comment. He knew he would presently, as Trustee, be paying the author's fuel bills.

Ralph died two years later, in the spring. Simon wrote to Dick. The twins, at Eleanor's suggestion, wrote to little Ralph and Cathy. Simon addressed his letter to 'Lord Kendall de Sterney'. The twins wrote to 'the Hon. Ralph and the Hon. Catherine Kendall'.

Dick wrote saying that his future research – insofar as he was going to have any time for research in his new life – would be in Europe, and that the Kendalls were at last planning to reoccupy their family home. He had written to the school where the twins went, knowing from Eleanor that it was eminently satisfactory in both an academic and a moral sense, and had entered Ralph and Cathy there. They would start in the fall. They were young enough to adapt to the problems of a different syllabus. Dick was in touch with the Trustees, and had apprised them of his intention, which was what they had expected. He devoutly hoped that he could count on Simon to continue his impeccable management of the estate. What Dick had to do, as he and Helen realised, was to give Simon and the twins time to find and settle into a home of their own. Preferably it should be a house on the estate; Simon would know what was suitable and available. The Kendalls expected to arrive in England some time in July. There was no question of evicting Simon and the twins, but obviously it would be convenient for all parties if they were resettled by then. Meanwhile the Kendalls were eternally grateful for Simon's stewardship of their patrimony, which they had observed with admiration and on which the Trustees had reported with approval.

'End of an era,' said Eleanor.

'Not before time,' said Simon. 'I've masqueraded long enough.'

'It'll be a jolt for the twins.'

'Not really. They'll still be able to sail on the lake and drive the trap and so forth.'

'But as guests.'

'They've been guests all along.'

The Dower House would have been the best place for Simon and the twins – where Simon and Melissa had started their married life, where he had had a tree-house built, and she had painted the skirting-boards. But Gregor and Rosie Montgomery had been there for nearly ten years, and Gregor's lease had another twenty years to run. He was still a solicitor in a partnership in Milchester. There was no chance of them leaving.

The Old Vicarage was not a serious possibility, with Simon's father in the state he was in.

Simon could not afford to buy a house, supposing a suitable one was available in the immediate vicinity. Living at Sterney had made it impossible to save, even though Ralph had paid the major bills. Even with the most generous mortgage, purchase was out of the question.

There was one decent house available for rent. It was partly furnished. There was an absolute embargo on dogs.

In practical terms that left the agent's house in which Simon had lived before his marriage. It was solid, and there was just room for them. There had been a series of short lets, and it would be available in June. It was the house that went with Simon's job. He had only flown as high as the Dower House because he married the boss's granddaughter.

He went to see over it, for the first time for years. He went into the stuffy little sitting-room. He nearly shouted aloud with agony. It was there that Melissa and he had come together; and in the bedroom he had used; and in the kitchen Melissa had cooked their supper wearing nothing but an apron.

The twins seemed philosophical, to Eleanor's relief. Probably they were still too young to have taken in the glories of Sterney, to have realized they were living in such beauty. There were no stables at the agent's house – no outbuildings at all. No doubt they would be able to keep their ponies and the trap at Sterney, and their boat on the lake.

They went with their father to look at the agent's house. Eleanor was there, bringing some linen from the Old Vicarage. The twins went quickly over the ugly little house. It seemed to make no particular impression on them, negative or positive; it was as though they were tourists being guided round a monument devoid of interest, reacting only out of politeness.

The Trustees could pay for structural alterations or repairs, since the house was on the estate, but not furniture or decoration. Some furniture could be spared from the Old Vicarage – chairs with patched and faded loose-covers, tables with unequal legs; Eleanor picked up some in the Milchester auction-rooms. Obviously nothing could come from Sterney – not one single object of furniture, china, silver or glass. None of it belonged to Simon. Nothing did, except his clothes, gun, rod, record collection and a few books.

'It comes of living in a museum,' he said. 'You don't acquire anything.'

Still from the Old Vicarage, Eleanor partly equipped the kitchen. There was a stove. Simon had to buy refrigerator and freezer. He bought old beds but he had to buy new mattresses.

It was infuriating that they had sold almost the entire contents of the Dower House to the Montgomerys; at the time it had obviously been the right thing to do. The Montgomerys would not sell any of it back, after living with it all those years.

It was like being first married, setting up a house *ab initio*: but without a wife, and without wedding presents.

The twins were indifferent about the colour of their bedroom. It was as though they were not really going to live there.

They were able to move in at the beginning of June. This gave Mrs Hawkins time to spring-clean Sterney, against the coming of its Lord.

Eleanor found a cook-general to come daily to the agent's house from the village. She was called Mrs Wild. She was old for the job. She left supper in the oven for Simon and the twins.

The twins' had their tenth birthday party in their new home. Nobody came except Eleanor. There was hardly room for five dogs and four people in the sitting-room.

The Kendalls came over immediately after the children finished school in the summer. Ralph was now eight and Cathy almost six. Dick was thirty-seven; he looked a good deal more, with his thinning hair, academic stoop, and formal manners. Helen was two years younger, and looked as though the difference was much greater than that. Simon saw Dick in the office but not in the house. Eleanor went to offer Helen any help with moving in, but Helen needed no help.

They moved in smoothly, because the house was a going concern.

After only four days they asked Simon and Eleanor both to dinner; just the four of them, but they were to change. Simon was startled to be admitted and announced by a butler; he had not seen a butler in a private house for twenty years. He remembered that Dick was very rich on his own account, from his slice of his mother's fortune, quite apart from having his bills paid by the Trust.

Simon felt peculiar, being welcomed into a room in which he had been the host for ten years: even though he had felt peculiar being a host in it.

They talked about all kinds of things. Helen had found

130

Huxtable the butler by remote control, using an agency in London. Dick was planning another book, but it was still at a gestatory stage. A hard tennis court – maybe a pair – was a priority. Would Simon sell Dick the sailboat on the pond?

Dick had become more obtrusively American since his last visit to England. That was all right – Simon liked Americans; but it was odd having such a very Yankee Lord Kendall de Sterney. Maybe he would gradually turn English, like the exotic houses and plants in his book, like Sterney itself. Helen had become more decisive, more dominant. She was not strident or bullying. She made it clear that she had strong and well-defined views about everything, and that she was right.

The evening ended early. Simon faced a heavy day, and Eleanor had to get back to her father.

The twins were asked for the day. Ralph and Cathy were active and attractive children, clamouring for attention and getting it. Ralph had learned how to sail a boat at summer camp; he offered to teach the twins. He told them about the tree-house, which was now his tree-house. He said they could come visit in his tree-house.

'Where are the birds?' Pandora asked suddenly.

'The chickens? Mommy had them taken away. They made an ucky mess in the stables and everyplace.'

'And the fantails?' asked Peter.

'All gone. Some guys went up in the middle of the night with a sack. They're all in the freezer now. My Daddy says a pigeon pie he had once in France is the best thing he ever ate. They made even more mess than the chickens. On the *cars*. What kind of cars do you have? We have a Merc and a Range-Rover and Mommy has a BMW. That bird stuff is acid. It makes holes in the roof of a car. It's real ucky. I don't know about pigeon pie, but my Daddy says it's the greatest.'

When Simon came to get the twins, Helen showed him some of the changes she planned in the garden.

CHAPTER 7

Dick was nothing if not conscientious. He made a serious and sustained effort to understand the management of the estate. With Simon he met everybody, making notes of names, jobs, lengths of service, numbers of children, wages, memberships of trades unions. With Simon, he plodded up and down hedgerows and headlands, making notes about the past and future of each field, what sprays or slurries had been put down, what fencing and drainage. He looked at the books, Simon taking him through them, interminably, item by item. It was all a new world to him. Nothing in his background equipped him to understand why one field required six land-drains, or why the periodic flooding of a stream could only be cured by the widening of a culvert two miles below. Not only his training but the cast of his mind, the type of intellect he had, was ill suited to rows of pigsties or rows of figures. He continued at it, doggedly. It was admirable: but it added shockingly to Simon's work. How ever many hours of his time Dick wanted, he still had to put in the necessary hours in the office, on the land, at market.

Dick was becoming used to being called 'my Lord'. He bought ready-made tweeds in Milchester. He looked like a don on a holiday which he was trying to enjoy.

Eleanor's intimacy with Helen and Dick was a little difficult to maintain, although they all still had all the same intellectual interests. Helen's unpretentious academic background had not changed, but her foreground had. It was no use either side pretending they could meet on terms of equality.

There was friction between Huxtable the new butler and Mrs Hawkins the housekeeper. There should have been a solid, solemn alliance between those two, attended by stately courtesy and protocol: Helen knew all about that from Vita Sackville-West. The reality in 1970 was different.

Mrs Hawkins left. She cried when she came to say goodbye to the twins.

The twins startled Mrs Hawkins by saying, 'We'll have you back.' It was as though they expected to be living once again at Sterney.

Simon tried to find a second-hand upright piano. Even the smallest grand would not fit into the agent's house. Even the smallest upright was a major outlay. The twins would practise at school when term started. The Steinway at the Court was kept locked.

The children at the private day-school were cautiously welcoming to Ralph and Cathy. Their accents were quite familiar, to English children, from television. It may not have been a disadvantage to them that they came from the great house. Ralph had played soccer in America; he was good at it. They were bright; they fitted into an unfamiliar syllabus. They were friendly, normal, and without vanity. Used to strict discipline at home, they adjusted happily to the discipline of the school.

Dick consulted Simon about the estate Christmas party. Simon told him what had been done in the old Lord's time, and faithfully repeated ever since. Dick was determined to adhere strictly to tradition.

The twins would not come. Peter said he had a splitting headache, and Pandora would not go without him. Eleanor came and sat with them. She had not been asked to the party. That was quite reasonable, as she did not work for Sterney. Simon could have mentioned the matter to his employer, but it would have been awkward.

Simon went to the party as one of the employees of the estate, no more, no less. He was rather relieved than otherwise; but he did not think Dick managed the party well. He was too shy to be bluffly welcoming; he gave an impression of cold reserve, stand-offishness, which as Simon knew was the last way he wanted to seem. Mistakenly he wore hairy, pale-coloured tweeds; all the men had put on their best dark suits.

For the first time in Simon's memory, one or two of the young men got drunk. He made sure there was somebody to drive them home.

At the end, Simon was given a present, like all the rest: a gift-wrapped bottle of whisky, like all the rest. He was given presents to take home to the twins. Peter's was a toy cannon which fired matchsticks, Pandora's a large stuffed Snoopy.

They wrote identical letters:

Dear Cousin Helen,
    Thank you very much for the beautiful present. I was so sorry not to be there, I'm sure it was a lovely partly.
    Thank you very much again.

The presents disappeared. Simon never knew what the twins did with them, and the twins were politely evasive.

Helen studied pictures and plans of the formal gardens of Palladian villas in the Veneto. She thought there must have been such parterres and avenues at Sterney; but no old print could be found that showed them.

The renaissance theory, she knew, was that formal gardens extended the lines and proportions of the building: it all formed a grand design. Palladio did not intend the graceful mansions he built for rich Venetians to be surrounded by informal countryside; his English disciple two centuries later would not have intended it either. Taste for the 'romantic' and the 'picturesque' came far later, with Parson Gilpin and Sir Walter Scott. The unbroken sward between the house and the lake, fringed informally by clumps of trees, made life easy for gardeners on big ride-on mowers, but it was wrong histor-ically and aesthetically.

Helen combined several sixteenth-century garden plans, and adapted the result to the proportions of Sterney and of the great lawn. It was her main preoccupation all that first winter.

She got huge sheets of graph paper, rulers, protractors, compasses. She hired computer-time to calculate parabolic and hyperbolic curves. She consulted experts about planting, showing them pictures of the real thing, seeking an Adriatic effect in a cold climate. She recruited surveyors with theodolites, drums of cord, and thousands of marker pegs.

There was a warm spell at the beginning of March. The mechanical cutters began to slice and lift the ancient turf. Truckloads of pot-grown plants began to arrive. Helen walked up and down with her charts, in her new green gumboots, sticking pegs into the bare red earth.

The twins were reading omniverously that winter, books from the school library, books Eleanor got them from the Public Library in Milchester. Their conversation became peppered with incongruous phrases, pompous or adult or archaic, which they had met and liked. 'A smiling day' they said when it was warm and sunny; they talked of 'forenoon' and 'sennight'; a stupid child was 'muttonheaded'; and a clever one 'satirical'.

It did not seem to Eleanor, who watched Simon's treatment of the twins with undiminished anxiety, that these verbal fancies were a private code, or designed to impress. The twins were not showing off; they were flexing their mental muscles and enjoying themselves.

One quite simple remark, perhaps falling into this new-learned category, conveyed nothing special to Eleanor at the time, but it obscurely worried her when she thought about it afterwards. She came on the twins at the edge of the park, for once apparently completely idle. She stopped her car and offered them a lift. They declined, polite as always. She asked them what they were doing.

'Biding our time,' said Peter.

Simon tried to make time to see his father as often as possible. It was difficult to get to the Old Vicarage often, with the demands of the job, the demands of Dick Kendall's agricultural education, and the demands of the twins. As to the last, it was not so much that the twins clamoured for more of their father's time, as that he clamoured for time for himself to be with them. It was not only his manifest duty, it was also his keenest pleasure. It was really his only pleasure. So much of the light had gone out of his life; and the twins looked so very like Melissa.

In fact, Simon recognized that his visits to his father had more to do with his own conscience than with his father's needs. The old man was eighty-one. He had had what the doctor called a 'mini-stroke', the effect of which was to leave him in permanent confusion about names, faces, where he was, when it was. Often Simon, sitting unhappily opposite him with a glass of sherry, found himself cast as his own long-dead uncle, or as some theological college contemporary, with a football match or a mid-term examination approaching. The old man would call querulously for his tea at three o'clock in the morning, or take himself laboriously to bed at noon. The burden fell heavily on Eleanor; it gave her less and less time to concern herself with the twins.

Simon and Eleanor could not, between them, possibly afford a private nursing home, nor the day and night nurses who were really wanted if he stayed at home. The geriatric ward of the Milchester hospital was despairingly inspected by Eleanor; she came away determined that under no circumstances would her father go there.

Life was no fun for him any more. Living in the remote past, he seemed always to be living in its most miserable moments of failure and betrayal. He could hardly be persuaded to eat. What he did eat, the doctor said, his system hardly made use of. He shrank to a little frail shadow, his collar enormous round his neck, his ears grotesquely large.

Simon and Eleanor agreed, nowadays, about almost nothing that related to the twins; but they agreed that it would distress the children needlessly to see their grandfather so shrunken and so mad.

It was impossible for them to keep the trap and the two ponies at the agent's house. Dick offered animals and vehicle permanent house-room at the Court, the twins to come and use them when they liked. The only condition was that his own children should have the use of them too.

Simon had hoped for this arrangement, and was thankful. But the twins were unaccountably apathetic. It was as though they had suddenly outgrown both riding and driving. They made all kinds of excuses – homework, the need for piano practice, reports of a hoopoe's nest on the river bank. Everybody knew that teenagers were apt to lose interest, overnight, in the whole world of the horse; but it was odd in ten-year-olds who had loved it so much, and been so good at it.

Helen bought trap, harness and both ponies from Simon. She bought the fibre-glass sailing dinghy. Simon put the money on deposit for the twins.

It occurred to Eleanor that the twins had not, in truth, outgrown the great joys of their childhood. It was that they did not want to be poor relations at Sterney; they did not want to share things that had once been altogether theirs. She was surprised and unhappy to find herself suspecting that they were becoming jealous and possessive. It was entirely counter to all that they had shown themselves to be – welcoming Ralph on that long previous visit, sharing everything with him, losing games on purpose. If it was so, it was the fault of the way Simon was spoiling them. Eleanor's conscience obliged her to say so; and she might have been talking to the marble pillars in the hall at Sterney.

The twins' eleventh birthday. They were given a kind of party at school. They would not have a party at home for anybody except themselves, their father, Eleanor, and the five dogs. They said there was no room for more people unless the dogs were turned out, and they would rather have the dogs than any other people.

In spite of this, they received generous and imaginative presents from Dick, Helen and their children. These did not disappear, like the field-gun and the Snoopy. They were put in a drawer, and stayed there. The twins wrote correct, identical letters to all their cousins.

Old Mr Collis died of pneumonia in the autumn. Everybody tried to remember him as he had been years before.

Everybody said that Eleanor should go right away, take a proper rest. She refused to consider any such thing. There were a thousand things to do, at home and in the neighbourhood, which she really wanted to do; and at last she had the freedom to do them.

From things she let drop, one of the things she was most bent on doing was safeguarding the twins from Simon's indulgence. But she did not find sympathetic listeners on this topic. People did not know, as she knew, the realities of life in the agent's house. People saw the twins' courage and kindness, their beauty and their beautiful manners. There was nothing much wrong with children like that. If more people brought their families up as Simon was evidently doing, the future world would be a much better place. What more did Eleanor want? What on earth was she talking about?

In dismay Eleanor realized the impression she was making. She was the nosey, frustrated spinster trying to interfere in someone's family because she did not have one of her own.

She thought she could talk to Helen about it.

Helen agreed that Melissa had been dangerously lax, laying up trouble for the twins in the future. She did not suppose Simon made the same mistake – he was so efficient, sensible, organized.

'But surely you've seen what I'm talking about? Surely you've seen it, in everything they do?'

'I've seen them hardly at all since we came here.'

'What?'

'It seems their lives are completely full. Friends of their own age, of course, which is as it should be. Their music. That nature-study which I think you got them on to. It's a fine thing, you know – it does them credit. Children should have so many projects on hand at any one moment that no day is long enough. If they don't have projects of their own, they should be led up to projects. Led, not pushed. But it's good to see kids self-reliant about what they do. I'd love to have them here, but I quite understand that we don't fit into their plans.'

Eleanor was astonished. She had assumed the twins came often to play and explore in the Sterney park and gardens, and to revisit the secret places they had.

Eleanor thought she understood, though she deplored, their not wanting to share their ponies and boat. She was amazed they did not want to enjoy all the glories of that magnificent place. Had they turned against Sterney? Out of sour grapes? Was that possible? Were they cutting off their noses to spite their silly little faces?

138

She put it to them, straight, that they were stupid not to enjoy Sterney when it was there to be enjoyed, and their cousins more than ready to welcome them.

'We're awfully busy just now,' the twins said. 'We'll go there later. Later we'll go there all the time.'

'I'll hold you to that.'

They assured her they would go there later. They were quite clear about it. Eleanor thought she ought to have been satisfied, but she was not.

Questions now arose about the future of the Old Vicarage, the agent's house, Eleanor, Simon and the twins. All these related problems were discussed by those involved, and by many who were not involved at all.

Eleanor could continue to pay the rent her father had paid to the estate; it was not much, and she had a little income from a trust. But it would obviously be to her great financial benefit to have Simon and the twins there, sharing expenses. Presumably it would suit them to have the benefit of her efficient housekeeping. Alternatively, she could move to the agent's house, where there was a bedroom for her as long as the twins shared a bedroom. Simon and the lawyers could then let the Old Vicarage, or even sell it.

Eleanor put this alternative to Simon. One or the other. Common sense insisted it was one or the other.

To Eleanor's despair, Simon said he must discuss it with the twins. They were at home more than he was; they were more affected; it was more important to them; he did not much care where he lived or with whom, but they did.

Eleanor exploded. Two caring and responsible adults could be trusted to come to a decision in the best interests of everybody – the estate, themselves, the twins – without being bound by the whims of eleven-year-olds.

Simon repeated, gently, that he would talk it all over with the twins.

Eleanor went to see Dick. She disliked going behind Simon's back, but it had to be recognized that there were areas in which he no longer made sense. His notions of his duty to the twins, his idea about the conduct of a one-parent family, might do his heart credit but they were playing havoc with his head.

Dick was extremely polite, in his stately, old-fashioned manner. He said that he had already discussed the matter with the Sterney Trustees – the curator, in such a question as this, entirely deferring to the lawyer. The lawyer had agreed with Dick's own view that everyone would prefer Eleanor to continue as tenant of the Old Vicarage, which she could be trusted to keep in perfect order; nobody liked the idea of letting it to an outsider; and there was no question in the short term of the sale of a property thought certain to appreciate. Meanwhile Simon could better discharge his duties from a base in the middle of the estate, rather than one completely outside its boundaries. Young children were better among fields than among streets. Simon was using part of his modest legacy from his father to buy an upright piano, and the agent's house was a small one to hold both a piano in constant use and someone who was, like herself, not deeply concerned with music. Eleanor could, subject to the approval of the Trustees, put the spare space in the Old Vicarage to such use as seemed to her good. She might consider, to give a single example off the top of Dick's head, taking selected paying guests, people of culture and refinement, who would find Sterney village an excellent centre for exploring an area of scenic beauty and historic interest. In sum, Simon would stay where he was, and Eleanor had best stay where she was.

The twins had got at Simon, and Simon had got at Dick.

Spring: the Easter holidays. Ralph and Cathy at the Court; Peter and Pandora everywhere but at the Court. They went off on the bicycles Simon had given them for Christmas. They went to spend days with friends; they went to watch the birds building in the Milchester Marshes nature reserve. In bad weather they played the piano; it was evident, even to Eleanor, that they were gifted and well taught. They did not want to play the Steinway at the Court.

'Not yet,' they explained. 'Not till we play better.'

They agreed seriously that one day they would play the glorious piano again, as one day they would explore all the fascinating books in the Sterney library.

140

'When we're old enough to understand them,' they said. 'Later, you know.'

They made no comment when Simon and Eleanor discussed Helen's extraordinary gardening. Eleanor herself felt torn about it. Helen was undoubtedly right, historically, judging by every picture Eleanor had ever seen of an Italian renaissance villa; but the great lawn had been so beautiful, calmly joining the house to the lake. Simon thought, with typical philistine practicality, that the amount of edging, trimming, planting, pruning and weeding would mean at least two more full-time gardeners.

'It can go back to grass,' said the twins indifferently, 'if anyone changes their minds.'

It seemed they had not even seen the new geometric parterres; that they were not interested. It was a question of time, they said. They had so much to do. They would visit the garden later.

Eleanor's voluntary social work rarely took her on to the Sterney estate, which looked after its own. Her concerns were in the cottages and council houses not covered by that paternalistic umbrella. But she was asked, by the people in the shop in the village, to go and see old Hilda Mockett, widow of a gamekeeper, who had been living alone in a tied cottage on one of the outlying farms. Lady Kendall had been to visit Hilda, all right and proper and doing her duty as she always did, but Hilda couldn't rightly understand that American talk. Hilda's great-niece was there looking after her, but the talk was that the old thing ought to be in the hospital. They were the sort that wouldn't be helped, but they'd maybe listen to Miss Eleanor.

They maybe would, Eleanor thought. A little wearily she accepted another burden. It was all she was good for, so she had better get on with it.

Eleanor had been to the gamekeeper's cottage, but seldom and not for a long time. It was isolated. It had no telephone, although Simon, in the period of his stewardship, had laid on main electricity. The patch of garden had been let go, but it was not squalid as some of them were, with tin cans and old tires and broken washbasins. The cottage was dark, overfurnished and cosy. There was really only one downstairs room, kitchen and parlour combined, smelling of woodsmoke. It was clean. Old Hilda Mockett, bent double in her chair by the range, cackled with greeting. Her eyesight and memory were fine. The great-niece was new to Eleanor. She looked old to be anybody's great-niece. She was a widow herself, stiffish but pretty active, called Mary Snaith. Neighbours dropped in the groceries and such. They managed pretty well, on their combined pensions. The milkman came as far as the farm, half a mile away. The postman came once or twice a week, whether there was any post or not, and there never was any. Lonely? Not a bit of it. They knew they couldn't go on as they were for ever, but they were all right for a good bit yet.

Eleanor saw a large, stuffed cuddly toy, a black and white dog with long ears. Snoopy. Snoopy was suddenly every-where, but it was funny to find him here.

Somebody had given it to them, as a kind of decoration. They couldn't rightly remember who it was. One of the kiddies from the farm? The dog was supposed to be a beagle, so somebody had said.

Mr Simon's twins? Lovely children, the image of their poor dear mother. Seems they might have looked in. Couldn't say when or how often.

Oh no, thought Eleanor, oh no. Those women are both as bright as buttons. They know exactly where that toy came from. They could tell you the origin of every single object in the cottage. They could tell you exactly who had been to see them, over the last half dozen years, and what was said, and whether the visitor had a cup of tea. They knew very well how often and how recently the twins had been there. Why the secrecy? Because the twins had asked them to keep it a secret. Why? What could be more innocent than calling on that ultra-respectable little household? It was even something to be proud of, to take credit for.

The twins would 'go to Sterney later'. The twins were going to Sterney already. They were going secretly. They were spying, using Hilda Mockett's cottage as a base.

Why go secretly to a place where you are sure of a welcome? A game? A kind of dare? It could be a perfectly innocent game, to see how close they could get to the house without being seen. Even to get into the house.

142

They had not stolen or damaged anything, as far as Eleanor knew; and she would surely have heard of any outrage, if only from the servants.

If an innocent game, why drag Hilda Mockett and Mary Snaith into a conspiracy of silence? The twins had bewitched them, of course, with their charm and their chatter. Charm - most dangerous of gifts, because it made life too easy. Melissa had been loaded with it. Dick, though handsome in his way, had little. Eleanor herself thought she had little. She could never have seduced a tough and beady-eyed old creature like Hilda Mockett to tell lies about where she had been.

The twins' indifference to Sterney was a complete pose. They were devoured with interest about every bit of it. But secretly. Why secretly?

'We're biding our time.'

Eleanor took hold of herself. She gave herself a mental shake, and told herself to stop being ridiculously fanciful. The Snoopy toy might have come from anywhere, from anybody. The women might really have forgotten who gave it to them. The twins might not have been near the cottage for years. Even if they did have a game of spying on Sterney, where was the harm? They were not trespassing, going to a place where they had a standing invitation.

'We'll go there later.'

Eleanor felt like a pendulum; and at the end of one swing she mocked at herself for fears and suspicions which were manufactured by her own middle-aged spinsterish busybody imagination; and at the end of the other swing she was puzzled and frightened.

'I've just understood. I can't live with it.'

What could Melissa not live with?

'We're biding our time.'

There was nobody Eleanor could share any of this with.

Until Pippa came.

It was the summer of the twins' twelfth birthday; the summer they were taken for the second time to see the boarding-school where they were to go in September; the last summer of childhood, perhaps, before the changes and challenges of adolescence. Certainly they were still children, their voices high and clear and identical, their hair bleached to tow in the sun. They were still young children, but their father treated them as adults – gave them complete freedom, complete trust; never made a household or a holiday decision without consulting them; even deferred to their opinions, Eleanor thought, about music and pictures and books. Still young children, but with a self-possession – a kind of quiet caution in the face of the world, for all their physical daring – which was absurdly precocious, almost middle-aged. Other people noticed this, and misnamed it. They called it manners, consideration; they gave credit to Simon for the old-fashioned excellence of the way he was raising the twins. It would have made Eleanor laugh, to hear the way people talked about the twins, if it did not sometimes make her want to scream. She could discuss none of this with anybody, until Pippa came.

It all happened because the County Council was re-aligning a bit of the road between Milchester and Sterney, and the bulldozers uncovered the ruins of a Roman villa. In doing so they mashed up a large mosaic; the result was a jumbo jigsaw puzzle with all the pieces square and no picture on the box to guide the solver. Thousands of squares of various-coloured stone were collected, tons of earth being hand-sieved as though by prospectors for gold, while the county waited for its new road. The Kendalls tried to constitute themselves patrons and directors of the project, but the Ministry of Works and the County Archaeological Association were there before them. The jigsaw went to the Milchester Museum, and a team of experts was recruited to put it back together.

Eleanor went, like hundreds of others, to stare respectfully at the meaningless heap of stones; like hundreds of others she despaired at the thought of recreating the design. While in the museum, she saw her friend the Curator. He asked her – as a friend, and as a Trustee of the Sterney Trust – if she had made any plans for the Old Vicarage. She had not, because she had not finished sorting through her father's things. But she agreed that the time for making plans was near.

A few days later a cool voice on the telephone announced itself as Philippa Davies, calling at the suggestion of the Curator of the Milchester Museum. Mrs Davies was an archaeologist, an expert on the Romano-British period. She had accepted an offer of employment from the County Council and the Museum, probably for two years, to work on the mosaic. She needed somewhere to live, near Milchester but preferably not in the city. Might she come and call on Miss Collis?

Her voice was pleasant. She sounded very nice. She sounded congenial to Eleanor. She would come to tea on Sunday.

She was nice. She was congenial to Eleanor.

The first surprise was her age. Eleanor had expected an expert on mosaics to be at least as old as herself, in the middle-to-late forties; but Philippa Davies was only thirty-three. The second surprise was her appearance. She was smart, chic, dressed simply but not cheaply. She wore a wedding ring and two other rings, a good diamond and a circle of sapphires. She was not exactly pretty but she was very nearly beautiful, having a wide mouth and high cheekbones that gave her a Slav look. She was of medium height. Her legs and figure were excellent – quite in Melissa's class. Her hair was light brown and wavy: Eleanor thought it had been expensively cut, but she knew she was not a good judge of the price of hair-dos.

Philippa was a widow. So much, but no more, Eleanor learned. She was being paid for re-assembling the mosaic, but modestly; she had an income from letting the house she had inherited in London to an American bank which lodged its executives there. Her father was dead, her mother alive and living in South Africa, which Philippa hated on moral grounds with which Eleanor totally agreed.

Eleanor showed her the house. There was never any doubt in either of their minds that Philippa would move in. She could have the spare room immediately, and old Mr Collis's room as soon as it had been redecorated. A figure was agreed for rent, without haggling. By this time they were on Christian-name terms.

Neither smoked. Both drank wine, neither spirits. Pippa would come to church once or twice a month, perhaps, but probably not every Sunday. Pippa looked forward to doing some of the cooking and to helping in the garden, both of which she enjoyed. She could of course entertain her own friends, and have people to stay.

It was extraordinary that such a large decision, affecting

two lives for two years, could be made with such speed and such certainty.

Pippa moved in the following weekend, relieved to be out of the poky little hotel in Milchester, relieved not to be paying its prices, especially for meals, deeply relieved to be away from the noise of the town. Almost at once it was as though she had always been there. With miraculous speed she learned where everything went, in kitchen and pantry and larder. She did enjoy cooking, and she was good at it. She was tidy without being obsessive about it. She could do shopping for the household in Milchester at lunchtime, where there was so much more variety than in the village grocery or newsagent.

Her husband had been killed in a car smash, four years before. Eleanor thought Pippa would one day want to tell her about it, and about him.

'She doesn't look in the least like an archaeologist,' said Eleanor to Simon. 'I expected something acted by Margaret Rutherford in an Ealing comedy. She's not a bit like that. It's a tremendous success.'

'It's a bit soon to be sure of that,' said Simon.

'No. If we do get on each others' nerves, there's plenty of room. But I don't think we will.'

'You might have talked to me about it.'

'Why? No, I don't mean that. But you haven't been guided by me very much. Anyway, you can see for yourself tomorrow.'

Simon did not much want to go out to dinner with Eleanor. He was still deeply fond of her; she still meant infinitely well; but she had become a bore on a number of subjects, and above all on the subject of the twins.

Simon had not, as Eleanor seemed to think, been pushed into any decision by the twins, or been so stupid as to have been guided entirely by them. He had consulted people whose judgement he respected – teachers, parsons, the Sterney Trustees whose employee in a qualified sense he was, and neighbours whose children were at, or had been to, boarding schools. He took advice from nobody who had not met the twins, because, without knowing them, nobody could understand the realities, the specialness of the twins' situation. The specialness of the twins themselves. Simon met differences of

146

opinion in detail, of course, but unanimity in one thing: the twins *were* special; their talent, their manners, their precocious but un-brat-like maturity, combined to demand from any school they went to, from any adults who had charge of them, the very highest qualities. The worst and most irresponsible thing would be failure to foster such startling potential. Everybody said so. Some of the sages Simon consulted were more influenced than others by the twins' beauty, Melissa's beauty; it would not have been possible, Simon thought, to have been totally uninfluenced by it.

Old Eleanor thought she ought to have been consulted, at all points, about everything. But there was no need to consult her – you got her advice whether you asked for it or not. The thought of an evening of Eleanor telling him how to bring up his children was depressing. The thought of Eleanor's new lodger was depressing, too. She did not resemble Margaret Rutherford. If that was the most that Eleanor could think of to recommend her, Simon thought he faced an evening of boredom on both flanks.

Wearily, exhausted by a day full of irritations caused by the stupidity of other people and the earnest conscientiousness of Dick, Simon put on a dark suit, and got a bottle of moderate claret out of the cupboard he called his wine-cellar. (The Sterney cellars were the size of a tennis court.) The twins were playing a renaissance suite as he left – Peter on the inadequate little piano, Pandora on the alto recorder, the best of the collection they were gradually assembling, inspired by a concert the Dolmetsch family had given in Milchester cathedral. Simon knew that, at some moment, they would swap instruments. It was a pity that they could neither afford nor house a harpsichord. It was a pity Simon could not stay to listen to the twins making their cool and elegant music.

The evening got off to a bad start – not disastrous, just awkward. Eleanor had put herself, it seemed to Simon, in an invidious social position. She was showing off Pippa to Simon, and Simon to Pippa. She was anxious to justify to Simon her recruitment of Pippa into her household; so she invited Simon to admire some flowers which Pippa had arranged and some cheese-straws which Pippa had made. She told Simon, with a sort of dogged effusiveness, that Pippa had herself made the dress she was wearing, and invited him to admire the style and workmanship. Simon was made to feel that he was being sold something by a doorstep salesman of unusual zeal and ineptitude. He did not perversely or mulishly refuse to admire flowers, cheese-straws or dress; but he was put on the defensive. He made the minimum of polite comments, and then found it difficult to think of anything to say.

Pippa, meanwhile, seemed to bridle at the praise being heaped upon her; she seemed gruff in manner and grudging in personality. It was impossible to guess whether she thought she was being praised too much, or not enough.

Simon was not disgusted by Pippa's flower arrangement. It was like any other bowl of early-summer flowers in any middle-class house in England. It might have been done by Eleanor, or any of the hostesses whose flowers he saw. It was conventional, symmetrical: philadephus, fruit-blossom, young leaves; the stems, he was sure, had been correctly crushed with pliers before being eased into the bunched chicken-wire which kept them as any good pupil of Constance Spry would wish them kept.

Melissa had hurled miscellaneous armfuls of flowers into vases, sung to them, caused them to dance to her singing, embarked on melodramas in which the flowers became characters in a puppet theatre, and walked away from dramatic and idiosyncratic successes.

Simon was not disgusted by Pippa's cheese-straws. They tasted like cheese-straws. He could not imagine Melissa making cheese-straws. He supposed she must have done so. They must have eaten cheese-straws in the days before they moved into Sterney, in the days when she did the cooking. She would not have thought it an activity interesting enough to talk about.

Pippa's dress, which Eleanor was so exclamatory about? Simon had lived with Melissa long enough to understand a little about fashion, and to learn – by comparing Melissa with the rest of the world – that if it did not express the personality of the wearer it was a fraud and a bore. Melissa dressed up as Melissa. She never looked like anybody else because she never was like anybody else. Of Pippa's personality the vaunted dress gave no hint. It looked all right; it looked like a dress.

They chatted before dinner, in the gathering dusk. Simon heard himself asking polite, conventional questions about Pippa's work at the museum. He heard her guarded replies. He heard in his mind's ear, with aching clarity, the twins playing the renaissance dances on piano and alto recorder.

'What does she look like, Daddy?' asked Pandora when Simon tucked them up.

'Look like? I honestly don't know.'

'You must know. You spent three hours with her. Didn't you ever look at her?'

'Yes, of course I did.'

Of course he had. He had not forgotten his manners because he was dining with his sister. What did she look like? Pandora's feminine curiosity was understandable, inevitable; and Simon found he was perfectly unable to satisfy it. He had difficulty summoning Pippa Davies's face and figure to his memory. She had made, it seemed, no impression on him at all.

'She must be pretty dim,' said Peter.

'No, I shouldn't think so. I was pretty dim this evening. I was tired. Probably I was so dull she was bored, and so neither of us said much.'

'I bet Aunt Eleanor made up for that.'

'Yes, she was full of gas.'

'We played a new recorder duet after you left. Elizabethan. I wish you'd been here.'

'I wish I had.'

'It needs accompaniment. We want another pianist. It's all right at school, but we need another one here.'

'It's absolutely maddening I was never taught,' said Simon.

'Yes,' said Pandora, 'especially because you love it so much.'

'I believe Pippa Davies plays.'

'You're not sure?'

'No.'

'You spent ten hours with her, and you never properly discovered the *one* important thing about her?'

Simon laughed. He kissed Pandora, briefly massaged Peter's shoulder, and turned the light out.

'I'm afraid old Simon wasn't at the top of his form this evening.'

'I'm afraid I wasn't either.'

'Hm?'

'I was on approval, on parade, like somebody's girlfriend meeting his family. I still remember that with horror, being driven down to Tunbridge Wells to meet Merlyn's family. That was ten years ago. I sat like a dummy, being cross-examined.'

'It never happened to me,' said Eleanor. 'We never got that far.'

'You were lucky,' said Pippa.

She said no more. They finished the washing-up talking about the washing-up.

To Pippa – as a stranger, as someone who had never so much as heard of Melissa – Eleanor was able to talk about the twins. Pippa did not have the habit, which all the locals had, of adoring the memory of Melissa. She did not have the habit of regarding Simon as the steadiest and most sensible man in England. She did not have the habit, otherwise apparently universal, of almost worshipping the beautiful, talented, gentle, motherless twins.

So long dammed, Eleanor's suspicions poured out.

Even in her ears, it all sounded pretty thin, unconnected, unconvincing stuff.

A kick on the ankle at a long-ago Christmas party. A serious accident on the school playground to a child who had been teasing Pandora. The destruction of two childish hiding-places. The disappearance of gifts from the Kendalls. Odd phrases, references, looks. Evasiveness, deceit.

'None of that,' said Pippa, 'adds up to a row of beans. I've kicked other children at parties. I've hidden presents I didn't want. I've avoided going to places I didn't want to go to, even when there wasn't a logical reason for not wanting to go. We're all evasive sometimes. We all have secrets. By your own account, neither of the twins could possibly have been involved in that poor child's accident. Or have started that fire.'

'You must think me insane, paranoid, unhinged by the change of life or something,' said Eleanor.

150

'I don't know. Melissa sounds insane.'

'No. Yes, in a special sense. She was not in the least like other people.'

'She committed suicide because the baby died. When she had two other young children.'

'Because of how the baby died. The fact of his death shattered her, but she was beginning to get over it. I think it was something to do with how the baby died. She blamed herself. She thought she was actually, physically responsible. But there was something she couldn't live with.'

'I'm not clear,' said Pippa, 'how the kind of temporary insanity that leads to suicide relates to what you've been saying about the twins.'

'Nor am I. But there's something about their self-possession that sends cold shivers up my spine.'

'That sounds the opposite of insanity.'

'It's not altogether the opposite of Melissa. What I'm talking about is strangeness, differentness. People said Melissa was a creature from another planet. Her grandfather said so. They said the same about her mother. The twins are creatures from another planet.'

'I'll bear all this in mind when I meet them,' said Pippa. 'Till then I'll suspend judgement.'

Of course Pippa met the twins almost immediately.

It was in the village shop, on Saturday morning. The twins propped their bicycles outside the shop, and waved to their Aunt Eleanor through the plate-glass window. When they came in she introduced them to the tall young lady who was Mrs Davies. The twins shook hands, smiled, asked and answered questions. They spent their pocket money carefully.

They were just twelve. Physically and in manner they looked exactly that age. Astonishing precocity, if any, appeared only in what Eleanor called their self-possession. They were dressed similarly, and absolutely normally, in jeans, T-shirts and sneakers; but not identically. They were very similar in feature and indistinguishable in voice. They did not rush away when they had finished their own shopping, but offered to carry Eleanor's and Pippa's groceries.

151

'You didn't say she was smashing,' said Pandora to her father at lunch.

'Who?'

'Aunt Eleanor's friend. Mrs Davies.'

'Is she smashing?'

'You said you'd looked at her, but you can't have done.'

'She is comely among the maidens,' said Peter. 'She looks like that ballet dancer who ran away from Russia.'

'Nureyev?'

'No, a girl. And she *does* play the piano.'

'We found out in one tenth of a second,' said Pandora, 'what you didn't find out after five hours.'

'And there isn't a piano at Aunt Eleanor's,' said Peter. 'So she's coming here.'

'Tomorrow afternoon,' said Pandora. 'We'll play for a bit, and have tea for a bit, and play for a bit, and then you can give her a drink.'

'Ah,' said Simon. 'Remind me to put some Vouvray on the ice.'

'Nothing you told me,' said Pippa. 'can I attach to those delightful children.'

'They've made another conquest,' said Eleanor.

'I wouldn't put it like that at all. I'm not in the habit of being seduced or suborned or bewitched. But I am in the habit of responding to warm, attractive people. And of being impressed by good manners, especially in children. And of admiring beauty.'

'Oh yes, they're beautiful,' said Eleanor. 'They're certainly beautiful.'

'I'll disappoint them tomorrow. I'm shockingly out of practice.'

'They won't say so.'

'I shall. As an excuse for playing so badly.'

'The twins don't make excuses for themselves, or accept them from other people.'

Pippa burst out laughing. 'That sounds like an obituary in *The Times*. Of a general they're trying to pretend was popular.'

Eleanor laughed too, reluctantly. 'It did come out rather pompous. Helen Kendall told me once that Melissa had told her that the twins had never been punished. Helen was dreadfully shocked, but Melissa said they'd never done anything to be punished for.'

'I see what you mean. Putting it another way, they don't make excuses because they don't need excusing.'

'You don't see what I mean. Putting it still another way . . .' said Eleanor: but she stopped. The truth was that the twins got away with things. But Pippa had already joined the army of those to whom it was no good saying this.

CHAPTER 8

Simon made an effort to look at Philippa Davies with new eyes, after what his children had told him. She climbed out of her small Renault in the middle of a fine Sunday afternoon; the action pushed her cotton skirt up her thighs, and it was impossible not to see that her legs were bare and that they were excellent – long, slender, shapely, smooth as peeled eggs.

Yes, she did look a little like a Russian dancer. Yes, you could say she was striking. It was odd that somebody had had to point this out to Simon. He would have backed himself to spot a handsome woman. Perhaps not so odd. If beauty was what Philippa Davies had, it was not of a kind that rang any bells with him. He had a personal and permanent standard of beauty, and it was still in front of his eyes, daily, recreated in the faces of the twins.

It was certainly true that Philippa Davies did not look like an archaeologist, like a character played by Margaret Rutherford.

Simon supposed that his failure to react to her in any way at their first meeting was a combination of his fatigue, which had been real, his half-conscious resentment at not having been consulted by Eleanor, and his habitual assessment of attractiveness being simply on a scale of similarity to Melissa.

The twins greeted her as an old friend. They drew her into the house and on to the piano stool, from which one of the five dogs was dislodged. She played a few chords and a scale, trying the piano, flexing her fingers. She immediately gave evidence of a confidence which inspired confidence. The twins were visibly relieved – there had been an obvious possibility that she was hopeless.

Pandora put a sheet of music in front of her. 'It's by Anon,' she said. 'A lot of our music is. It's rather a pity – we'd like to give credit. I hope it's what you like. It's so simple it may be boring.'

'Heavens, are you asking me to sight-read?'

'We've played it with the piano and one recorder,' said Peter, 'and with the piano and the other recorder, and both recorders, but never with the piano and both recorders. We don't know exactly how it'll sound.'

Philippa began picking out the notes. It was simple, a slow dance, perhaps a pavane, but with ornaments in the recorder parts that to Simon did not sound simple at all. Philippa played self-effacingly, without pedal, when either or both recorders were playing; she let herself go a little more when the piano was alone. She once or twice had to stop and go back. Simon was struck, as often before, by the way the recorders always came in absolutely together, and never lost one another in the contrapuntal passages.

Simon was sitting in a corner with a dog in his lap. He should have been busy in his small garden.

They played non-stop for three hours. All four of them forgot completely about tea. The players paused only to turn to a new piece; they spoke only to agree on a tempo or a place to restart. At six o'clock Simon, rapt, became aware of dogs' noses being pressed into his knees. They were right. It was past their dinner-time. He waited until the end of the trio they were playing, which the twins had transcribed from part of a suite by Dowland for the lute. Rising, he broke the spell.

'I'm exhausted,' said Philippa. 'My fingers are falling off.'

The twins were contrite. They apologised for their thoughtlessness.

'I've adored every moment,' she said. 'Did you have to transpose as well as transcribe?'

Simon fed the dogs and uncorked the Vouvray.

He came into the sitting-room and into the middle of a conversation about the transposing instruments, which you played in a different key to that of the score. In spite of his love of music and knowledge of the classical repertoire, he was out of his depth in these professional technicalities.

155

Philippa was animated. Simon had seen her bored and embarrassed, he thought, at Eleanor's; he had seen her face set in total concentration, sight-reading unfamiliar music, much of it in the twins' manuscript; now he saw her eager, interested, laughing with the twins.

He could see that, for many eyes if not for his own, her face when animated could have a kind of beauty.

Once begun, there was no stopping this arrangement that gave so much pleasure. Pippa came once or twice a week in the evening, when she got back from the museum. She said it was marvellous relaxation after frustrating hours with her gigantic jigsaw. She came for two or three hours every weekend; sometimes, in wet weather, she came both Saturday and Sunday.

Simon thought that Eleanor should be delighted that her lodger, who was also her friend, was finding something so congenial to do. But he suspected that Eleanor's nose was actually out of joint. Especially because Eleanor had never taken music seriously as an artistic activity; especially because she had ideas about interfering in the lives of the twins; especially because she was a shade proprietorial about Pippa, as she was about the lame ducks she kept an eye on, as she had been – still would be, given the chance – about Simon himself.

The twins taught Pippa to play the various recorders which they had saved up their pocket-money to buy. (Eleanor thought they got too much pocket-money.) She caught on immediately. They were not difficult instruments to learn to play, but they were difficult to play well. After weeks she was still far short of the twins' skill.

They wanted to try madrigals, but it was impossible locally to find a tenor who could sight-read. Simon could, after a fashion, having sung in the choir at Marlborough, but he was a baritone. The ensemble sounded wrong and hollow without a tenor. Also Pippa was a natural soprano, like the twins; she could make very little noise at the bottom of the mezzo or alto parts. They gave up madrigals. Simon was relieved. He had been slowing them up. He preferred listening.

The three of them embarked on musical explorations, Pippa having found bundles of uncatalogued old music in the museum. They extended their range from Elizabethan and renaissance into baroque. They sighed for virginal, spinet, clavichord and harpsichord.

Simon was there when they played, whenever possible. It was often impossible, because of conferences with Dick or necessary journeys. He would come back to find an absorbed threesome. They stopped to greet him, but it was a quick greeting, and they turned back at once to their music. It was impossible not to feel a little left out.

Pippa became a member of Simon's family, but Simon never established a relationship with her. Most of her visits were shorter than any of them would have wished, because she had a duty to Eleanor and the Old Vicarage. It would not have been sensible, or fair to the twins, to ask her to sit and talk to Simon instead of making music. So they never did sit and talk. Simon wondered whether, if they had sat and talked, they would actually have found anything to talk about. His job? Hers? Local gossip? World affairs? Any talk there was when she was there was musical, and Simon could only contribute at the level of preferring one piece to another.

The summer suited Pippa. He light brown hair was lighter, and her skin a pleasing golden-brown. Thin summer clothes showed off her excellent figure.

She never talked about her husband, or how he had died.

Simon was entitled to four weeks' paid holiday, but he had never taken as much. He had hardly been abroad since he came out of the Army, and he had no taste for British holiday beaches. Melissa's favourite place in the world had been Sterney: and as she had seen so many other places she was in a position to judge. She had wanted no more travelling. After her death, Simon had recoiled from the thought of travelling alone, or with two young children. Now, perhaps, when the twins could look after themselves, they should be offered a change.

They did not want a change. They might find themselves somewhere where there was no piano, where music would be forbidden because it disturbed people. They would lose a third of their trio. The Sterney estate (if not, as it seemed, the house) was their favourite place, too.

Simon was convinced they really meant it, and thankfully agreed.

157

Eleanor thought this ridiculous and wrong, although she hardly ever went away herself.

No kind of intimacy developed between Pippa and the Kendalls of Sterney. It might have done. Dick was an academic as well as a titled landowner; Helen was academic-bred, and half a don; Pippa was a kind of practical academic, using her learning in three dimensions. But a spark, though lit and blown upon, never achieved more than a dull glow.

That Eleanor introduced Pippa to Sterney was inevitable but not, perhaps, helpful. A certain social awkwardness continued to distance Helen from Eleanor. A correct relationship, slightly feudal in character, had replaced what had promised to be a real friendship. Pippa came in half-way down the feudal ladder.

Eleanor saw that, from the first moment, Helen was making a conscientious effort to be friendly to this presentable young widow who had come to the village; but that the words that came out were patronising.

To Eleanor's dismay, Pippa was visibly astonished that such a cultured household should be so totally unmusical. She was astonished to see a Steinway grand with the cover locked. Eleanor grieved that Pippa's surprise should be so evident.

Helen showed Pippa the transformation she had wrought between the house and the lake: the infinity of geometrical parterres, the little box hedges that would be, the masses of bedding-plants that already were. Helen did not say, 'Look at what I've done,' but simply, 'Look at the formal gardens.'

Pippa's response was unfortunate. She said, 'What a nightmare to inherit. Who does the weeding?'

Eleanor had admired Pippa's honesty. She did not do so at that moment.

They did not, on their first and almost last visit, see Ralph and Cathy, except in the distance. 'They're running wild somewhere,' said Helen. 'We encourage self-reliance.'

Pippa did see them, from the car, as they drove away after tea. They were sitting in the shade of a tree, on chairs, reading. They were under the eye of a large woman who was knitting.

Simon knew some of the things the twins did during the long bright days of those summer holidays. They went great distances on their bicycles, to beautiful places, bird sanctuaries, famous gardens. They spent days and sometimes nights with friends, especially those who had pianos and those who had swimming pools. They still read a lot, but not in chairs under trees. They took the five dogs for gigantic walks, with their lunch in their pockets. They were out of doors most of every day when it was fine, and often when it was not. Their faces and arms were brown and their hair bleached. In the evenings, they played the piano and other instruments, and copied and transcribed music. As far as Simon knew, they never went to Sterney Court. He was entirely disinclined to pry into things they did that he did not know about. He trusted them to behave sensibly and to look after one another. They got into no trouble of any kind, and came to no harm. Simon's experience in the Army and on the estate convinced him that people became more trustworthy through being trusted; and he was far too busy to combine being an estate manager with being a nanny.

The twins went off to their new school in September. In spite of the older Ralph Kendall's generosity, Simon foresaw years of small drinks and leather patches on the elbows of his coats. He thought he was morally obliged to do at least as well by the twins as his father had done by him, and to make if necessary at least as many sacrifices. He more and more strongly believed that the talent and intelligence of his children merited the best. And he believed with them that they should be together. After Smiler's death they had supported their mother, and one another. After Melissa's death they had supported him, and one another. If their paths were ever to diverge, it was not yet.

He missed them terribly. He hated his solitary breakfasts and solitary suppers. He missed the music which had so often filled the little house.

Since there was no longer any reason for Pippa to come, she did not come.

The twins were good about writing. They wrote occasionally to Eleanor and Pippa, and weekly to Simon. If they were homesick they did not show it in their letters. They said they

159

saw a lot of each other, although they were in different houses. They got on fine with most of the pupils and most of the teachers. The school had a good reputation for music and the arts: they had the use of a harpsichord and a church organ.

They came home for one long weekend at half-term. They spent their first half-hour at home on the floor of the sitting room, being trodden on and slobbered over by the dogs. They were cheerful about their school. The food was all right, the work interesting, the beds tolerable, the people nice. They had made many friends. They admitted to homesickness in the first three weeks or so, but Simon had the odd feeling that they did so out of politeness.

The weather that weekend was revolting. They filled the house with music again. Pippa came.

It would have been absurd to expect a visible change in the twins after only a few weeks, but Simon sensed a change. The twins seemed if possible closer: perhaps because at school they were living for the first time in their lives under separate roofs.

They went to have tea with Eleanor. They did not go to Sterney.

'They're keeping more back,' said Eleanor to Pippa. 'They're more secret.'

'They seem extrovert enough to me. More than I was at that age. More than I've ever been since.

'Oh well, they're affectionate, and they chatter away. But have you noticed how they never talk about themselves?'

'They're not boastful, if that's what you mean.'

'They're opaque. They're elusive. They always were. They always had the knack of not answering questions. Now they somehow put you off even asking them. It's not that they've withdrawn into themselves, in the sense of becoming two introverted individuals. They're a partnership which doesn't need anybody else.'

'They need me, to play the piano.'

'Yes, to play the piano.'

'When children are very young,' said Pippa slowly, 'they live their whole lives in public. In their families, anyway. Nothing is secret. It can't be – they're too dependent. But as

160

they grow, they gradually become more private. You do things in private and your thoughts are private. As you grow up you're *entitled* to privacy. I don't see anything sinister in that. Secrets are not necessarily guilty. I'd almost call it a question of manners, of seemliness. Very young children shove everything about themselves down your throat, however boring or disgusting. They're the complete egoists. Growing up is not only needing privacy, it's also learning restraint. Learning manners. By the same token, an adult in charge of a young child has to know everything about the child, in order to look after it, in order to keep it safe. As the child grows up, that's no longer either a duty or a right. Restraint works both ways. Manners work both ways.'

Eleanor clearly saw the implications of what Pippa was saying, in regard to herself. She regretted having started the conversation.

Opening off the library at Sterney there was a small room traditionally known as the library office. It was assumed that it had, indeed, been occupied at one time by a person cataloguing the library, or repairing bindings and pasting in bookplates. Within living memory it had been used as an overflow book store, housing shelves of volumes which were without interest in either physical form or literary content. (Books had to be unattractive, unreadable and valueless – all three – to qualify for the library office, a rule made about the turn of the century.) There were two steel-engravings of classical antiquity, in style a long way after Piranesi, between the shelves, a pine table and two upright chairs, and the only rug in Sterney with a bare patch and frayed edges. There was a radiator; the room was warm. There was a window very large for the room, owing to the demands of exterior symmetry; it was light. The mouldings of ceiling and fireplace carried on, more delicately, those of the library.

It was a backwater: a section of the house which was unused and, as it stood, useless.

Helen Kendall's energies, now that she had her doctorate and as many children as she intended, needed an outlet. The New England puritan work-ethic was as strong in her academic background as in her mother-in-law's commercial background. The new formal gardens had occupied her; they were finished. She examined the house. There was much that she might have changed, in the interests of historical purism, but she knew herself insufficiently learned, as yet, to recreate with absolute fidelity, and she was too honest a scholar to make guesses. Her restless eye fell on the library office. She decided to make it an oasis within the oasis that was Sterney. It was to be the jewel in Sterney's crown. It was to be her office, and to express her personality.

The first thing was to get rid of the useless books. They were offered to Eleanor, Pippa and other literate neighbours; they could cart away any that they wanted, not free but at a modest price. There were almost no takers. The books were given to the Red Cross library in Milchester, and taken there in a van. Eleanor, who helped in the Red Cross library two mornings a week, went through them with a colleague. All but a few were sent for recycling.

The removal of the Victorian pine bookshelves revealed panels, also of pine. Helen had part of the panelling stripped. But the grain was not pretty. Obviously the panelling had always been painted, and must be painted again. It was all painted white, pending decisions on a more elaborate scheme. The large white panels, framed in delicate woodcarving, shouted for embellishment. They would show off superbly a series of matched pictures, such as those of high-school horsemanship which Helen had seen at Wilton House, or the Longhi studies of Venetian life in the Ca' Rezzonico.

Or murals. It came to Helen, as she contemplated the panelling in the autumn sunshine. A sequence of murals, depicting the history of Sterney and perhaps aspects of its life today. The model would be the Fragonard room at the Frick.

What a pity it was Rex Whistler was dead.

And then, in early November, a girl came to Sterney village. She was observed in the village shop. She was seen to have a sharp nose, large round spectacles, an active, wiry figure, and a very sweet smile. She was heard to have an educated voice, or (in other but compatible accounts) to sound like one of the toffs. She was to stay for some weeks with old Major Newbury in Fig Tree Cottage, near the church; he was her great-uncle. Her parents were in the process of being acrimoniously

162

divorced, and she was fleeing the horrible atmosphere, the horror of which was entirely brought about by money. Everybody knew all this immediately, because Sterney was that kind of village. The girl was called Charlotte Downing. She was twenty-seven. She had been to the Ruskin and the Royal Academy Schools. Yes, she was an artist.

She became within days a familiar figure in the village: in the picturesque main street, in the churchyard, in the fields and orchards nearby, with sketchbook or easel, in woolly hat and layers of Husky jackets recognised as Major Newbury's. She met and was befriended by Eleanor, inevitably, almost before she met anybody else. Eleanor saw her work. She thought the drawings showed more skill than originality, but they were undoubtedly accomplished. Charlotte was a professional; she really drew beautifully, even if the results were in sum conventional. She had a nice colour-sense, too, more dramatic than her draughtsmanship, unmistakably influenced to Eleanor's eye by John Piper's startling atmospherics.

Eleanor suggested a painting of Sterney: even, perhaps, a series from different angles, since Palladian designs are meant to be admired from all sides. Charlotte approached Helen Kendall, after a telephone call from Eleanor. She brought a portfolio of drawings and small paintings.

Helen had found her muralist.

They went into committee at once, to decide the subjects that would adorn the panels of the library office. Medieval Sterney, in the time of the first Talbots, as a basis for which Helen could produce woodcuts of thirteenth-century castles and antiquarian accounts, to which Eleanor had steered her, of the local countryside. The Talbots of Sterney entertaining King Edward IV about 1460, tame fallow-deer being coursed in the park for the king's amusement. Queen Elizabeth's visit, to a house rebuilt with large windows replacing the slits for arrows, and using masonry from a dissolved and demolished monastery. The building of the present house, after the model of the Villa Razzari near Padua. The triumphal return of the first Lord Kendall de Sterney after his introduction into the House of Lords. The Kendalls entertaining King Edward VII to tea, under awnings on the south terrace, an occasion of which there was in the library a whole album of photographs. Sterney at war, with air-raid shelters and student nurses.

Sterney today – perhaps the children in the pony-trap, with the house and lake in the distance.

Charlotte was to prepare sketches of the overall design of each panel; innumerable studies of the detail; then larger sketches in colour; all stages to be scrutinised by her patroness. The scale of commission was discussed, but a final decision not taken. They both knew that Charlotte was selling in a buyer's market.

Charlotte met Ralph and Cathy as she left; they had just been brought back from school. They took her to see the pony-trap, and Pooter the Shetland, now elderly and of uncertain temper. Charlotte was charmed to put this little equipage, with its youthful and attractive passengers, in the foreground of the final panel.

Helen swore Charlotte, and her own family, to secrecy about the whole project. She liked the idea of unveiling it to an astonished world only when it was all complete. Nobody was to see or hear about work in progress. If asked why she was spending so much time at Sterney, Charlotte was to say she had been commissioned to paint views of the house and gardens.

The twins came back for the Christmas holidays, looking a little taller and stronger, looking a little more different from one another. They dressed more differently, although they were still pre-adolescent. It seemed, from their conversation and observed activities, and from their school reports, that they were developing differently in tastes and talents. Music they still shared, but outside that Peter was more verbal, Pandora more visual. Both were said, in the reports of tutors and form-teachers, to be scholarship material, to be likeable and popular and co-operative. There was a hint that they found it a bit too easy, with the consequent danger that they might later under-achieve.

Eleanor tried to extract from the twins an admission that they had been miserably homesick, or that they were being so little extended by the progressive schooling that their father was wasting his money. She was not mischief-making; she was deeply concerned about the twins; she was worried about them and worried by them.

'Oh well of course,' said Peter, 'Pandora cried on my

shoulder a few times, so a master beat her, because there's a strict rule against crying, and then of course the bigger girls bullied her and pulled her hair and teased her –'

'*What?*'

Pandora giggled. She had not wept, and nobody had bullied either of them. They would work hard when the time came.

Pippa's visits were resumed. Peter had started the oboe and Pandora the flute, and they had been encouraged to bring home instruments belonging to the school. They did not discard their recorders and early music, but they were advancing towards Haydn and Mozart. Simon was there whenever possible. He noticed objectively – almost fleetingly – that Pippa looked well in the winter. The cold air gave her cheeks a high, healthy colour. She and the twins had a great deal to talk about; she and Simon had nothing to talk about, and no time to talk in the intensity of music-making.

Eleanor's nose, unlike Pippa's, was always red in the winter. Charlotte Downing's little sharp nose was red, too; the difference was that she knew and laughed about it. She came to tea to meet the twins, and said immediately that she wanted to draw them. She did no portrait drawings but a lot of sketches, studies. She got the twins to sit side by side on the sofa as though on the seat of the pony-trap, and sketched them so. She did not say why. She did not breathe a word about the murals.

Simon thought the likenesses excellent but the drawings a little obvious and sentimental, like those of most child portraits, especially the most fashionable. Pandora's long fair hair, untidy that afternoon because of a walk with the dogs, became an impossibly disciplined Hollywood mane. The twins were romanticised in the drawings, which was the last thing they needed.

Charlotte took the sketches away with her; but she said she would want the twins as models again.

'No,' said Helen. 'The idea's ridiculous. We live here. My children are part of Sterney as it is today. They're the Kendalls, the new generation of the family that belongs here. You want to put the Collis kids in because they're blond. It simply isn't a good enough reason. The trap belongs to us, and the pony, and the park. The twins never even come here.

165

Having them in this mural would simply be misrepresentation. I want people to look at this panel in a hundred years' time and say, "*Those* are the very children that lived in *this* house in 1973." You must see the force of that.'

Charlotte argued in vain. She could not say that the twins were more beautiful than the Kendall children. She was still selling in a buyer's market.

'"According to local tradition, Queen Elizabeth visited Sterney in the time of Sir Fulke Talbot",' said Pandora, reading aloud from the Victorian volume of local history which Eleanor had found in the second-hand bookshop in the shadow of Milchester cathedral. '"Though such a visit is not inhere – inherently improbable, there is no documentary evidence that it ever actually occurred".' She looked up from the book. 'Charlotte's just guessing, then.'

'Guessing at what?' asked Eleanor. 'Why on earth should Charlotte guess that Queen Elizabeth visited Sterney?'

Pandora glanced at Peter. She suddenly blushed, vividly, painfully. Eleanor was startled. The twins were so remarkably, so almost unnaturally self-possessed, that neither had ever been seen to blush.

Peter looked angry for a moment. Then his face relaxed into its usual blandness.

Eleanor thought Pandora had given something away. It had never happened before, as far as Eleanor knew. She had spoken without thinking, interested in what she was reading, her guard for once momentarily down. She had blushed out of guilt, shame, embarrassment, apology to Peter. He had been transparent for a split second, showing an anger which normally he totally concealed, if he ever felt it.

'Has Charlotte been insisting that Queen Elizabeth visited Sterney?' said Eleanor, determined to learn something from these unprecedented chinks in the twins' armour.

'I was talking about Charlotte Webster,' said Pandora. 'A girl at school. She said Queen Elizabeth stayed at Sterney.'

This was possible, but Eleanor was quite certain it was a lie. A reference to a girl at school was no kind of dangerously revealing slip; it would not have caused Pandora's blush or Peter's flash of anger. Pandora had meant Charlotte

Downing. Eleanor's antennae vibrated. The twins did have secrets, a lot of secrets. That blush was a guilty blush.

Pandora, now in total control of herself, mildly repeated that Charlotte Webster, in the form above them at school, had claimed to have read somewhere that Queen Elizabeth had visited Sterney Court. Eleanor could get no more out of either of them.

'I did talk to Lady Kendall about it,' said Charlotte Downing.

It seemed to Eleanor that she blushed, across the dinner table at the Old Vicarage.

'Were the twins there?'

'No.'

'How on earth did the subject come up?'

'I can't talk about it. You'll know one day.'

'Why should Pandora think you thought Queen Elizabeth had been there?'

'I don't know. Unless. . . .'

'What?'

'Really I can't talk about it.'

More secrets, now between Charlotte and Helen. Obviously not guilty ones. Charlotte's blush might have been embarrassed, self-conscious; it was not a guilty blush. Possibly Helen was commissioning Charlotte to do a picture of Queen Elizabeth's apocryphal visit to Sterney, and for some reason they were keeping quiet about it. Possibly because they knew the visit *was* apocryphal. How did Pandora know anything about any of it?

'This conversation has left me miles behind,' said Pippa Davies. 'Why on earth should it matter if one of those children got an idea that Charlotte got an idea about Queen Elizabeth's country-house visiting?'

'It might matter very much,' said Eleanor. 'Something very odd and worrying has been going on for years.'

Eleanor caught the glance which Pippa and Charlotte exchanged. It was a glance which conveyed a shrug of the shoulders. Charlotte had joined Simon, Pippa and the rest of the world in unquestioning adoration of the twins, and in tolerant mockery of herself and her suspicions.

'You didn't see Pandora blush,' she said. 'You didn't see the guilty way she looked at Peter.'

'I blushed all the time when I was Pandora's age,' said Pippa.

'I still do,' said Charlotte.

'Pandora doesn't,' said Eleanor.

'Rubbish,' said Pippa. 'All twelve-year-old girls blush.'

'Pandora isn't all twelve-year-old girls,' said Eleanor.

'No,' said Pippa. 'She's better looking and better mannered and more talented.'

More than ever, Eleanor was a voice crying in the wilderness. Less than ever did she really know what she was crying about.

Eleanor was one of those asked in March to the unveiling of the murals in the library office. Quite a large party assembled in the library. Groups of half a dozen at a time were admitted to the office; more, in that little room, would have made it impossible to see Charlotte's painstaking work.

The Curator of the Museum was there; a photographer from the *Milchester Argus*; some critics lured into the depth of the countryside by the promise of seeing the rest of the house and of being fed by the Kendalls; Pippa, Simon, the artist herself, and the more discriminating local gentry.

The general effect was pleasing. The elegant little room had the air of an enamelled jewel-box. The pictures were well-composed, interesting in subject, skilfully drawn, and in colour dramatic without being overpowering. The most successful, to Eleanor's eye, was the single contemporary scene: Ralph and Cathy Kendall in the park in their pony-trap, with house and lake and bridge and topiary yews in the distance. The least successful was a fanciful gala in which Queen Elizabeth I, in unsuitable clothes copied from a Nicholas Hillyard miniature, was watching some fallow-deer being coursed by greyhounds.

'Charlotte's just guessing.'

Helen Kendall, in a little speech of greeting, had admitted the childishness of keeping the whole thing a secret until it was done. Charlotte's embarrassment in the winter was explained, and her reticence. They *had* kept the secret. Not Eleanor, not anybody else, had had the least idea about the murals.

And the twins kept their secrets.

168

In June the twins were given a thirteenth birthday party at school. They were both now in the junior orchestra, with flute and oboe, and also members of a wind ensemble and a recorder band. Peter was playing the organ and Pandora the harpsichord. They played Viola and Sebastian in a production of *Twelfth Night*, the casting being automatic as they still so resembled one another; their performances were given an almost swooning notice in the school magazine. They were both, that term, awarded internal scholarships. Peter won a prize for a poem about a willow tree; Pandora won a prize for a pen-and-ink drawing of the same tree. Poem and drawing were printed together in the school magazine. It was remarked that Peter's poem was as much about the drawing as about the tree, and Pandora's drawing was as much an illustration of the poem as a representation of the physical tree. It was supposed that they would one day collaborate on a book, if music and drama and all their other activities ever gave them time.

'You must be proud,' said Pippa.

'I'm bursting with pride,' said Simon. 'I have to make a conscious effort not to talk about them all the time.'

They had met by chance on one of the farms. It was odd that such a meeting had not happened before, but it had not. It was early evening. Pippa was stretching her legs after a stuffy day in the museum; Simon had been visiting a tractor-driver who had broken his foot in an accident. Her way home took her past his door. She fell into step beside him, her stride matching his. She was wearing a cotton skirt and shirt; her legs were bare and she wore sandals. The air was oppressive: it felt like thunder.

'We'd better get a move on,' said Simon. 'We might just beat it.'

It beat them – thunder, then a midsummer cloudburst that drenched them both to the skin within seconds.

It was warm. It was no great hardship to be wet.

Pippa's wavy hair was straightened by the inundation, and pasted flat to her head. Her thin clothes were glued to her body, revealing as though she were naked the shape of her breasts and buttocks and thighs. If she minded there was nothing she could do about it.

There was no point in running the last two hundred yards. They could get no wetter.

They joined hands as they walked. Simon did not know how this came about. He did not think Pippa was frightened of the thunder.

They stood dripping in the narrow hall of his cottage. Pippa began to laugh, and Simon found himself laughing.

Suddenly Pippa stopped laughing, and suddenly she was in his arms and he was kissing her passionately. He was startled by the strength of her response. It was as though she had been waiting for this moment, and could barely control herself now that it had come. With one another's help they struggled out of their wet clothes. Naked, Simon went to the bathroom, and returned with two bath-towels. They made a pretence of drying one another between their kisses. Pippa showed no embarrassment and Simon felt none.

Her body was beautiful, and suddenly he fell in love with the unusual beauty of her face.

'This is my first time for five years,' said Pippa, on Simon's bed.

'Mine for six.'

'I expect we'll remember.'

'I expect we will.'

They lay afterwards face to face, locked together.

'How on earth did I do without it?' murmured Pippa.

The thunderstorm had passed. Sunshine blazed on a saturated world. Pippa lay back against pillows. Simon stroked her, marvelling.

'I wonder how long I've been in love with you,' he said.

'I was wondering if you ever would be.'

'Did you want me to be?'

'Yes.'

'What a slob I must be. More than a year. Stupid, blind. And you've been here so often.'

'That was the trouble. You got used to me. I became part of the furniture.'

'Better legs,' said Simon, stroking them.

'I was beginning to think this would never happen. Thank God for rain. I suppose even now it would never have happened if we hadn't been all stuck together with wet. I've wanted you like mad.'

170

'You never showed it.'

'Of course not. I had a struggle not to. I probably did show it, only you didn't notice.'

'What a dolt. What a boring, thick-skinned, thick-headed clod.'

'You're as far from a clod as anyone I ever knew. Or I wouldn't be here.'

'I suppose I was looking at the twins all the time.'

'That's easy to do. I like doing it myself.'

'This is not just because of the twins?'

'They're part of you, of course. They wouldn't be what they are with a different father. You wouldn't be what you are with different children. They're one of the ways I've got of knowing about you. I love them. You know that. They're part of what I love about you. Not the only part I love. I love this part, too.'

Now she was stroking him.

Naked, Pippa telephoned to Eleanor to tell her not to worry. It was exciting to watch her, doing something so usual as telephoning but looking so unusual while she did it. Simon saw that she was proud of her body, proud to show it to him. He was not displeased with his own: he thought it was passable for forty-four, neither flabby nor scrawny. Pippa showed him she thought it was passable.

Simon fetched wine from the ice. He poured glasses.

'Before you decide anything about me,' said Pippa, 'there's something I've got to tell you. Nobody here knows, not Eleanor, nobody. A few people once knew. A few people have never forgiven me, and never will, and never should.'

'You don't have to tell me anything,' said Simon. 'I know everything I need to know.'

'No. You don't. Yes, I must tell you. Nobody else. I must tell you. About Merlyn, my husband. I killed him.'

Simon looked at her blankly. It was impossible to react at once to this statement, made in a flat, quiet voice.

'I had two children,' said Pippa. 'Nobody here knows about them. I had a boy of four and a girl of eighteen months. I killed them.'

Simon felt stifled. He felt insane. He could not be hearing the words he was hearing.

171

'We were going up the M1, to Merlyn's parents, for Christmas,' said Pippa. 'I was driving because he was drunk. After his office party on Christmas Eve. I was going too fast, much too fast, because he'd made us late. The children were hungry and exhausted. I was fed up with Merlyn. I was angry. I was driving aggressively because I was angry. There was a lot of traffic. I hit another car as I was overtaking it. We skidded and turned over. It was dark. It was raining. A car ran into us, when we were upside down. That's how the children were killed. Merlyn died in the ambulance, on the way to the hospital. I was in the hospital for ten days, then I was perfectly all right. I've never been all right since. For one whole hour, this evening, I didn't think about it once. It's the first whole hour I've spent without thinking about it, ever since it happened. You can see why I had to tell you.'

Tears began to roll down her cheeks. She was not sobbing, hiccupping, sniffing: just weeping quietly and openly. A tear fell from her chin, and glistened on her breast.

Simon took her in his arms and she wept on his bare shoulder.

'I twice nearly married again,' said Pippa. 'Two years ago and four years ago.'

'Why didn't you?'

'They didn't make me forget anything. They didn't have your healing touch.'

'You didn't go to bed with them.'

'No. When it came to the point I didn't want to. They weren't as pretty as you. Nice and slim, and all those nice muscles. And there wasn't any rain. It's going to be hours before my clothes are dry. Can you give me dinner?'

'Yes, of course. I wish you could stay the night.'

'I wish I could, too. But of course I can't, not here, not with you so public and important. Beady eyes and galloping tongues. There's something to be said for living in London. Fancy starting all over again at my age.'

'Thirty?'

'Ha bloody ha. Thirty-four.'

'There's plenty of time.'

She knew what he meant. 'One of each,' she said. 'Paying back what I took out.'

'You must stop blaming yourself.'

'What I must stop doing is drinking this wine.'

'Pause for a bit, maybe,' said Simon, caressing her.

'My God. I never felt less like an archaeologist.'

'What do you feel like?'

'Insatiable. Like you, you dirty beast. Yes yes yes. You must have been missing it as badly as I was.'

'Yes, but I didn't realize it. I felt numb for years.'

'What do you feel?'

'Lascivious.'

'So you do. Did I hear you propose to me?'

'Yes. Did I hear you accept?'

'Yes.'

They agreed to tell nobody until they had told the twins. They thought the twins would be happy about it. Effectively they had been the matchmakers.

The twins came back from school in triumph, with their scholarships and prizes, with golden opinions in their reports, Peter with a tennis cup and Pandora with a swimming cup. They pretended reluctance to talk about all this.

Peter's voice was beginning to break. He sometimes alternated squeaks and growls. He announced that he was giving up talking, completely, until the following Christmas, by which time it could be assumed that the process would be complete.

As soon as they got home, before they changed or unpacked or did anything at all, they rolled about on the sitting-room floor for half an hour with the dogs. Then they opened the piano.

Simon told them his news at supper time. They seemed much less affected, one way or the other, than he expected.

'It won't make much difference to us,' Peter explained. 'We see such a lot of Pippa as it is.'

'I don't suppose she'll play the piano any more or any less,' said Pandora.

'Our food will be better. She's a super cook,' said Peter.

'I refuse to get fat or spotty,' said Pandora.

At almost the same moment Pippa told Eleanor.

Eleanor's reaction was a total surprise.

'Oh my God,' she said. 'Be careful.'

CHAPTER 9

Among connections and neighbours the news fell oddly flat. All those interested – and many not interested at all – knew that Pippa Davies had for months spent hours a week with the Collises. Nobody believed that all those hours had been given to music: Helen Kendall, herself unmusical, least of all. It was said that the twins were always there, all the time, when Pippa was there; nobody believed this. Something had been going on for a year between Pippa and Simon; the announcement of their engagement was to some a relief, to some an anti-climax, to none a surprise.

Pippa telephoned to her mother in South Africa with the news. Her mother said she was coming to England in September – could Pippa postpone the wedding until then? It was only two months. Pippa could.

Naturally, Pippa was that summer even more often at the Collises', cooking lunch and sometimes dinner, gardening, spending relaxed hours with Simon as well as busy musical hours with the twins. The twins now kissed her, in greeting and at parting. They praised her cooking. Pandora did not get fat or spotty.

'You're right about one thing,' said Pippa to Eleanor. 'The twins are spoilt.'

'Try telling that to Simon,' said Eleanor.

'I've got to try. I owe it to them and to him and to myself. They've got to go to bed at proper times and get up at proper times and eat what's put in front of them. And treat their father with more respect.'

'They actually do adore their father.'

'They adore their dogs, too, and they treat Simon and the dogs in exactly the same way. And Simon comes running and sits down and plays dead just as obediently as the dogs do. He almost wags his tail, when the twins pat him on the head. It makes me mad sometimes. I didn't realise when I was playing the piano every minute I was there. It didn't show. I didn't see what was going on. Now that I do . . . I wouldn't worry if I didn't care about them all so much. I've got to think of myself. I've got to take over running that house, but I'll still be putting the mosaic together. I've got to make it possible for myself. I don't think I'm a dragon about punctuality and tidiness and so forth, but it's got to *work*.'

'Don't do it,' said Eleanor. 'Don't do any of it.'

'What on earth are you saying? You've been banging on and banging on about the twins –'

'Don't even mention any of it.'

'I can't marry Simon if things go on as they are.'

'Then don't.'

'But I *need* him. He needs me. The twins need me. You know they do. I'm *agreeing* with you, for God's sake. I'm saying that you were right and I was wrong. Are you telling me to be frightened of something?'

'Melissa said she couldn't live with whatever it was she knew.'

'I'm deeply sorry for Melissa. I've never felt close to suicide, even after. . . . But I can imagine what they call a dark night of the soul. She was tormented by that baby's cot-death. Everybody says she was divine, but from what I hear I don't think she was emotionally tough. I'm not divine in her way, but I am tough. Emotionally, mentally. You know that. I'm in love, Eleanor. I see the man I'm in love with playing puppy-dog to his children. I can't stand it. I love them, too. I can't stand what the set-up is going to do to them. All this is what you've been telling me for over a year. Now you're telling me to go along with – with the self-destruction of their characters, the characters of beautiful, charming, talented, potentially

176

excellent children. . . . Or else to walk away from it. How could I do that? I'm the only person who *can* put things right in that family. I'm in a unique position. I'm there. I will be there. Simon loves me and trusts me. I think the twins do. I know they do. I don't understand you. I simply don't understand. What is it I'm supposed to be frightened of?'

'Melissa couldn't live with it,' said Eleanor. 'But I don't know what it was.'

Charlotte Downing had gone away after the unveiling of her murals. She came back in July to spend a few days with her great-uncle, and to see her Sterney friends.

Photographs of the murals had been published, and had done her a great deal of good. She had been working for a month on *trompe l'oeil* landscapes round an indoor swimming-pool near Ascot.

She congratulated Simon and Pippa. Because she had spent those months at Sterney, she joined the ranks of the unastonished.

The twins came to see her. She was charmed to see them, so friendly, so attractive, Peter amusingly self-conscious about his new and unreliable baritone voice, Pandora more aware of her appearance, and with the beginnings of what promised to be a lovely figure.

They wanted her address. They wanted to be sure of being able to get hold of her, at some future date.

Pippa knew that she had to go very carefully. This was not because she was influenced by Eleanor's nameless fears. Until the fears were given a name, they had to be dismissed as neurotic vapourings. Eleanor was not in other ways neurotic, but she had this one absurd fixation. She had fastened on what was genuinely wrong in the Collis household, and blown it upwards and sideways into some kind of nightmare. No – Pippa's caution was dictated purely by the need not to antagonise the twins. To have them resentful, hostile, would be a ghastly start to married life with Simon. Indeed, if she made enemies of the twins she might not have a life with Simon at all, so overwhelmingly were they the reason for his life.

The thing that had to be changed was Simon's attitude. Gradually, almost subliminally, he must be made to see that having himself as their adoring slave was calamitous, not for him but for them.

Pippa heard from her mother, who gave dates. It was thus possible to fix the date of the wedding with the Vicar of Sterney, and to begin to think about engraved cards and a notice in *The Times*. Helen Kendall offered Sterney Court for the reception. Eleanor offered the old Vicarage, but the offer was neither seriously meant nor seriously considered.

Everything was suddenly actual. Pippa felt a sense of urgency.

Pippa was spending a Sunday in early August with her fiancé and his children. They had had for lunch only a huge salad of the American type – lettuce, blue cheese, tiny fried croutons, raisins, chopped apples and bananas, fragments of crisp bacon. Simon and Pippa had drunk most of a bottle of chilled Rosé d'Anjou, of which the twins had each had a glass half-in-half with Malvern water.

After lunch they sat or lay relaxed on the small lawn. Simon and Pippa were in deck chairs with the Sunday papers. Peter was writing. He did not say what, and nobody asked. Pandora was drawing: pencil, on a pad of cartridge paper: her subject was Peter, sitting cross-legged in shorts with his notebook on his lap, in a tattered straw sombrero which had been brought back from somewhere, before he was born, by his mother. Pandora's hair hung like a bright curtain, almost silver, each side of her small, sun-browned face. She washed her hair three times a week now, and brushed it interminably. Gone for her was the tomboy carelessness of childhood. She had become used – all too used, all her life – to being told she was beautiful; now she knew it, of her own judgment.

Pippa pulled her mind away from annoying comparisons between Pandora now and herself at Pandora's age. She returned to the paper on her lap. She was almost asleep, lulled by sunshine and bees and the deeply soporific book reviews in the *Observer*.

'Ten thousand thunders,' said Pandora. 'I left my pencil sharpener upstairs.'

Pippa waited sleepily for Pandora to scramble to her feet: or for Peter to do so: perhaps for Pandora to abandon her drawing, or make do with a blunt pencil.

Simon heaved himself out of his deck chair.

'In your bedroom?' he said to Pandora.

'Oh Daddy, you're an angel. On my desk, I think. Or somewhere else. It's a blue plastic squirrel.'

'An object,' said Peter, in his ever-more-reliable light baritone, 'of the most excruciating vulgarity.'

'Given to me,' said Pandora, 'by a repulsive female at school who is, or was, besotted by the boy-bard squatting yonder with his doggerel scribbles. She gave me this offering with a view to ingratiating herself.'

'Did she ingratiate herself?' asked Simon, laughing.

'Of course she did,' said Pandora. 'Nobody has lived who has not loved their very own plastic squirrel.'

'"Nobody" is not followed by "their",' said Peter. 'You should say, "Nobody has lived who has not loved his or her very own plastic squirrel".'

Simon laughed again. He stretched. He looked very well but tired. Pippa knew he was exhausted by the harvest, and that he would be back at work – probably unnecessarily but driven by conscience and the desire to set a good example – later in the afternoon.

Possibly Pippa had had a glass too many of the heady rosé wine.

She suddenly found it intolerable, obscene. Simon worked Homerically hard. He spent more than he could afford on this brat's education and on expensive musical toys, records, sheet-music, instruments, her paper and paints and crayons and mounts and frames. Pandora was as active as a flea when it suited her. But now she sat placidly, motionless as a sack, content that her exhausted father should run her errands. It was how life was, for herself and for Simon. It was to both of them the natural order of things, and it was obscene and intolerable.

'Don't you dare go!' Pippa exploded at Simon.

He looked at her with almost comical astonishment.

'I'm going in anyway,' said Simon mildly. 'I want a hat. Shall I get you one?'

Pippa got up and followed him indoors.

The sound of their voices could be heard out on the lawn, though not what was said. The twins did not look at one another. Neither had looked up, at Pippa's outburst or at her

179

departure. Peter crossed out a word on his pad, and wrote in another. Pandora, with her blunt pencil and her fingertip, deepened in her drawing the shadow cast by Peter's tattered sombrero.

The wedding was six weeks off.

'It's funny Pippa never had children,' said Pandora at supper. 'Aunt Eleanor told me she was married for six years.'

'Why do you say that?' said Simon.

'If she did have any,' said Peter, 'where are they?'

'Only Pippa can tell you about that,' said Simon slowly. 'And she only will if she wants to.'

Simon realized afterwards that he admitted to the twins that Pippa had a secret and that she had probably had children. He did not see how he could have answered differently. He was not prepared to lie outright to his own children; he was not prepared to betray Pippa's confidence, even to them. He did not have their inherited genius for avoiding answers, preventing questions.

The old Pekinese which had been Melissa's developed an ulcer of the eye. It did not respond to treatment, and the old dog was obviously in agony. The twins agreed, as sombre as Simon had ever seen them, that he must be put to sleep. They came with him to the vet. They said it was to comfort the Peke in his last minutes. Simon knew that it was also to comfort him.

After the merciful final injection, Simon stayed in the surgery for a few minutes, confirming dates for the vet's visits to the farms. Peter and Pandora chatted to Ginnie the vet's receptionist, an old friend.

'I always say,' said Ginnie, 'get another dog the minute you lose one. Otherwise there's kind of like a hole in the air in the house.'

'We agree,' said Peter. 'Although the holes in the air in our house are pretty well filled.'

'You do have a pack o' dogs, it's true. Too many, some say.'

'Who say?'

'That nice Mrs Davies they do say is moving in with you lot. She come in a day or two back with your auntie. Trouble

180

with that Norwich terrier. Her third or fourth, isn't it? We was talking about your poor little Peke, and I said, confidential, you'd have to be cruel to be kind. Mrs Davies, she says, "I'm sorry for the little dog and I'm sorry for them, but one fewer still leaves plenty. That house," she says, "it's like the Battersea Dogs' Home. It's not run for people at all," she says.'

The Vicar of Sterney, third incumbent since the retirement of the Reverend Jonathan Collis, received an anonymous letter. He saw that it was anonymous before he read a word of it. He nearly threw it away unread, having seen such things before. Some of those he received during a long ministry were obscene, some vituperative, some expressive of religious or anticlerical mania, all nasty and all pretty well mad.

It might be a plea for help. The vicar inspected it. Typed, on quarto paper of the kind used in offices, a cheap brown envelope with his name and address typed. Postmarked Milchester. The vicar, who read detective stories, knew that the paper would bear excellent fingerprints, but that fingerprints on the envelope would have been obscured by those of sorters and postmen. He knew that the individual typewriter could in theory, eventually, be traced. This was all academic, because whatever the contents of the letter it was not likely to be either criminal or in the least important. (He had once received an anonymous death-threat; it had come from an elderly spinster member of his congregation, obtrusively pious, instantly identified, who had decided that he was the Antichrist.)

He read the letter, at last, reluctantly:

39 Buttermarket Street
Milchester
13th August 1973

Dear Sir,
It has come to my knowledge that a Mrs Philippa Davies is proposing to remarry in your church, saying that she is a widow. I know her to be divorced and her husband living. I imagine she will deny this. But if you require proof of what I say I can provide it. I am not motivated in writing this letter by any malice, but by the words of Our Lord in the Sermon on the Mount (St Matthew's Gospel, Chapter 5, Verse 32): 'Whosoever shall marry her that is divorced

committeth adultery.' We are also in Holy Scripture commanded not to be liars.

A Humble Brother in God.

The vicar tore the letter in half: then put the two halves together again. Proof. If there was a living ex-husband that could, indeed, be easily proved. The vicar dithered. He was in a horrid position. He liked Mrs Davies. He had accepted unquestioningly, like everybody else, that she was a widow. He was pleased that poor Simon Collis had found someone so attractive and so suitable; he was pleased for the twins, too.

Obviously the only person he could talk to about this was Mrs Davies herself. He telephoned Eleanor Collis, and left a message for Mrs Davies to contact him as soon as he got back from Milchester.

'This is ridiculous,' said Pippa. 'It's pure mischief-making, I suppose.'

'If what he says is true,' said the vicar unhappily, 'he can easily prove it. If it's false, you can easily disprove it.'

'I can prove what I say, naturally. I must say I'm a bit upset to be asked to.'

'I can see your point most readily, Mrs Davies. I am sure you can just as readily see mine. There are rules in these matters which, as things stand, allow me no discretion whatever. No doubt this is, as you say, pure mischief-making, but since the charge has been levelled and proof offered I am bound to assure myself of its falsity.'

'You can go to the Milchester library and look at *The Times* of the twenty-eighth of December 1968. The announcement of my husband's death on the back page. And a brief report of the accident in which he died on an inside page. Nobody else here knows anything about this, except Simon of course, and I'd rather they didn't. I've got a small pension from my husband's firm. That's documented, I suppose. And you can ask my mother when she gets here next month. I'd rather you didn't, but you can. What I'm going to do is find your Humble Brother in God. Can I have that address?'

The house in Buttermarket Street was a newsagent-tobacconist. Yes, they were used as an accommodation address by people of no fixed abode, and by people who didn't want their wives to see their letters. Because of such people, real or suspected, the names were confidential. Of course the police would be given a list, if they asked. They never had asked. A small charge was made. It was all quite normal and legal. It was actually more trouble than it was worth, but they did it to oblige.

Pippa considered going to the police. The letter was defamatory. They would presumably act, if she asked them to. And a lot of miserable ancient history would come out. And even if nothing came out, it was another thing more trouble than it was worth.

The vicar was surprised to get a telephone call from Peter Collis. The twins came to church, but not often in the summer. Peter asked to see him privately. He asked him not to tell anybody he was coming. The vicar would understand about that when he came.

The vicar supposed that Peter had some problem of puberty which he was ashamed to discuss with his father.

From his study window, only a few minutes after the telephone call, the vicar saw the twins arriving together on their bicycles. Pandora went away on hers. Peter leaned his against the garden wall, and came to the front door.

The vicar was struck once again by their startling blond good looks, and by the similarity which was surviving into adolescence. He was struck by Peter's new air of maturity, and by Pandora's promise of an adult beauty which would equal that of her mother. Her mother's death was before the vicar's time, but she was a legend in the village.

Peter said, 'Thank you for seeing me, sir. Sorry to be so solemn and secretive on the telephone. A letter came out of the blue, addressed to our father and us. He'd already gone off to work when the post arrived, and Pandora was out somewhere, so I opened it. It's about Pippa, Mrs Davies. I haven't shown it to my father and I haven't shown it to her, and when you read it you'll see why.'

It was the same sort of paper and envelope, and it looked like the same typewriter. It came from the same address, but it was dated two days later.

It made the same accusation, offering proof in the same

183

terms, and quoted the same verse from St Matthew. It was signed 'A Believer in the Sanctity of Vows'.

'So you see the spot I'm in,' said Peter. 'The last thing I want to do is distress Daddy or Pippa, but I can't get away from the fact that this person says he's got proof.'

'You did right to come to me,' said the Vicar. He was upset that a young boy should be subjected to an adult moral dilemma; but he was relieved not to have to give a homily on masturbation.

'Obviously what I want,' said Peter, 'is something to convince me that Pippa really is a widow. But I want to get it without her knowing. Don't you see, sir? She might get the idea that we didn't trust her, that we were ready to believe crazy lies about her, if we asked her for proof. We shouldn't have to ask her. We should just take her word. But for our father's sake . . . Just suppose . . . He *does* say he can prove it . . . Do you think I'm being unreasonable, sir?'

The vicar did not. He thought that Peter had so far behaved with absolute correctness. If Pippa was divorced and her husband living, Simon must be told. Presumably it would make no difference to him – they would marry in the Milchester Registry Office, and have a Service of Blessing afterwards in the chuch. But there must be truth between them. Peter was reacting as he himself had reacted – the truth must be established. But the boy was showing compassion and wisdom beyond his years – it *would* hurt Pippa Davies to think the twins could doubt for a moment that she was telling the truth about herself. She should begin life as their stepmother believing they trusted her.

'Mrs Davies can prove she is a widow,' said the vicar.

'Has she done so, to you?'

'She has offered to do so, and explained by what means.'

Peter frowned. 'Why did she? I mean, how did the subject come up?'

'I received a letter similar to yours.'

'Oh.' Peter looked shocked. 'So you asked her about it?'

'With reluctance. But it was my clear duty.'

'And she's offered to prove it to you, so you could marry them in church. But she hasn't actually done so yet?'

'She gave me chapter and verse, like our anonymous correspondent.'

184

'Is that good enough for you? I hope that's not impertinent, sir. I'm really bothered about this. I'm trying to do the right thing.'

'It ought to be good enough for me,' said the vicar, who had been asking himself the same question.

'Yes, it ought to be,' said Peter slowly. 'But it's my father she's marrying. . . .'

The vicar told Peter about *The Times*. He did not remember the precise date; he should have written it down, but he had not done so. There were two relevant items in the same issue, soon after Christmas five or six or seven years previously.

'Oh well,' said Peter, 'if she gave you chapter and verse, as you say, it must be exactly as she says. I mean, nobody would be so silly as to make something like that up. What a relief. Thank you very much indeed, sir. It would be best if we didn't say anything to anybody, wouldn't it?'

'Much the best,' said the vicar. 'And if you or I get any more of these notes, we might communicate, I think?'

'We'll tell you straight away,' said Peter.

Peter spent the morning at the Vicarage. Pandora had gone into Milchester on the bus, to go shopping. Much as he loved his sister, Peter said, he did not want to spend a fine morning watching her buying underclothes. What he wanted to do was to borrow the vicar's edition of Horace with the Connington crib. He was supposed to be construing some odes as a holiday task, and they were a bit beyond him.

So Peter sat in the Vicarage garden until almost one o'clock, under the windows of the vicar's study, with Horace and a dictionary and a notebook, while the vicar composed his sermon for the following Sunday.

The Milchester Public Library had *The Times* on microfilm. An assistant librarian was pleased to show the attractive teenager how to select the issues she wanted and scan the pages in the magnifier. Late December, 1967, 1968, 1969. The girl said she was looking for reports of a puma that had got out of somebody's wildlife park; the assistant dimly remembered that there had been some kind of panic, some years back. The girl found what she wanted quite soon. She made careful notes. She was very polite and grateful.

The next few days the twins spent, most unusually, at Sterney Court. There were things they wanted to look up in the wonderful library. Helen and Dick made them extremely welcome. Ralph and Cathy were more cautiously welcoming, because the twins were becoming so dauntingly grown up.

The twins did not look at the murals in the library office.

Nobody knew how the rumour started, but in a village like Sterney, once started, it went everywhere immediately. In the grocer's, the post office, the newsagent, the pubs, the bus-stop, the Women's Institute, the Young Wives' Group, the garages and filling-stations, the lanes where people walked their dogs, the pavilion of the village cricket ground, the thing was discussed.

Pippa went into the grocer's on Saturday morning, and was aware of a conversation suddenly stifled. Two women turned their backs. Two stared. The girl behind the counter, usually so chatty, filled Pippa's order in silence.

She heard a gabble of conversation resumed as soon as the door had jangled shut behind her.

Her greetings, all down the village street, were ignored or given the minimum of almost frightened acknowledgement.

Old Mrs Maddocks refused a lift in Pippa's car, which meant a three-mile walk for her, home from her daughter's.

Pippa was puzzled and angry, though she pretended not to be even to Eleanor and Simon and the twins.

She was on call on Sunday for Communicare, to take people to hospitals in her car. The Communicare Duty Officer rang up to say she would not be called on as a driver.

To Ivy Kirkley, Eleanor's faithful daily help, early on Monday morning, Pippa said, 'Ivy, what is all this?'

'If you don't know, nobody does,' said Ivy.

It came out as blunt as that – not insolent, exactly, but not friendly.

Every Monday morning Pippa gave a lift to three children who attended a school in Milchester as weekly boarders. She went to pick them up by the bus-stop. They said they had been told not to go in her car. They would go on the bus, although it would make them late.

'Why?' she said.

They said simply that they had been told never to go in her car.

On Wednesday Pippa broke down so far as to ask Eleanor.

'I'd rather not talk about it,' said Eleanor. 'Obviously you don't want to, or you would have by now.'

'I'm going mad.'

'You really don't know what's being said?'

'No.'

'I wish somebody else would tell you. Get Simon to tell you.'

'Simon won't have paid any attention to whatever this is. He won't even have heard it.'

'He may not have paid any attention, but he's heard it. He must have. He sees people all the time.'

'And they all tell each other. *What do they tell each other?* For pity's sake, Eleanor . . .'

'All right. What's being said is that you killed your husband and two children in a car smash, when you were drunk. You got off on a manslaughter charge by saying your husband was driving. Which meant you had to move him into the driving seat after the crash. When he was dead or dying. I'm sorry. There are variations, but that's the gist. Is it complete fabrication?'

'The damaging bits are. Anybody who says I . . . Where did this vicious rubbish start?'

'I suppose you could say it started when you crashed that car. If you did. Did you?'

'I wasn't in the least drunk.'

'Christmas Eve, they say it happened. You'd been to an office party in London.'

'*Who* say?'

'I don't know. Everybody.'

'Why do they?'

'I suppose they think it's true. I suppose somebody has some grounds for thinking so. I don't know who, or what grounds. They wonder who you'll kill next.'

'Oh my God. A little bit of truth, given this obscene twist. . . . A tragedy perverted into. . . .'

Pippa burst into tears, which Eleanor had never seen her do before.

Ivy Kirkley, listening next door, reported later to a crowd in the grocer's: Mrs Davies, tackled straight by Miss Collis, came near admitting the whole thing right out.

'For you not to believe me is the end of everything,' said Pippa.

'I'm trying to believe you,' said Simon.

'Read the report in *The Times*.'

'Had you had a drink?'

'Before a three-hour drive at six in the evening on Christmas Eve? Of course I had. You know how much I drink.'

'I know how much you drink now.'

'Oh my God. The whole countryside's poisoned. You're poisoned. Go and read *The Times*.'

'If you do that, it'll show you don't trust Pippa,' said Pandora.

Pippa started violently. She had not heard Pandora come in.

'Do *you* trust me?' Pippa asked Pandora.

'Yes, of course. But I don't know what you're talking about. What do you want Daddy to read in *The Times*?'

'You must have heard.'

'No. We've hardly seen anybody, except at Sterney. Besides if it's something about you they probably wouldn't tell us.'

There was a silence. Simon looked acutely unhappy.

Finally Pippa said to Pandora, 'You're having tea with Eleanor, aren't you? I'll give you a lift.'

'No, thank you,' said Pandora. 'We'd rather bicycle.'

They had heard. They wondered who she'd kill next.

There was a sudden silence in the newsagent's. Pippa flushed. She was trying to rise above it, to get used to it, to ride it out until it was forgotten.

She knew that in a village like Sterney it never would be forgotten.

People were saying her driving licence ought to be taken away.

'I'd sue if I could nail anything down,' said Pippa.

'Who?' asked Eleanor.

'Anybody repeating this vicious, distorted story.'

'They're passing on a rumour as a rumour. This is a *village*.

I think suing would be a very bad idea. They haven't got the money to pay damages, or your costs.'

'I don't want damages. I want to rub their noses in the truth.'

'Oh dear. They won't like that. You know what would happen if it came into court? All the village would get up, one after the other, and mumble that they couldn't rightly remember the details, they never properly believed it, they didn't know who told them.'

'Including you?'

'No. You'd get the truth from me, and from Simon. What truth? I can't remember where I heard this part of the story or that, the bits you say are true and the bits you say are lies. I don't suppose Simon can. Who *would* you sue? And how *would* you pay for it?'

Pippa said nothing. Her sick anger had no outlet.

She stood it for another two weeks.

Simon, this is the most difficult letter I've ever had to write. But I think you know as well as I do that it won't do. You don't completely trust me. At least, I shall never be sure that you completely trust me. We can't live with it. So by the time you get this I shall have left Eleanor's and Sterney for good. I've given them notice at the museum. Don't try to follow me or find me or get me to change my mind, because I won't.

Anyway my life in the village had become pretty well intolerable, as you probably know. I could have stood it with you, but not alone. It's a rotten shame, isn't it?

Love, but a bit qualified, Pippa.

'Oh no, Aunt Eleanor,' said the twins. 'We did hear a rumour, but it was completely different. We heard Pippa was divorced and her husband was still alive. But the vicar told Peter he had proof that what he heard was a complete lie. We didn't start a rumour. We didn't tell anybody.'

'Yes,' said the vicar to Eleanor. 'Peter came to me, alone, in some distress. I reassured him that Mrs Davies had offered to prove to me, categorically, that her husband was dead. She referred me to a back number of *The Times,* which I was to consult if I wished to in Milchester.'

'You told Peter that?'

'Yes, to set his mind at rest. He spent all morning here, reading, if you will believe it, Horace.'

'Where was Pandora?'

'Peter told me she was bound for Milchester. She was shopping, I believe.'

Feeling self-conscious about behaving like a private detective, Eleanor went to the Milchester Public Library. She asked about recent users of the microfilms of *The Times.* An assistant librarian was produced who remembered Pandora well, recognizing her immediately from Eleanor's description. The girl was in the greatest contrast to the other users of the microfilm, who were in any case very few. She had only come that once. She was interested in reports of an escaped wild animal, which she had apparently found. No fair-haired thirteen-year-old boy had used the microfilm.

Continuing detective, Eleanor established that, on the day she went to Milchester, Pandora had been home in time for a late lunch. And that both twins had been at Sterney Court for most of each of the four days after that.

Therefore, whatever Pandora was looking for in the back numbers of *The Times,* she could not have been steered to it by anything the vicar said to Peter.

Eleanor, with rigorous intellectual honesty, saw that her suspicions were baseless. But they would not go away.

The twins got on to one of the music-teachers from the day school they had attended. He was glad to come once or twice a week to accompany them. They managed without Pippa.

Simon bought a Pekinese puppy, to replace the old one that had been put down.

CHAPTER 10

Ever since the twins had started sleeping in separate rooms, the cottage had really been too small for the family. They would have been cramped even without the swarm of dogs. There was no room for anybody to come and stay. If school-friends of the twins came, they had to have sleeping bags on the floor (the dogs owned the sofas), or be put up by Eleanor.

There was simply no other available house. Gregor Montgomery and his family in the Dower House showed no signs of moving; it would have been neither possible nor fair for the estate to have evicted them. The idea of Simon and the twins moving in with Eleanor never now arose. It might have been expected to do so, especially after the departure of Pippa, but it never did. The twins had somehow killed it.

Building a new house on the estate was a possibility occasionally discussed. Planning permission would not be easy, but in the light of Simon's responsibility for the estate it was considered possible. The neighbourhood had been desig-nated an 'Area of Outstanding Natural Beauty'; it was protected against development by every kind of official label and by action groups and environmental societies. Dick Kendall had himself lent his voice and given his money to prevent even in-filling between houses in the village, and he would have turned down out of hand offers to carve up any of his land into building plots, however massive the profits. He could hardly without hypocrisy take the other side when it came to housing his own employee. Thus application was never made to the Planning Committee of the County Council. Simon and the twins would not have liked living in a new house anyway.

Luckily the twins were pretty tidy for their age. They seemed to be all right for the time being. They seemed content.

Eleanor should have been reassured by their acceptance of it all.

Eleanor lost her spare latchkey, the one Pippa had returned to her when she left. She thought it was simply lost – one Yale key, not on a ring, probably now in a crack between floorboards. She wondered whether to change the lock. She decided against it, and instead had another spare cut. She had very little to attract a burglar, and the house, as befitted an erstwhile vicarage, was in the middle of the village, overlooked from all sides.

If the key had been stolen, any of dozens of people could have taken it, people who had been coming in and out of the house ever since Pippa's departure. Nobody had come that she did not know – no new meter-readers or strange plumbers or telephone engineers or Special Delivery messengers. If one of her friends or colleagues had picked up the key by mistake, he was probably wondering what door it fitted.

Like many big and long-established agricultural estates, Sterney was dotted with isolated, inconspicuous, indestructible, and generally useless little farm buildings. They were built as though to withstand siege, with squat, massive walls of local stone. The walls were windowless, but most were pierced here and there with small holes. The Kendalls had romantically taken these holes for arrow-slits, and pictured the levies of ancient lords of Sterney defending their children and livestock against vagrant bandits. Simon told them that the holes were meant to take the ends of beams, on which racks had been put for drying and storing crops. The relevance of the barns had been to the much smaller tenant farms – many no more than smallholdings – into which much of the estate had been divided until the late eighteenth century. Few were now used for anything, being inconveniently small and remote. They could never be converted into habitable dwellings. Their occupants were owls, starlings, and occasional tramps.

Some of the barns had stone roofs; some had been thatched. Some of the thatch had been unbeautifully replaced by Victorian slates; some, tattered and disreputable, had survived. As soon as Dick Kendall put on the mantle of his grandfather – worn so long and so uncomfortably by Simon – he began a gradual process of rehabilitating the little barns. They might not be much use for anything, but they were part of the ancient empire which he held in trust for posterity. One by one, over the years, the thatched barns were given new Norfolk-reed roofs. The results were charming, if a little consciously picturesque. Helen took a lot of photographs. Simon thought the expense ridiculous, and felt it his duty to say so at least once. But Dick's sense of duty overrode Simon's, and the Trust was paying.

In the April of 1974 Bob Wykes the thatcher turned to the unnamed little fortress between Clay's Wood and the steep flank called Bigglehill. In size it was scarcely more than a shed, some twenty feet by twelve. It was very old; its walls were almost a yard thick. They were not pierced for beams. The door was four inches of oak in an oak frame; the enormous hinges were rusty but perfectly serviceable. The wood had weathered to the consistency of iron. The door was secured not by a lock or latch, but by a bar of oak which fitted into iron brackets in the door-frame. The floor was trodden earth. The timbers of the roof looked eroded and worm-eaten, but experts said they were good for a few hundred years yet. The thatch was a mess.

The barn could be reached by a rough track along the valley between the wood and the hill. This was a relief to Bob Wykes. Bob was amazed that his Lordship was bothering with this remote, invisible bit of ancient masonry; but he cheerfully inspected the roof from the top of his ladder, and made his plans for a job that would see him through the summer.

They called the place Clay's Barn, arbitrarily, simply to give the job a name to put costs and man-hours against.

Simon told the twins about the rehabilitation of Clay's Barn, because they were usually as interested in all the doings of the estate as if they owned it. Their interest on this occasion seemed no more than the polite minimum. As far as Simon knew they never went to see the place, although they liked Bob Wykes and had sometimes helped him.

There was to be a song recital in the school hall, organized by the piano teacher who had become the twins' accompanist. The singer and pianist were giving their services; tickets were a pound; the beneficiaries were the Red Cross and the County Association of Boys' Clubs.

Simon bought tickets for himself and the twins, though it was always possible that, at the last minute, he would not be able to go. Dick and Helen Kendall bought tickets, but Simon knew they were unlikely to go. Eleanor bought a ticket, and would probably be driven by duty to make her appearance. The response was good; the hall would be nearly full.

'Aunt Eleanor will subject herself to something that bores her blue,' said Pandora. 'Somebody ought to tell her she really needn't.'

'She flies flags,' said Peter. 'She's a perambulating flagpole of good works. Will Cousin Dick and Helen come?'

'No,' said Simon. 'They've done their bit by buying tickets.'

'Are you sure, Daddy?' asked Pandora.

'Yes. Dick was talking about it in the office today. He asked me if I thought people would notice their absence, and if they noticed whether they'd mind. I said nobody would think the worse of them for not wanting to sit through the *Winterreise*.'

'It's funny,' said Peter, 'he still needs reassuring about things like that. After all this time. With all that money.'

'Yes. He still feels a bit of an outsider, desperately anxious to do the right thing and not always certain what it is. Helen doesn't feel like that. She never did. But I suppose he always will.'

'Perhaps not for long,' said Peter.

Simon only half-heard this remark. In a moment he had forgotten it.

Simon drove Pandora to the concert at 6.30. Peter had gone

194

on ahead on his bicycle; he was borrowing a book from the vicar and returning one to Eleanor.

Peter walked with Eleanor the short distance from the Old Vicarage to the school. The sun had set. It was a cool April evening, with a gusty wind from the west. There was no feeling of impending rain.

When they reached the hall, Peter excused himself from Eleanor with the precocious correctness which characterized the twins' manners, and which was oddly, even ironically, reminiscent of Dick Kendall's punctilious style. Peter went to talk to the teacher who had organized the concert. He got from him a copy of the Roneo'd programme; Eleanor watched them discussing it, knowing that she would not have understood the conversation. They were at the back of the hall, near one of the emergency fire-exits.

Simon arrived with Pandora. Simon came to talk to Eleanor; Pandora saw a group of friends with whom she had been at this school. She was engulfed by them. Some story she was telling cracked them all up with laughter. She was easily the best-looking of the girls in the group – the most beautiful girl of her age in those parts, the most beautiful, since Melissa, that Eleanor had ever seen. It was not beauty of face and figure only: it was carriage, grace, a lovely elegance of movement; it was grooming – Pandora took trouble with her appearance, without in the least trying to look older than she was; her hair shone so that it had platinum highlights in the overhead strip-lighting. It was, outside all these things, vivacity, devastating charm, a smile of great warmth and a most infectious laugh.

Peter was in almost comic contrast to his sister, still in deeply serious discussion with the teacher about the music they were to hear. This was the other side of the coin. Each side was inherent in the other. Before the evening was over, Pandora would without any doubt be having a conversation about the music, with an adult or a contemporary, fully as serious as Peter's. Before the evening was out, Peter would be as ebullient and extrovert as Pandora. It was all there, all the time, in both of them. Eleanor looked from one to the other, marvelling, frightened.

People found seats. Simon and Eleanor were together, near the central gangway, a third of the way back from the

195

platform. Pandora was a few rows in front of them, in the midst of her attractive young friends. Peter was somewhere at the back.

Eleanor sat down carefully, remembering the hazards of these school-hall chairs. They were not of the modern plastic stacking sort, but old-fashioned wooden folding ones. They were not very secure. They tended to wobble and they had been known to collapse, especially under wriggling children.

The teacher was on the platform. He welcomed the audience to the school hall, and announced the money which would be going to the Red Cross and the Boys' Clubs. There was applause; the audience clapped itself for its generosity. The speaker introduced, with proper respect and gratitude, the distinguished artists who were about to delight them – a soprano of growing reputation, her self-effacing regular accompanist. Programmes rustled. The teacher left the platform and sat down in the front row. The accompanist sat at the piano, and adjusted the position of his stool. The soprano took station beside the piano. Silence fell.

Almost as the pianist raised his hands over the keyboard and the singer filled her lungs, there was a crash in the midst of the audience. A scream. One of the untrustworthy chairs had collapsed. Pandora's chair. It was her involuntary scream. She was up in a moment, laughing, apologetic. She called an apology to the singer. The singer laughed. Everybody laughed, except the accompanist, who looked glum. Pandora had not been hurt in the least. Her hair was less perfectly tidy, but otherwise she was unscathed. It was lucky in a way that the accident should have happened to Pandora, if it had to happen – another teenager might have been acutely distressed by this sudden prominence, by the general laughter – might have been overwhelmed by a sense of awkwardness and humiliation. Pandora made a show of resurrecting her chair and sitting on it with exaggerated caution.

'All secure?' called the singer, who was being very sporting and jolly about the whole thing.

'I hope so,' said Pandora.

Silence fell again. The reverential atmosphere returned. The recital began.

The telephone rang at Sterney Court. Dick Kendall answered it, as the butler was out. He could not at first understand the excited voice at the other end, which was gabbling in an unusually broad local accent.

The man gave his name. It sounded to Dick like Zekiel Gummidge, which was scarcely possible even in that rural backwater. Probably it was something normal enough, but oddly pronounced. Dick let the name go for the moment. The caller was the nephew of Bob Wykes the thatcher. He had been helping his uncle get squared up at Clay's Barn for to get peeling off her old roof. Dick had not known that Bob Wykes had a nephew, but there was nothing odd about that. Probably the nephew was being trained in the thatcher's arcane and traditional skills; Dick hoped so.

'Us maun lift ol' roof off her first peep o' dawn,' said the caller. 'Uncle set on 'at 'cause o' change in weather. I say he maun wait till your Lordship ben come for t'see pictur 'at do cover one o' they walls. If she's open t'wind an' rain, 'at won't do her no sight o' good.'

'Picture?' said Dick. 'A picture in the barn?'

'Ay, wall ben plastered a sight o' years back, an' a gurt great paintin' laid all over of her. She do look to me like she were a holy sort o' paintin', folks wi' wings like angels, see, an' they goldy hats they do call haloes.'

'Listen,' said Dick urgently, 'don't on any account let Bob Wykes take off that roof until we've looked at this painting.'

'Ay, but Uncle ben set t'take lid off her peep o'day tomorrow. Ain't no means we can talk to un tonight – he'm gone off somewheres t'pub, mebbe, an' I maun be t'Milchester first thing.'

'Where are you now?'

'Tes a liddle house. Tes Massr Gummidge's house. He bain't yere.'

Gummidge again. Impossible. The point was unimportant. Heaven knew what telephone the caller was using.

'I'll come to Clay's Barn right away,' said Dick. 'Will you meet me there?'

'Ay. I do b'lieve your Lordship ben in for a gurt surprise.'

As excited as the caller, Dick told Helen and Ralph what he had just heard. Helen was immediately and equally excited. The painting could be the valueless daub of some modern

197

child, but it could be an artistic discovery of incalculable importance. Perhaps the barn had really been some kind of shrine or chapel. It was isolated enough to have housed a hermit. Could it have been intended as a tomb, a mausoleum? Had it been used as one? What grave-goods might not be found under that trodden-earth floor? The building itself was undatable, but it might be Norman. If so, what might not that painting be? Painted on plaster? A fresco? Medieval or renaissance? Had the barn been used by recusant Catholics during the Commonwealth? Was it, conceivably, still consecrated? Might the Kendalls not restore it as a place of artistic and religious pilgrimage?

Nobody who knew Helen would have doubted that, when Dick hurried out to the car, she would be with him. Little Ralph came too. Medieval paintings were not yet much in his line – he was not quite twelve – but he was infected by his parents' excitement. Cathy would perhaps not have come, even if she had been at home. Helen understood the negative effects of ramming culture down the throats of nine-year-olds. The question did not arise, because Cathy was with her aunt Andrea Ivens in Martha's Vineyard.

In the school hall, the singer announced a change in the programme. She was to sing not one group of Schubert songs but another. It was all one to most of the people here. It was all one to Eleanor, who was finding her chair excruciatingly hard, as well as unstable. It was good news for Simon – he knew the advertised songs from a record he had bought a year before, but not the ones he was going to hear. To Pandora it was apparently either good news or bad, but it was hard to say which. She became abstracted, as though brooding on what she was to have heard, or what she was to hear. For a minute or two she was lost in contemplation of something, her eyes empty and her face expressionless.

It was almost full dark. Dick drove the Range-Rover carefully down the track between Clay's Wood and Bigglehill. The ground was pretty dry. It was rutty and bumpy, but there was no risk of getting bogged.

Clay's Barn was actually much nearer to the village than to Sterney Court, though divided from the former by the steep,

198

tree-crowned ridge of Bigglehill. By road the distances were about the same, but there was a footpath over the hill. The path descended steeply on the Clay's Wood side, so that it was sport for the village children to bicycle down it at hair-raising speeds. Dick had at one time tried to stop this, owing to the danger to pedestrians. He failed to do so, so he stopped trying; a continued effort would only have undermined his local authority in other and more important directions. In any case, no pedestrians ever did use the footpath, since it led to nowhere except Clay's Barn.

The Kendalls kept telling one another not to expect too much. They had brought powerful flashlights, in order to get at least an idea of the wall-painting. If there was even an outside chance of the painting being even of the slightest interest, they would head off Bob Wykes before he started pulling off the old roof.

Dick drew up in front of the barn, his headlights glaring on the massive little old building. The old thatch looked particularly disreputable, lit from the side and from below. It looked as though it had harboured thousands of birds' nests, armies of small rodents. Bob Wyke's ladder was leaning against the barn flat to the pitch of the roof. They had come in the nick of time. There was no sign of the young man who had called; no doubt he was on his way from whatever telephone he had used. Young? Yes, he must be quite young to be Bob Wykes's nephew; and to Dick his voice had sounded young for all its rural burr.

The door of the barn was open, the oak bar that secured it propped against the door-frame. That was bad, wrong, if what they were about was protecting a painting. Presumably Bob's nephew had been too excited to remember to fasten it.

Dick left the headlights on; they might help a little to make the interior visible. The Kendalls got out of the Range-Rover with their flashlights.

'Hey,' said Ralph, 'how come nobody saw this picture before?'

'Nobody's had a light inside there all these years,' said Dick. 'And maybe some whitewash on top of it had powdered away. That's happened in a few places, revealing some extraordinary things.'

'I'm telling myself not to expect any extraordinary things,' said Helen.

Dick stopped suddenly as they neared the door of the barn. He sniffed.

'Gasoline,' he said.

'Ours,' suggested Helen.

'I don't think so. The Rover never smelled of gas before.'

'Then Bob Wykes's truck, or the nephew's.'

'I don't like the idea of a lot of gasoline spilled around a thatched building.'

'If it is spilled it'll evaporate in this wind,' said Ralph.

'That's true, son.'

They went on into the barn, flashlights lancing the dark ahead of them. Ralph ran in first, then Helen, for whom Dick stood aside. The beams of their flash-lights zigzagged, dancing, running from wall to wall. There was no plaster. There was no painting. There was nothing.

There was, inside, a stronger smell of gasoline.

The heavy oak door slammed shut. Dick heard, outside, the bar slotted into place across it.

'Hey!' shouted Ralph.

'If this is a joke,' said Helen, 'I don't care for it.'

Dick did not care for it either. Obviously it was a joke, a tiresome, crude, thoughtless practical joke of the kind some of his mother's Californian friends had liked. He had examined the door, door-frame, hinges, bar and brackets, in order to see if any of it had to be replaced, and he knew that only with explosives, or big sharp tools they did not have, could they get out. Until, presumably Bob Wykes arrived in the morning. They would be cold, twelve hours in the barn on the bare floor. They would be hungry and thirsty. They would lie hard. They would not suffocate – there were gaps, as Dick remembered, where the thatch had rotted away over the eaves. He could see gleams of light from some of these gaps, at the top of the wall over the door, from the headlights of the Range-Rover. There was a thread of light at the bottom of the door. There was no sound.

'I'll kill whoever did this,' said Ralph.

'You can have him when I've finished with him,' said Helen. Dick had never heard such anger in her voice. He was very angry himself. Maybe one day they would laugh about this, but he thought not.

The streaks of light above the wall and under the door disappeared. The prankster had turned off the headlights of the Range-Rover. Maybe that was a good thing. Those little spots of light had been no help to them, and the battery would be saved.

Dick yelled. They yelled in unison. They expected no reply and they got none.

There was a rustling above them. Bird? Animal? Somebody on the ladder, on the roof over their heads. They all turned their flashlights uselessly to the roof. Except here and there at its tattered edges, the thatch was enormously thick.

There was a new sound. A kind of crackling. There was a new smell. Smoke.

Interval in the school hall. Prolonged applause. People stood, chatted, stretched, milled about, went to the serving-hatch at the back of the hall for coffee or wine in paper cups. Eleanor decided to skip the second half. She said so to Simon, who nodded, understanding. She would stay to say hullo to friends she had not greeted, then slip away before the music started again. The second half of the programme named composers she had never heard of, which, for her, was always a bad sign. The ones she had heard of were boring enough.

Pandora and two of her friends were on the platform, talking to the singer, who had come back into the hall after making her curtseying exit. They were serious. They were not laughing about Pandora's collapsing chair, but discussing the music past or to come. To Eleanor's surpise, Pandora sat on the piano-stool and played a short passage to the singer. The singer nodded, squeezed herself on to the stool beside Pandora, and played a few bars also. Pandora's friends, and now the organizer of the concert, leaned over the piano, intent on the discussion.

Pandora had slipped, without any sense of change, into Peter's serious musical mood. Had they exchanged? Was Peter now causing explosions of laughter with that anarchic drollery so very like Melissa's?

No. Peter was standing in the emergency exit, now open, with Gregor Montgomery. The reason for this was that

Gregor was smoking. Other people, in order to smoke, had gone out of that door or some other into the car park, but Gregor thought it enough to puff his smoke out of doors while keeping most of his body in the warm.

Peter went towards the hatch, presumably for some of the disgusting school-hall coffee.

Some instinct made Eleanor hurry across to Gregor Montgomery.

'What were you and Peter talking about?' she said.

He looked startled. Well he might. Her question must have sounded odd, even impertinent.

'I'm sorry,' she said, 'but I do have a reason for asking.'

What reason? She did not know herself. But there was a reason. Something was odd and wrong. She did not know what was wrong, or how she knew.

'We were talking about the change of programme,' said Gregor. 'Peter, as you'd expect, knows the songs she was going to sing, but he said he didn't know the ones she did sing. So he was glad she changed. I didn't know either lot of songs, so I didn't mind either way.'

'Which of you first mentioned the change of programme?' asked Eleanor. 'I know it sounds a crazy question.'

It was a crazy question. She did not know why, in logic, she had asked it. It seemed urgently necessary to know the answer.

'Peter brought it up,' said Gregor at once.

'You're sure?'

'Absolutely. The whole subject is far more his line of country than mine. I would probably have been rabbiting on about the county cricket championships, but of course at a concert a lad like Peter is going to want to talk about the music. And look at Pandora! She seems to be performing to the performer.'

The singer could be seen to be talking volubly to Pandora on the platform, then to embrace her quickly and to disappear behind a curtain. Somebody pressed a buzzer. Eleanor slipped away. The last thing she saw was Peter, his face serious, expectant.

Eleanor let herself into her house, turned on some lights, and

202

dealt with the exuberant greeting of her terrier. She let him out into the garden.

Going into the drawing-room she stopped short, frowning. She knew, for an absolute and certain fact, that she had left a string-glove on the telephone. The telephone was on a table of its own near her writing table. It was out of reach of any jump of which the terrier was capable. Partly for this reason, it had been her habit for years to use the telephone and its table to remind her of things. The glove was on the telephone to remind her to retrieve its fellow, which she thought she had left in the newsagent's. Right across the telephone, where she could not fail to see it in the morning. She had put it there before following Peter out of the house on the way to the concert.

No draught existed – not in that room – that could have blown the glove off the telephone on to the table beside it.

Peter had not nudged it off, unthinking, on his way out of the house. He was through the door before she put it there.

She had not herself nudged it off, coming in or greeting the dog or letting him out. She had not set foot in the drawing-room while doing these things.

She had a quick, nervous look around, upstairs and downstairs. Nothing had been disturbed. The house might have been entered, but obviously it had not been burgled.

As far as she could see, only the telephone had been touched. That *had* been touched.

Somebody, perhaps, did have her spare latch-key. Somebody had used it, perhaps, to come in and use her telephone.

She sat down, her head spinning. Somebody took a frightful risk, in order to save a few pence? But if the call were to Australia? Suppose the intruder had to make his call not in the visible, spotlit circumstances of a public box, but in secret, unseen? He wanted to avoid being overheard? He was threatening or blackmailing or planning a crime? If a criminal, why sneak into a house and take nothing? If not a criminal, why sneak into the house?

Eleanor told herself there was another reason for the glove having fallen off the telephone. She conducted a series of experiments, tugging the flex at floor level, in various directions, as though the dog had run into it in the dark. No. Only by physically lifting the glove, or lifting the telephone, could she budge the glove from where she had put it.

The servants at Sterney were nonplussed when, at eight, dinner was announced with no one to announce it to. There had been a telephone call, earlier in the evening, just when it was getting dark. The bell had been heard on the many extensions. The conversation had not been heard. Immediately afterwards, it seemed, his Lordship and her Ladyship and Master Ralph had gone off in the car. The indoor servants, busy cooking and laying dinner, or busy with the television in the servants' hall, had not known about the car until a parlour-maid ran out to the stables.

Since they had said nothing, they had obviously expected to be back in time for dinner. His Lordship was never one to forget consideration for his servants. They had never, in four years, simply swanned off into the blue, and come back late for a meal. Gone off, yes, as it might be to a cocktail party or a meeting, but always back at a proper time. Gone off saying they'd be late, yes, so folks knew where they stood.

The servants twittered, reaching out hands to the telephone to call the police, then drawing them back again.

The butler came back at 8.45 from his day in Milchester. He dithered, too, the moment he heard the news.

At nine he called the police. At 9.12 the police were at Sterney. Description of car. Number. Clothes of party when last seen. This information telephoned to the station. The telephone used to get accident reports, hospital admissions. Nothing. They had been gone for two and three-quarter hours. Alert broadcast over a wide area for crashed or disabled Range-Rover.

Two of the servants stayed up all night. The police kept in touch, with nothing to keep in touch about. Hopes turned to fears and fears to complete bewilderment.

Bob Wykes did not get to Clay's Barn at the peep of day, but he was there by 8.30. He was astonished to see, from a distance, his Lordship's Range-Rover parked by the barn. He thought it must be his Lordship's – he didn't know of another on the estate. Bob parked beside the Range-Rover. He climbed out of his truck and stood goggling at the smoking shell. The walls were still there. Part of the door was still there. All the roof had fallen in, beams and battens as well as thatch. A westerly breeze gusted through the gap where part of the door had burned away. The breeze fanned the smouldering remnants of the collapsed beams. The ash of the burned thatch was piled into drifts, with pieces of smouldering wood sticking out of it like the timbers of an ancient wreck half swallowed by seaside sand. Only half Bob's ladder was left.

His Lordship. He must have come after 5.30, when Bob had left the previous evening. Why in God's name would he do that? Suppose he was smoking his pipe. How could the fire in a pipe-bowl send up a spark to light the thatch? Or the flame of a match or a lighter? A gas-lighter with an adjustable flame could make quite a tongue of fire, but not ten feet of it.

He must have gone up the ladder. Lit his pipe or knocked it out while he was up there. Maybe tried to beat the fire out, and fell through the roof.

Yes, because the bar was across the door, singed but not destroyed. Bob had left the door open, wanting a bit of air to sweeten the damp interior of the barn. His Lordship must have shut and barred the door, then gone up the ladder. There was no sign of the body, under all that ash.

There were other possibilities. It might be a different Range-Rover. It might be his Lordship's Range-Rover with a different driver. It might be that some yob pinched the Range-Rover, drove it here, started the fire on purpose or by accident, and ran away leaving the car behind.

Bob tried poking about in the smouldering ruins with a pole. The heat drove him back.

The thing to do was to get to the Court. If his Lordship was there, report to him. If he wasn't, report to the police.

At the Court he was met by shocked, blank faces. He heard the appalling news: all three of them. He used the telephone.

Within minutes he was back at the barn. Firemen and police were there. There was not much left of the bodies. They would have to be formally identified, presumably by dental work, but there was no doubt in anybody's mind who they were.

It was horrible and completely puzzling, until a fireman made an intelligent suggestion. The kid was ten or twelve. Boys at that age are mischievous. He had locked his parents in, as a joke. He had climbed the ladder. Boys that age climbed any ladder they saw. And then, somehow, he had set fire to the thatch. It was dark by then – he had lit a match to see by.

But by all three bodies there were the recognizable remains of flashlights, more proof than flesh against fire or asphyxiation. Yes, but the kid's didn't work. No way of knowing now whether it worked last night or not, but suppose he got to the top of the ladder, found his torch didn't work, lit a match to see by. . . . To see what by? To see his torch by, to see why it wasn't working. Match burns his fingers, he drops it, still alight, boom goes the old dry thatch, he tried to beat it out, goes down through the burning thatch, still holding the useless torch. . . .

But why in the name of God did Lord and Lady Kendall and their son visit Clay's Barn in the dark?

The telephone call. The police knew about that. The servants heard the telephone ring. Nobody was sure of the exact time, but when it was getting dark. Nobody knew who called or what was said. The car maybe came straight to the barn, maybe not. But the visit to the barn must have been the result of the call.

What could the call have been about, to get the three of them out here in the dark?

The fireman's theory remained objectively possible, as to the door being locked and the fire starting. But another theory began to look more likely. Hoax call gets them out of the house, on to the road, into the barn. Somebody comes quietly round the corner, shuts and bars the door, goes up the ladder, starts the fire, and then nips away out of it.

Why? What enemies did the Kendalls have? Who stood to gain?

Cathy Kendall stood to gain, if you could accept that she wanted to be a nine-year-old orphan. She was sure enough now the owner of Sterney Court and its estate. She was 3,000 miles away. The late Lord Kendall's sisters stood to gain to a moderate extent. They had already been provided for financially, by their father's dispositions. They and their husbands were specifically excluded by the terms of the Trust from inheriting Sterney. A picture or two, a few sticks of furniture, were what they stood to gain. One of the sisters was 3,000 miles away and one 6,000. Their husbands and children were with them. There were a number of other beneficiaries of Lord Kendall's will. None was to inherit a massive sum. With three exceptions, none were within 3,000 miles of Sterney on the night of Lord Kendall's death.

The three exceptions were Simon Collis and his children. Simon was left £5,000 in recognition of his devoted service to the estate. His children, first cousins once removed of the deceased, were left the same sum, each, in trust until their twenty-first birthdays. Simon and the twins had been in the school hall from about 6.30 until nearly nine, and then in each other's company in the car and then at home. Simon had spoken to his sister on the telephone almost immediately after getting home. She had rung. It was something about a glove and a telephone. Simon had not known what he was supposed to do about a wandering glove on his sister's telephone-table. Both twins had spoken briefly to their aunt on the telephone.

One of the three, or any two of them, or all three together, could have gone out after that, and burned the Kendalls alive, for £15,000.

No. The Kendalls had left Sterney about 6.30. Did they wait for three hours, in the barn, like sacrificial goats, until it suited their murderers to come and burn them alive?

Intensive enquiries produced a man who from his bicycle had seen a glow at a great distance, from the right direction, at about 7.30. Nobody had lit any other fires. When the fire was lit the Collis family, all three of them, were in the school hall.

Were they?

A new doubt. Weird, far-fetched, hardly to be taken seriously. But, the statement having been made, enquiries had to be made.

Miss Eleanor Collis and her glove and her telephone. And her doubts and instincts. And her nephew and niece 'biding their time'. And her certainty that they had been getting secretly into Sterney Court. And her idea – quite a good one – that young Peter Collis had slipped away from the concert under cover of the commotion when his sister fell off her chair. And much else of more doubtful credibility or relevance.

Had anybody actually seen Peter Collis in the school hall

during the first half of the concert? Before it began, as it was about to begin, yes. In the interval, yes. In between, perhaps not. Inconclusive. People were paying attention to the music, the singer. He was right at the back. He had been talking there to the organizer of the concert. He said he was sitting not in a row but behind all the rows. This was because he tended to wriggle; he tended to get cramp, and needed to stretch his legs suddenly. Conclusive: he knew about the change in the programme, announced not at the beginning of the recital but at the time: knew not just that there had been a change, but what songs were on the programme and what were in the event performed. Nobody told him. He knew because he was there. Nobody told him? Anybody might have innocently told him, by way of discussion, not knowing that he did not know already. Everybody at the concert (all local people, their names listed by the organizer as an aid to the mounting of future events) could be contacted and questioned. Four people could swear to having spoken to Peter Collis in the interval. All the rest could swear to not having done so. One of the four could swear to have discussed the change of programme with Peter, and to Peter's having known all about it without being told. The other three could swear to the subject not having been mentioned.

Miss Eleanor Collis could swear that there was no contact, during the interval, between Peter Collis and his sister.

Motive? Not obvious but imaginable. Local knowledge, knowledge of Clay's Barn, knowledge of the short cut over Bigglehill, knowledge of the Kendalls, knowledge of Miss Collis's telephone and of her empty house. Bicycle on the spot at the school hall. Unexplained episodes in the past, surely not susceptible of Miss Collis's explanations, but – still – unexplained. But he knew, without being told, what he could not have known unless he had been in the school hall throughout the first half of the concert. It was an unusual alibi, but it was watertight. The police were thankful. They had been a little shaken by Miss Collis's passionate certainty. But Peter Collis was such a nice lad that they were delighted to prove him totally innocent.

Dick Kendall's sisters, Andrea and Stella, came over for the funeral. Andrea brought her husband Bob Ivens, and little

Cathy. Helen's parents, Professor and Mrs Denniston, were not able to contemplate the journey.

Cathy was heiress of Sterney, but there was no question of her living there. She must live with Andrea and Bob most of the time, Stella part of the time. That was the only family she had. Obviously, therefore, she would be educated in America. When she was old enough she would decide about herself and about Sterney.

In order to look after these mourners while they were in England, in order to keep things going, Simon and the twins moved temporarily back into Sterney Court. The Trustees commanded this; there was no alternative; it had to be.

The day after the funeral there was a meeting: the two kindly and solemn Trustees; the two sisters of the deceased, moist-eyed but brave and businesslike; and Simon Collis.

What was at issue was the preservation of Sterney Court, which implied its occupancy. The Trustees were legally obliged to ensure, as far as possible, the well-being of the house and its marvellous contents; the others were morally so obliged.

Simon was required by those present to take post once again as caretaker of Sterney Court, on behalf of his late wife's young cousin. The older Ralph Kendall's arguments were produced again, dusted off, and found to be as compelling as ever. As before, Simon protested, but his protests were weaker – since he had done it before, to everybody's entire satisfaction, he could certainly do it again. He would be acting Lord of Sterney with dignity, humanity, and conscientiousness. In the fullness of time, presumably, he would surrender the keys to Cathy Kendall.

The twins took the news calmly. They unlocked the Steinway and played a duet.

Fantails reoccupied the dovecote, and bantams pecked for crumbs when, that summer of the twins' fourteenth birthday, the family had tea under the cedar.

Immense numbers of roses and small shrubs were distributed to the gardens of a wide area. Several hundred square yards of turf were delivered to Sterney, cut into curious shapes, and laid. Sprinklers gushed; rollers trundled; there was again an enormous unbroken lawn between the house and the lake.

Charlotte Downing, the little bespectacled artist, came at the twins' invitation. She set to work in the library office.

The final panel of the murals still had pony, pony-trap, and house and lake in the background. In the trap were now depicted two fair children, beautiful, closely similar, a boy and girl.

CHAPTER I I

The summer vacation of 1980. Peter had finished his first year of reading history at Magdalen, Pandora hers of studying art at the Ruskin. They had decided, in the end, against careers in music, though they still played a lot and went to many concerts. Professionally, academically, their paths had diverged; but they were together at Oxford.

Eleanor constantly heard about and read about the twins at the university. They had blazed on small stages. Now they blazed on a big one.

They had hundreds of friends of all kinds, in the university and outside it. They knew dons, undergraduates, actors, musicians, journalists, great landowners and small shopkeepers. They were not snobbish. They required only excellence of their friends, which could be excellence of character – goodness, good nature – as well as of talent or intellect or wit. This was what was written about them in the gossip columns, and this was what everybody said.

They were celebrities. At the age of twenty they should not have been, but they were. It was evident to Eleanor that the whole world was bent on spoiling them as calamitously as their father had always done. Peter's poems had been published in serious magazines, and Pandora's paintings were being exhibited. Editors were spoiling Peter, gallery managers Pandora; critics and public were spoiling both. Eleanor recognized that they were outstandingly talented, but the scale of their precocious celebrity had at least as much to do with their beauty and charm, with their being twins, with their living at a place like Sterney, as with talent.

At odd moments they were collaborating on a children's book. It was called *The Tree House*. It evoked in words and pictures the spirit of Melissa and of their own golden childhood. The book already had a commission from a publisher.

Pandora had done some modelling, but she refused to contemplate being a professional model.

Peter said it would be five years before he wrote his first novel. Pandora said it would be fifty years before she had her first one-woman show. Nobody believed either of them.

They took a full part in local life when they were at home. They went to staid little drinks and dinner parties, usually with their father. They went to church, not weekly. They were patient with the elderly and companionable with children. They were immensely popular.

Their friends came to Sterney, in dribbles or droves, all that summer. Eleanor met some of them. They were excellent. They were beautiful and funny and gifted. They were considerate to the servants and respectful to Simon. They were the twins' court. People said it was superb to see Sterney used exactly as its builder had intended, as Palladio, designing its original, had intended. Music, masques, candlelit suppers by the lake, the music of a lute over the water, laughter among the clattering wings of the fantail pigeons. Already the gossip-writers were talking of the 'Sterney Set', in which brilliance was matched by beauty and culture by kindness.

Eleanor remembered something said long before by somebody: the twins deserved to have Sterney as their frame.

Cathy Kendall came for two weeks in August. She came with her aunt Andrea Ivens. Andrea stayed a weekend, then left to join friends in St Tropez.

Cathy at fifteen might have turned out to be anything, given the horror of six years before, given an adolescence in the household of a glib, trendy advertising man like Bob Ivens. As might have been expected, she was beautiful, small-boned, dark; a heart-shaped face with high cheek-bones, a slender and flexible figure. As might have been expected, she was clever, well-read, responsive, amusing.

Of course she remembered Sterney perfectly. She wandered round it with visible elation. It might be full of tragic memories and anguished ghosts, but it was home and she adored it.

She preferred the great lawn as an uninterrupted lawn. She was delighted to see bantams strutting in the stable-yard and fantails cooing in the doors of the dovecote.

The twins made her warmly welcome. They treated her as an equal and an intimate. They made her free both of the tree-house and of *The Tree House*. She loved both. She had the taste and education to appreciate the house and estate she owned; she had the sense and spirit to take advantage of it all.

When she was twenty-one, in 1986, she would be very rich.

She would undoubtedly live at Sterney. If she married, her husband would live at Sterney.

Simon in 1986 would be fifty-seven, nearing retirement.

'I shall put a statue at the end of that walk,' said Cathy. 'With a lavender hedge each side of the walk.'

'What kind of statue?' asked Eleanor.

'I guess it should look Venetian,' said Cathy. 'I don't know where to go for a Venetian statue.'

'Venice,' suggested Peter.

'Off the front of St Mark's,' said Pandora. 'Go the whole hog – get one of the horses.'

Eleanor saw that the idea was a good one – not the joke about the horse, but a small bronze statue against the old stone of the wall behind, and an avenue of foaming lavender to lead the eye towards it.

She saw that Cathy saw herself as mistress of Sterney and custodian of its excellence.

She saw that Cathy was blandly signing her own death warrant.

'I have no standing in the matter at all,' said Eleanor to the Trustee who was the lawyer. 'You can put me down as a nosey old bore. But I am concerned about my brother's future, and his children's. And as you know I've always cared deeply about Sterney.'

213

'What is it exactly you want to know? I don't think there are any secrets. I don't think there's any provision of the Trust or decision of the Trustees that couldn't be published. As a matter of fact, I doubt if there's anything of any consequence that hasn't been published. Sterney always seems to be news.'

'Well. Catherine Kendall will take up residence at Sterney soon after her twenty-first birthday.'

'Probably not. She will still be pursuing her studies at the university which she, and we, confidently expect her to attend. Almost certainly an American university.'

'After her graduation, then.'

'Yes. In, I suppose, about eight years' time. She will be twenty-two or three. Having graduated, we expect Catherine to take over Sterney. The duties of the Trustees, having been light, will suddenly become onerous. But from what we have seen of her, young as she is, we will warmly welcome her succession.'

'Suppose she doesn't come?' said Eleanor. 'Suppose she marries a man who has to stay in America?'

'Then the present arrangement will presumably continue.'

'What happens if – forgive me, but I do want to be clear – what happens if Catherine dies, either before she takes over Sterney or soon afterwards?'

'If she is married and has children, her oldest son will of course inherit.'

'If not?'

'To a qualified extent the answer lies within the discretion of the Trustees. Your brother is in all respects a completely satisfactory tenant of Sterney.'

'And if he dies? Looking much further ahead, I hope, *when* he dies?'

'Let me be clear, Miss Collis. The hypothesis is that Miss Catherine Kendall has died without issue, and Mr Simon Collis has died. As you know, the effect of Ralph Lord Kendall's will, and of the terms of the Trust, specifically exclude the sisters of Richard Lord Kendall from the inheritance, this provision having been made with their full knowledge. Who then inherits Sterney? Is that your question?'

'Yes.'

'Any other descendants of the body of old Lord Kendall,

as we still think of him. There are two such descendants. His grand-daughter's children.'

'The twins.'

'Of course.'

'Will actually own Sterney.'

'Certainly. If they were both to die without issue, there would be problems.'

'Oh, they won't do that,' said Eleanor. 'Whoever dies it won't be them.'

Of course the twins knew that if Cathy died without issue, they would be owners of Sterney. Joint owners, presumably. And if Simon were still alive he would be their tenant, or their guest, or their employee, or their pensioner.

Simon was reconciled now to living at Sterney, because it made a frame for the twins.

Of course the twins knew the Trust had been sufficiently funded by the elder Ralph Kendall for Sterney to be maintained in all regards: for its consequence and its duty of hospitality to be maintained. There would always be fires laid, meals cooked, lawns mowed.

There Peter would have his study, Pandora her studio. Music would fill the rooms, and the laughter of beautiful people.

Except that Eleanor would kill the twins rather than let it happen.

The second weekend of Cathy's visit, the house was once again full. There was a young don from Peter's college, the leading oboist of a London orchestra, an actress about to go into rehearsal with the RSC, as well as Oxford contemporaries of the twins. None of the guests was yet well known. Some might never be. The don spoke with a broad Yorkshire accent. It was a good mixture, and it worked. They had a happy time, at once lazy and stimulating. Simon was never made to feel left out; nor was Cathy, to whom (Eleanor thought) the conversation must have been heady stuff.

They played ludicrous charades after dinner on Saturday. The oboist was the back legs of a pantomime horse who had lost his front legs.

Eleanor was there for tea on Sunday. The party sat or lay

215

on the flawless lawn, under the cedar tree; the bantams and their clockwork-toy chicks foraged for crumbs of shortbread, picking their way between people and dogs.

Cathy was talking to Peter about *The Tree House*, which she wanted finished and published before she was too old to enjoy it.

'Have an owl go live in the tree-house,' she said. 'It can teach the children.'

'To fly?' said Peter, smiling with affection and goodwill. 'Or to say "To-wit to-woo". That was all Thurber's owl could do. I don't mean the one in the attic.'

'Owls are wise,' said Cathy. 'It could teach them about ecology and conservation. I don't mean the book has to be teachy.'

Other people contributed bizarre subjects in which the owl could instruct the children who lived in the tree-house in the twins' book. They amused one another; they amused Simon and Cathy; they amused Eleanor, although she was painfully conscious of a duty to look after Cathy.

Pandora said to Cathy, 'What's this owl of yours called?'

Cathy had no immediate suggestions. But all the others had ideas.

In the middle of the night Eleanor was struck – as though by a hand coming out of the darkness and smiting her face – by a memory of the golden afternoon.

Pandora on the Chinese bridge, showing something to another girl, far away from the party under the tree, far out of earshot of the conversation about the owl.

Pandora and the girl strolling two hundred yards from the bridge to the rest of the party, to the people and dogs and bantams and tea things.

Pandora aware that Cathy had introduced the owl into the conversation. Aware how?

Quite certainly the owl was a new idea. It had not been discussed, not thought of.

It was possible, even probable, that Pandora joining the conversation could have become almost immediately aware that an owl was being suggested as a character in the book.

It was completely impossible that Pandora should have known that the idea was Cathy's.

216

Eleanor understood about the twins.

Eleanor had most of her life kept a kind of diary. Not a day-to-day record. She knew very well that her life was too humdrum and repetitive for daily reporting. She was no Parson Wood-forde, to pin rural life on to the page for future generations. Eleanor recorded events of interest, the small excitements and the large tragedies of her life. The hoopoe on the river bank. The wild orchids in the water meadows. The feuds in the Red Cross Committee. Special exhibitions in the Milchester Art Gallery. Her single love; the death of her love. The milestones in Simon's life. The Kendalls. Melissa. Smiler. The twins.

Early, early on Monday morning, Eleanor pulled the stacks of her diary out of the drawer in her writing-table. Her handwriting was firm and clear; she always used an old-fashioned pen with permanent blue-black ink. Everything was legible. She made notes as she read. It took her three days. She hardly ate in that time. At all the places where she was expected, people were told that she had a go of summer 'flu.

More or less chronologically:

When they were small, the twins had chattered freely to other people as soon as they had learned to talk. But when they were alone they never spoke to one another. They did not need to.

When he was two and a half, Peter viciously kicked a little boy, really hurting him, meaning to hurt him. He was capable of violence, cruelty, at least on behalf of Pandora.

From having been always together, the twins took to separating themselves by tracts of countryside, on pony and in trap. They were practising. They were seeing how far the range of the instruments extended, and whether they could go through woods and hills. They found they could.

A small boy who had teased Pandora had suffered a serious accident in the school playground. Peter was not suspected because he knew, in detail, an impromptu story being told at the other end of the playground. Pandora was listening to that story.

That old shed in the garden was a kind of shrine, in a secret game of the twins. It was, as it were, desecrated by little Ralph Kendall. It was burned to the ground. Peter was not suspected because he reported, accurately, words just spoken by the nurse. Pandora had heard those words.

Smiler had been a great nuisance to the twins, silencing the piano, stopping their mother from reading to them, appropriating their pony-trap, depriving them of their tree-house. Smiler exhausted their mother to collapse, and was exhausting her increasingly. When Smiler died, it was proved that Peter was in the hay-loft, because he knew the cover photograph of a magazine which had only just arrived, and which he could only have seen in the hay-loft. Pandora had seen the magazine.

Melissa, recovering, had been in the pony-trap with Peter. Pandora was riding. From that outing, Melissa came back in despair, and within thirty-six hours she was dead. She had discovered something she could not live with.

The twins pretended indifference to Sterney. They were avidly interested in it. They visited it secretly. They were biding their time.

They knew the subject of a mural they could not have heard about, because they had seen it.

Pandora had gone to the microfilms of back numbers of *The Times*, knowing exactly where to look, knowing to look in *The Times* and not elsewhere. She could not at the time have known. Peter knew, because the vicar told him. They had thereby driven Pippa Davies out of their lives, because she was going to stop their father spoiling them, because she was going to have fewer dogs.

They bided their time, and their time arrived. The concert, the Kendalls at home, Clay's Barn, Eleanor's house empty and its key in Peter's possession. Peter could not be suspected even of making the telephone call, let alone of setting light to the thatch, because he had known that the singer had announced a change in her programme, half-way through the first half of the concert. Pandora had known because she had been there.

It fell into place with Pandora's remark to Cathy: 'What is your owl called?' Probably Eleanor would not have taken in the significance of this, if she had not been hypersensitive to everything concerning the twins and Cathy. Even so it had taken six hours for the penny to drop.

The telepathy test, meticulously conducted by Helen

Kendall and herself. The twins had cheated in reverse – deliberately switched off transmitters and receivers, reduced their results to the mathematical average, and pretended to be disappointed by the results.

Melissa, in the pony-trap with Peter, had suddenly understood all this. Presumably the twins had given themselves away, as they had to Eleanor on the lawn. Melissa had understood that Peter had killed Smiler. She understood how, and why, and how Peter had avoided all suspicion. She accused herself of giving birth to monsters. She knew that there were strange things about her mother and her grandmother, and about herself. She thought she should not have had any children. She could not live with what she knew or with the future. The twins killed Melissa.

On Thursday Andrea Ivens came in a hired car. She took Cathy away to London Airport.

It was conceivable that Cathy would stay away, whatever she felt at the moment; if, for example, she married a man who could not or would not leave America. It was not terribly likely. She would not marry such a man. Anyone she married would come to England whether he started off wanting to or not. Cathy struck Eleanor as being as strong-willed as her mother.

There would be another 'accidental death', the coroner full of sympathy. There would be another cast-iron, fraudulent alibi.

It was not only a question of saving Cathy. Retribution came into it. It was obscene, unthinkable that anyone should get clean away with such atrocities. Eleanor remembered with a sort of dizziness what Melissa had said long before – the twins had never been punished because they had never done anything that deserved punishment.

Ways and means. The essence was to demonstrate, to an impartial witness, that the twins were between themselves telepathic. All the evidence of twenty years, assembled and re-examined by Eleanor, suggested that they had not radios but telephones – they received signals not from the world at large but only from one another. Eleanor herself – anyone else – was opaque, silent, emitting only such messages as anybody could receive, by voice or facial expression or observed actions.

The twins could therefore be deceived. Even without their special gift they were very clever, perceptive and quick: but they could be deceived. They would have to be tricked into revealing the talent that had made their crimes possible.

It would break Simon's heart, already broken twice. And bruised again, when the twins got rid of Pippa. Eleanor could not allow herself to be deflected by that.

Eleanor knew exactly what to do, and presently she knew how to do it.

An early nineteenth-century Vicar of Sterney, the Reverend Joseph Blackadder, had compiled, and published by local subscription, an *Antiquities and Curiosities of Sterney*, a book so grossly unreliable as to be useful only for amusement. No more than a few copies had been printed; it had become extremely rare. There was one in the British Museum, one in the Bodleian, one in the Milchester Museum, and one at Sterney Court. All the family had at one time or another glanced at Blackadder; Eleanor was sure she was the only person, now that Helen was dead, who had read it all the way through.

Eleanor went to Sterney when she knew Simon and the twins were out. She told the servants she wanted to consult one book in the library. She was left in peace there. She put Blackadder in her bag and went away with it.

She told Simon by telephone, in the evening, that she had come to look up something in Blackadder. She had wanted to re-read his account of the marriage of Arabella Talbot to the Earl of Crondall in about 1620, which included the menu of the banquet. She was quite sure nobody would remember that menu. Simon admitted that he did not. Asides, audible to Eleanor at the other end of the telephone, revealed that the twins did not. Well, said Eleanor, she had failed to find the book in its proper place. Had the twins been using it, or one of their friends? Had someone borrowed it?

Immediate, fruitless search for Blackadder. Consternation. The book might be historically almost useless, but it was rare and valuable. It was Cathy Kendall's property. And Eleanor was no nearer finding the menu of Arabella Talbot's marriage banquet.

It was entirely consonant with Eleanor's interests and

activities, as known to Simon and the twins, that she should be concerned with this arcane rubbish. She had had an argument with the Curator of the Milchester Museum; or she was writing an article for the Diocesan Newsletter or the Parish Magazine, *A Millennium of Menus* or *Food of our Forefathers*. It was harmless, a bit boring, entirely typical. It was old Eleanor again.

What Eleanor must not do, she knew, was appear at any point out of character. She must be dear old Eleanor, interfering, a bit bossy, no less the ageing spinster, no more privy to the twins' secret.

She recruited Sir Edwin Drummond, a retired High Court judge who lived with a martyred wife at the edge of the village. She told him no more than the necessary minimum; enough so that he would see the proof when it appeared, see it for what it was, understand the implications, say nothing to anybody before but everything to everybody afterwards, and be, more or less, available on demand.

Eleanor bided her time, patient as the twins had been.

The time came. It was the Christmas vacation of the twins' second year at Oxford. Simon was in London – rare circumstance – unable to confuse things by his presence, spared the shock of being on the spot when the truth came out. Pandora was in Milchester, driving herself in the twins' Mini, doing last-minute Christmas shopping, expected back about four. Peter was out to lunch, but committed to being back by three to take a call from a friend in America. Sir Edwin Drummond was free and agog for a chase he only dimly understood.

Eleanor collected Sir Edwin in her car at 2.15. Blackadder was in her bag. They drove to the Court. They went to the library, where the servants left them. Eleanor opened Blackadder to the page with the bill-of-fare of Arabella Talbot's marriage banquet.

The centrepiece of the banquet was 'venison pasty with green geese roasted'. Sir Edwin, joyously declaiming the phrase, said it was like a line of poetry.

Peter came back at ten minutes to three. He came to the library, having been told that Eleanor and Sir Edwin were there. He would take his call from the extension in the library office. He was delighted that Blackadder had surfaced; Eleanor showed him where she said she had found it – a piece of the purest serendipity, since she and Sir Edwin had been looking for one of the old herbals.

There was no obvious reason why Sir Edwin should not have been interested in old herbals.

Eleanor was cock-a-hoop that she had found Arabella's marriage menu.

'Venison pasty with green geese roasted,' intoned Sir Edwin. 'Two anapaests, a spondee and a trochee. Does that metre accord with any model in classical prosody?'

'Probably,' said Peter, laughing.

The telephone rang. Peter went into the library office, leaving the door open. It was his call from New York. They heard him agreeing to meet his friend at Heathrow two days after Christmas, and to bring him down to Sterney. They gestured farewells to Peter through the open office door. He waved back with his free hand even as he spoke to the telephone. He was standing against the last of Charlotte Downing's murals, which showed Pandora and himself in the pony-trap, with the house and lake in the background.

'This will be a cold bit,' said Eleanor, as she drove Sir Edwin to and through the village and out on the Milchester road.

They waited for a white Mini, by the hump-backed bridge four miles out of Sterney where cars slowed down even when driven by the twins. Eleanor's car was parked thirty yards short of the bridge, or beyond it as Pandora would come. Eleanor took out and hid her ignition key. It was almost dark. The place was isolated. There were no light from any windows within sight. It was moderately cold.

After forty minutes the Mini snarled round a corner, then slowed for the bridge. Eleanor and Sir Edwin waved madly, in the manner of stranded motorists.

Explanations. Eleanor's stupid mistake. A duplicate key at home. Would Pandora mind?

'I lose my key when I'm not driving,' said Pandora, 'but I don't see how you can lose it when you are.'

'We left the car for a moment,' said Eleanor, ready for this. 'There was an owl in the middle of the road.'

Another owl. It had the ring of truth. Eleanor had once seen an owl standing in the middle of the road, giving back the glare of her headlights with bottomless, illuminated eyes.

Pandora pitched armfuls of parcels into a corner of the Mini's back seat. Eleanor got into the front beside Pandora, Sir Edwin into the back. He leaned forward, his head almost between the shoulders of the others. Whatever was said, he would hear it.

'Venison pasty, with capons roasted,' said Eleanor.

'Hum?' said Pandora, sounding startled.

Eleanor repeated the phrase. Pandora remained blank. Eleanor reported finding Blackadder, and Arabella Talbot's menu. Pandora said she was glad.

'I wonder what the pastry of a pasty was like,' said Pandora, starting her engine and getting into gear. 'Pretty doughy, I should think. What did they take for indigestion? Do a monograph on that, Aunt Eleanor.'

'Venison pasty with green capons roasted,' said Eleanor.

'Green capons as well as ordinary capons?' said Pandora. 'What pigs the Talbots were. Does 'green' mean the capons were bad, or young, or had green feathers like a parrot? Green parrots roasted. If you ate them you'd talk better, like eating nightingales' tongues. Sympathetic magic. Shall I drop you here, Sir Edwin?'

The coup had failed. The twins had not been communicating at the operative moment. Presumably, Eleanor thought, they could get through to one another if need arose. They were not buzzing with one another's thoughts and experiences the whole time. At the operative moment, Peter had been waiting for his American call, Pandora driving in near-darkness. They were keeping radio silence, as it were, so both could concentrate.

Very well. Eleanor had increased her knowledge. The attempt was a failure but it was not wasted, and all that was lost was a little time. There was plenty of that. There was all the time until Cathy's return to Sterney.

Pandora drove Eleanor to the Old Vicarage. Eleanor found her spare ignition key, and Pandora took her back to the hump-backed bridge.

'All right now?' said Pandora. 'I must whizz home.'

She snarled away, very fast, back towards the palace where she liked living so very much.

Eleanor drove home more slowly, already trying to formulate another plan. She was confident of ultimate success. Knowledge was power.

She drove up the short drive of the Old Vicarage, between her neighbour's shed and her own front lawn, and into her garage.

Almost before the car came to a stop she was aware of a rear door opening. She twisted round, impeded by her seat-belt. Immediately something besides the seat-belt was imprisoning her – a cord round her waist, holding her back more tightly into the driving seat, imprisoning her arms at the elbow. The rope went round her breast, round her waist again, round and round. It was not so tight as to hurt, through her thick winter clothes and sheepskin coat, but it held her completely helpless. She began to scream. The very beginning of her scream was cut off by a gag which felt like a silk scarf. A cord went round her ankles, outside her calf-length boots, pinning her legs to the front of the seat. An invisible hand switched off lights and ignition.

'It's your own clothes-lines, in case you were wondering,' said Pandora. 'It won't leave any marks, because you're so nicely padded up. I couldn't have done this in the summer. I don't think anybody will see my car. And I don't think anybody will hear your engine running, once I've closed the garage door. And I'll take away the clothes-line and the scarf, as soon as I'm sure you don't need them any more. I don't know why they'll think you did it. We won't have any idea. Sir Edwin may think it's because you were so sick you didn't trap us, after taking all that trouble. I don't think he'll say so. I'm sorry about this, really. "Venison pasty and green geese roasted." I was supposed to correct you, wasn't I, when you said "capon"? Just blurt it out, without thinking. I have done that once or twice, as you know, but we've got a lot more careful. I do wish you'd left well alone. We've been worried about you ever since you did that sleuthing in the Milchester Library. We know you've been watching us, but we've been watching you, too. You might have become a menace. You had become a menace, but only a little one, as you can see now. We couldn't wait much longer, in case you became a big menace. I shall have been back at home, you know, an hour before you could have started to gas youself. I shall be able to

224

prove it, because I shall know if anyone's been there, or rung up, and I shall know what records Peter's put on, before I have a chance to talk to him. I think you understand all that. But I don't think anyone else does, or ever will. Goodbye, Aunt Eleanor. We are sorry, truly. It's such a shame you brought this on yourself. It's such a shame Cathy likes Sterney. We love her. We love you, too. But people keep forcing our hands, so what can we do? Goodbye. Happy landings. It won't hurt.'

The ignition was switched on. The starter whirred and the engine fired. Still warm, it ticked over cheerfully without the accelerator. Pandora left the back door of the car open, and opened the front door. The garage was very small and quite airtight. There was already a smell of exhaust. Eleanor heard the garage door shut.